THE CRIMINAL WORLD
OF SHERLOCK HOLMES

A Guide to The Crime and Criminal Enquiries
of Sherlock Holmes

Volume Two

By Kelvin I. Jones

Hardcover ISBN 978-1-78705-868-2
Paperback ISBN 978-1-78705-869-9
ePub ISBN 978-1-78705-870-5
PDF ISBN 978-1-78705-871-2

Published by MX Publishing
335 Princess Park Manor, Royal Drive, London, N11 3GX
www.mxpublishing.co.uk

Cover design by Brian Belanger

My great thanks are due to those fellow Sherlockians who have unfettered me from dark places recently; to Jo and Mark of The Fat Frog Cafe, Liskeard, for their unfailing support; and to my friend and fellow philosopher, Anthony Langdon; to the intrepid Jack Ryder of Jack Ryder Antiquarian Books of Liskeard, for being the wisest, friendliest and most bookish man I've ever known; to Roger Johnson, the Immortal Sage of Baker Street, for his kindness and generosity. Special thanks and gratitude, to the generous website, www.arthur-conan-doyle.com. And last, but not least to that fearless campaigner, and man of Gothic imagination, Arthur Conan Doyle.

THE CRIMINAL WORLD
OF SHERLOCK HOLMES
VOLUME TWO

MX BOOKS 2022

THE CRIMINAL WORLD OF SHERLOCK HOLMES

CONTENTS OF VOLUME TWO. (For list of illustrations, see p. 279
PREFACE by Roger Johnson. 1.
1.The Ubiquitous Jack The Ripper. Part the Third. 5.
2.The Ubiquitous Jack The Ripper. Part the Fourth, Concluding. 50.
3. Sherlock Holmes' use of drugs. 65.
4.Freudian Holmes. 104.
5.The Madman of Dartmoor. 117.
7. Half man, Half Beast; Psychopathology of Grimesby Roylott. 132.
8. Those Baker Street Boys. 148.

APPENDICES 163.
9. The Use of Disguise & Art of Deception by Holmes & Gross. 163.
10. Bibliography relating to Victorian Crime. 184.
11. Newspapers of Sherlock Holmes. 186.
12. Primary Sources for Crime Research. 190.
13. Classic crime cases in Holmes' 'Good Old Index.'193.
14. Criminological Writings of Sherlock Holmes. 194.
15. Coiners and Coining. 198.
16. A Dictionary of Victorian Criminal Slang. 203.
17. Upon Tattoo Marks by Sherlock Holmes. 231.
18. Scene of Crime Investigation by Holmes; notes by H. Gross. 235.
19. The Curious Case of Camden Place. 249.
20. The Murder Lab: An analysis of Murder in the Holmes Saga. 258.
21. Thieves, Locks & Safes. 264.
22. List of Illustrations. 276.
23. Index. 279.

1 Bush Villas, Southsea, Portsmouth, 1880s, here young Conan Doyle pursued his medical practice. And here it was when he began to learn about the murderer, Jack The Ripper. Doyle's practice rooms were between the huge Bush Hotel and the equally imposing Baptist Church.
From an advert in the Portsmouth Central Library Conan Doyle Archive.

\

Arthur Conan Doyle, photographed here in 1902. Perhaps the most famous and successful of crime fiction writers the world has ever known. But not so well known is the fact that not only did he possess a large library of books on criminology, but he also used his knowledge of criminal investigative methods to free two falsely accused men and published several articles about real-life crime. And he had his own intriguing theory about the identity of Jack the Ripper.

PREFACE TO VOLUME TWO OF
'THE CRIMINAL WORLD OF SHERLOCK HOLMES'
BY ROGER JOHNSON,
COMMISSIONING EDITOR OF
THE SHERLOCK HOLMES JOURNAL

"The Dark Jungle of Criminal London"

One of the great pleasures of our particular pastime is that Arthur Conan Doyle's stories (or John H Watson's reports, if you prefer) are full of details that that provoke our curiosity. Time and place, for example, are not always defined in the stories – hence the many attempts to draw up a chronology of Holmes's exploits, and the even larger number of books and essays that endeavour to establish where those exploits took place. However, the period, from 1881 to 1914, is accurately and atmospherically evoked. The first readers of Holmes's adventures in The Strand Magazine recognised his London and the locations outside the capital as their own, even if some specifics were disguised.

The apparel, means of communication, means of transport, social conventions, science, art and so much more that is depicted or merely mentioned in the stories were everyday matters to those first readers. More than a century on, we may be aware of the essentials, but we want to know more – not necessarily every detail of every element, of course, but because we love Holmes and Watson, we want to be familiar with their world. And an essential element of that world, Sherlock Holmes being not merely a detective but the "only unofficial consulting detective,"[1] is crime.

When Holmes told Watson of his intellectual duel with ex-Professor Moriarty, he remarked, "As you are aware, Watson, there is no one who knows the higher criminal world of London so well as I do."[2] If he was less familiar with the capital's lower-level malefactors, it may be because they were so numerous that he couldn't possibly know them all individually. It was the crime – or perhaps more accurately, the puzzle – that appealed to him, and a baffling crime usually means a very cunning perpetrator. Dr Watson tells us that "he frequently refused his help to the powerful and wealthy where the problem made no appeal to his sympathies, while he would devote weeks of most intense application to the affairs of some humble client whose case presented those strange and dramatic qualities which appealed to his imagination and challenged his ingenuity."3

However, despite Watson's assertion that among the seventy-odd cases he shared during his first eight years with Holmes, there were "many tragic, some comic, a large number merely strange, but none commonplace,"4 we know that some of his investigations did uncover misdeeds that to him were merely mundane, such as the "very commonplace little murder" revealed by the reaction of litmus paper.5 That one, it seems, was easily solved, but on several occasions Holmes remarked on the difficulties that the unexceptional crime presents: "The most commonplace crime is often the most mysterious because it presents no new or special features from which deductions may be drawn."6 The police, of course, were obliged to tackle such crimes every day, and among them were many that proved not to be commonplace after all.

The first police detectives we encounter in the Holmes canon are Gregson and Lestrade, not yet promoted to Inspector but already recognised by the press as "well-known Scotland Yard officials".7 The best that Sherlock Holmes could say of them is that they were "both quick and energetic, but conventional – shockingly so." Being out of their depth, he said, was their normal state. In various of the earlier cases, he twice used the word "imbecile" to describe a police detective,8 but in time his attitude mellowed, and he came to recognise the great qualities of the police. "There may be an occasional want of imaginative intuition at Scotland Yard," he said in a late case, "but they lead the world for thoroughness and method."9 And on at least one investigation, Holmes found himself working alongside a police detective who was unarguably his equal!10

So, what were the British police really like in that fin-de-siècle period? What were the private detectives like? And the criminals and the crimes – what were they like? Among Holmes' passing references to the likes of "Von

Bischoff at Frankfort … Mason of Bradford, and the notorious Muller, and Lefevre of Montpellier, and Samson of New Orleans,"11 we do encounter the names of a few verifiably real malefactors, such as Palmer and Pritchard,12 Charlie Peace,13 and Wainwright.14

Arthur Conan Doyle was genuinely interested in crime and detection. The character of Sherlock Holmes was inspired by the remarkable talents of Dr Joseph Bell, his teacher in the Medical School at Edinburgh University, who did on occasion provide expert assistance in a criminal investigation, and it has been convincingly argued that Holmes' first recorded case was inspired by the disappearance and probable murder of Urban Napoleon Stanger in 1881.15

Conan Doyle followed the news reports of the most notorious crimes of the period, the Whitechapel murders of 1888, and he and formed his own theory as to the identity of the killer known as Jack the Ripper. In 1903 he was a founder-member of the Crimes Club, now called Our Society, whose members share a common interest in crime, especially murder. Later, he turned detective himself, playing an essential part in exonerating two men wrongly convicted of serious crimes.

The world of Sherlock Holmes is not born entirely of the author's imagination. Invented details, imagined characters, plots devised by a master storyteller, fictional crimes – they all convince because they fit perfectly into a world that is as real to us today as it was to those early readers of The Strand Magazine who knew it at first hand.

Read on, and follow Kelvin Jones into "the dark jungle of criminal London…"16

Roger Johnson, BSI, ASH Editor: The Sherlock Holmes Journal

NOTES:
1.The Sign of Four.
2."The Final Problem".
3."Black Peter".
4."The Speckled Band".
5."The Naval Treaty".

6.A Study in Scarlet.

7.A Study in Scarlet.

8.Peter Jones in "The Red-Headed League" and Lestrade in "The Boscombe Valley Mystery".

9."The Three Garridebs".

10.Inspector Baynes of the Surrey Constabulary in "Wisteria Lodge".

11.A Study in Scarlet.

12."The Speckled Band".

13."The Illustrious Client".

14."The Illustrious Client." The reference is to Thomas Griffiths Wainewright, rather than Henry Wainwright.

15.A Study in Surmise by Michael Harrison (Bloomington, IN: Gaslight Publications, 1984).

16."The Empty House".

Fig. 2. Conan Doyle here with his visitor from Lipppincott's Magazine, USA, looking very much the prosperous author.

1.THE UBIQUITOUS JACK THE RIPPER
Part the third

The following article appeared in Doyle's copy of The Portsmouth Evening News, and it is most likely that Doyle and his wife Louise would have read the entire, graphic account which now follows.

Conan Doyle and his wife Louise were still living in suburban correctness, in Southsea, a suburb of Portsmouth, where Doyle sustained a small but flourishing GP practice, but by March they would be gone from

Southsea since the writer had decided, boldly, to move to London, where he decided he would try his hand at being an ophthalmic consultant.

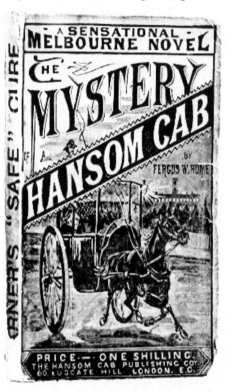

Fig 3. The book by Fergus Hume, 'The Mystery of the hansom Cab,' was one of the first best-selling murder mysteries since Wilkie Collins' The Moonstone.'

The Doyles had experienced some perturbing and frustrating times. Late in the November of 1890, they had travelled to Berlin, where Doyle had heard that a certain Dr Koch had found a cure for tuberculosis, his wife being much afflicted by this degenerative and distressing condition.

Doyle had rather foolishly failed to get tickets for the lecture Koch gave on the subject, so he had to admit defeat, and instead of hearing the lecture, made copies of a colleague's notes who had gained admittance to it. In the January of 1891 he and his wife stayed in Vienna. Here Doyle had decided to study and further enhance his knowledge of ophthalmology, but again, his plans didn't work out.

All this time he was diligently applying himself to the business of being not only an expert in the field of general medical practice and ophthalmology

But also, in what he hoped he would one day achieve: that of becoming a full-time writer. He knew he might achieve his objective. After all, had he not just published his historical, medieval romance, *The White Company*? Then there had been his second Holmes novel, *The Sign of Four*, which had been published by the American magazine, Lippincotts' Magazine, in the autumn of the previous year, then subsequently by Smith, Elder, and Co., which had collected encouraging reviews comparing it to the successful, and best-selling crime novel by Fergus Hume, *The Mystery of the Hansom Cab*. The book had been most successful in Australia, selling 100,000 copies in the first two print runs. It was then published in Britain, selling over half a million copies worldwide, and outselling the first of Doyle's Holmes novels, *A Study in Scarlet* (1887) and there can be little doubt that Doyle hoped that his rationalist detective might enjoy a similar success.

The Strand Magazine, which would mark his real success, in the form of the classic and innovative crime short story genre, had only started to surface in the novel's first edition, published in December 1890. Doyle was at a threshold of the unseen. But soon he would be reconfiguring his notion of who the psychopathic maniac, Jack the Ripper truly was, and not least, when he read an enormous article, published about Jack in his local newspaper, *The Portsmouth Evening News*, on the third of January 1890.

In fact, not many people may be aware that the aspiring writer's interest in the Jack the Ripper case can be traced back at least to the December of 1892 , when as an enthusiastic and regular member of the Crime Club he happened to visit the famous Black Museum, then held at what is now Old Scotland Yard, standing still today on the Thames Embankment where it no longer serves its purpose as a headquarters to the Metropolitan Police. Conan Doyle travelled there in the company of his brother-in-law, the writer E. W. Hornung, who shared Doyle's huge interest in real-life crime and criminology, and who was responsible for a series of amusing stories about a moralistically reverse Sherlock Holmes type and highly devious burglar and jewel thief, Raffles, 'the amateur cracksman,' these amusing tales having been inspired by the character of Sherlock Holmes.

These compatriots of Conan Doyle were accompanied by yet another humorous writer, Jerome K. Jerome, author of the comic novel, *Three Men in a Boat*.

The small company of Crime Crime Club members met Dr Gilbert, in Whitechapel, who had been the attending surgeon in the case of Mary Kelly, a Whitechapel prostitute, whose disembowelled and dissected corpse had been discovered in a small room which was part of a tenement building near to the Thames Embankment.

The group on this unusually ghoulish outing were also shown a postcard and a letter which many police detectives believed were the work of the Ripper. These items were originally housed in the Black Museum and had for some while been on public view there, but when Sir Robert Anderson became the new Commissioner of Police after the Ripper murders were thought to have been concluded, he had them removed, much to the disappointment of some detectives, since Anderson did not share the general view that they were genuine.

Conan Doyle and his friends were not the only people with a high public profile to attend on this day in the capital; in fact it had been staged as something approaching a public relations event by the Commissioner of police and the party included a subsequent leading barrister, Ingleby Oddie, the City of London police surgeon Dr Frederick Brown, who was something of an expert about the Ripper's victims, and several Scotland Yard detectives, who had been involved in the Ripper investigations at the end of the previous decade.

PORTSMOUTH EVENING NEWS. 13th February, 1891.

REAPPEARANCE OF JACK THE RIPPER. ANOTHER HORRIBLE CRIME.

WHITECIIAPEL.WOMAN BRUTALLY MURDERED IN THE STREET.

'London, Friday, 6 a.m.—

Shortly after this morning, a woman was found in Chamber Street, Leman Street, Whitechapel, with her throat cut and other injuries. The body was first found by the policeman B on the beat, who immediately raised the alarm. Assistance at lodging houses was made in a search for a clue to the murderer, and the body was removed to the mortuary, The Ripper's Work.

Fig. 4. Master of horror and the crime story, Doyle was
greatly influenced by the dark fantasy tales of Edgar Allan Poe.

On March 9th, 1909, Conan Doyle gave a speech in London, honouring this writer, who had so deeply influenced his own crime writing and who he admitted, Poe's cerebral and Bohemian detective, the melancholy Auguste Dupin, had formed the inspiration for his own 'rational and empirical' detective. The Poe detective stories, though few in number, had a profound effect upon him as a young writer. In both writers, the concept of the metropolis is always a preoccupation; for in both, the city is seen as corrupt, manifestly evil, and beyond redemption. In the Holmes stories, Doyle goes even further than Poe with this metaphor, appointing Professor Moriarty as the overlord of the dark and vampiric city, where all who fall beneath his shadow are then corrupted.

Telegraphing at 6.30, the Press Association said:

'The murder is evidently another in a series of crimes associated with East London, although in this case the revolting features which have characterised the former atrocious murder, are happily absent'.

Nevertheless, the circumstances of the crime, the character of the victim, and the mysterious features by which the deceased is environed, undoubtedly place it in the same category; though the time chosen by the murderer, locality, and the precautions taken to escape detection are in all respects similar to those followed on previous occasions.

It appears that shortly after two o'clock morning, fifteen minutes past the hour, or as nearly to it as can be ascertained, Constable X., when passing through an archway of the Great Eastern Railway, which leads from Swallow Gardens, Orman Street, a thoroughfare running parallel with the Whitechapel Road, but lying towards the river, observed a woman who had extended her back into the centre of the thoroughfare.

A Horrible Scene.

The constable had passed the spot fifteen minutes previously, and there was no one there. On turning his lamp on the prostrate figure, he was horrified to find to the throat, a cut extending literally from ear to ear. He immediately sounded his whistle for assistance, and within ten minutes he was joined by a Constable whose beat was adjoining.

The woman gave no sign of life, but the body was quite warm, and the constable felt that the pulse was beating faintly. A messenger was despatched to the residence of Dr. Philip, surgeon to the police, who resided near at hand.

Action of the Police.

In the meantime, the police allowed the woman's body to remain undisturbed, in accordance with instructions. The deceased woman was 27, and lay in the roadway, her feet being towards the footpath and crossed one over the other. One arm was bent over her breast, while the other lay extended by her side. A black crape hat lay beside her, and several pieces of crape or black lace were found in her pocket.

The Doctor's Verdict.

On the arrival of Dr. Phillips, the police surgeon, he pronounced, after a brief examination, that the woman, although not quite dead, was fast expiring. In fact, before preparations could be made to remove her, a stretcher which was brought from Leman-Street Station, under direction of the medical man. The body was then conveyed to the Whitechapel mortuary to await an inquest. Intelligence of the crime was telegraphed to adjacent police-stations as soon as possible. Supt. Arnold, a detective inspector, and several other detectives along with uniformed police were soon on the scene, investigating the crime.

The Scene of the Crime.

Swallow-gardens and Ormon street are badly lighted thoroughfares, and not much frequented after midnight. The arch under where the body was actually discovered, is about five yards in length, and lighted by lamps at one end, but the centre, where the deed was committed, is dark. One side of the arch, which is boarded off, is used as a builder's store.

Women of the unfortunate class frequent this spot, and last night two women were apprehended for loitering there. Deceased was known to the police in the locality and had been during the evening about Leman-street. The Great Northern railway shunter passed the archway a few minutes past two o'clock, and a city detective passed here some minutes later.

The Police Theory

The theory of the police is that the deceased was lured into the archway and that the murderer was scared by someone approaching before he could go on.

Further outrage on the body

No money was found on the deceased, but on searching the ground, two shillings were found behind a pipe for carrying off rainwater from the railway. Shortly before five o'clock Chief Inspector Swanson, of Scotland Yard, arrived, with Inspector Arnold, who made a searching examination of the spot, and the walls and hoarding surrounding it. No marks of any kind were, however, found.

A portion of the blood in the road was, by direction of Mr. Swanson, collected and preserved for analysis. The archway was then opened for traffic by the Chief Inspector, charged with the further investigation of the crime. Early information of the murder was sent to Mr. Macnaghten, the Chief Superintendent of the Eastern Police District, who arrived at Leman Street soon after five o'clock. After consultation with Superintendent Arnold, the instructions as to the course to be followed were set for the subsequent inquiry.

Description of the Deceased

The official description of the woman was as follows: Age, about 25, height, five feet, eyes and hair, brown; complexion pale, dress black, diagonal jacket and skirt, black, satin bodice, white chemise and drawers; button boots, ribbon round the neck, black vulcanite earring, black crape hat, and ditto round folds of dress. In dress pocket—three pieces of black crape, one striped stocking, and comb. The clothing was considerably worn and dirty, and the lobe of her left ear bore a mark of an earring having been torn from it. The body was fairly well nourished.

ANOTHER ACCOUNT

The Central News Agency said:—

Whitechapel; this morning

Again, the scene of one of the terrible tragedies which has made its name notorious throughout the world. As in previous cases, the victim today is a woman, apparently of the age of twenty-five. From the appearance of the deceased, and the circumstances surrounding the case, the police infer that the woman was leading an abandoned life. The place selected for the crime was one similar to those previously selected by the fiend of Whitechapel for the perpetration of his horrible deeds, and the only reason for doubting whether this latest crime is really the one by Jack the Ripper, is the fact that beyond a terrible gash in the throat, there are no mutilations on the body.

This, however, may well be accounted for by the probable fear on the part of the murderer of interference in his work. The special representative of the Central News learns, from full inquiries made on the spot, that Police-constable H., a young officer of only a fortnight's service in the Metropolitan Police Force, saw lying in a dark archway the body of the woman. "Its position was not clear against me then, but I just thought at first, naturally enough, that it was a drunken case," said he, and he went on to say how he had proceeded to rouse the woman.

A second glance showed him that blood lay beneath her, and that the woman had been brutally murdered, a terrible gash having been inflicted in the throat.

So great had been the force with which the knife had been drawn across her throat, that the head was almost severed from her body. The deed could only have been committed a short time previously, for the body was warm, as also was the blood which lay in the pool. The hair of the deceased was dishevelled, and there was a wound at the back of the head, but the dress, of rather a superior kind to that of the generality of women of her class in that neighbourhood, was not disordered.

There were no signs of struggle, and it is conjectured that the poor creature must have been willing as an accessory, up to the moment that the knife was drawn across her throat. At all hours of the night police are now passing this archway, but no screams were heard or any sounds to excite suspicion.

The particular locality which the crime was committed in is known as Swallows Gardens.

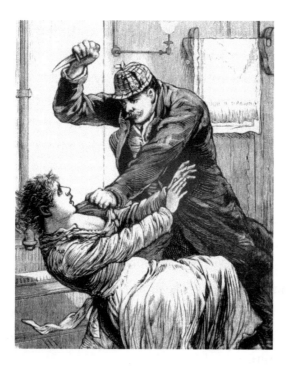

Fig. 5. Sensational view of a Ripper murder from
The Illustrated Police Gazette.

Sensational drawings like this one, from The Illustrated Police Gazette, (see above) did nothing to help allay the public's fears, and the horror and desperation felt by them was echoed in Queen Victoria's frequent complaints to Scotland Yard regarding their lack of success in establishing the identity of this psychotic killer who often mocked them.   For example, when Mary Jane Kelly was killed on November 9, the Queen went straight to the Prime Minister, the Marquess of Salisbury, and wrote: 'This new most ghastly murder shows the absolute necessity for some very decided action. All these courts must be lit, and our detectives improved. They are not what they should be. You promised when the first murder took place, to consult with your colleagues about it.'

It is an undeniable certainty that Holmes, like his creator, would have applauded the Monarch's critical view of The Yard. Ironically, perhaps, in the 20th and 21st centuries, several writers have attempted to establish a link between the Monarch and some of the people known to her. There are a number of alleged but unproven links. First is Sir William Gull, the physician who cared for the Royal Family. Writers like Stephen Knight have accused him of helping get rid of the alleged prostitutes' bodies, while others claim he was the Ripper himself.

Two others have named Queen Victoria's surgeon Sir John Williams who ran a surgery in Whitechapel at the time of the murders, while another theory much more convincingly links the murders with Queen Victoria's grandson, Prince Albert Victor, the Duke of Clarence. And as we shall see, in my examination of Sherlock Holmes' involvement in The Cleveland Street Affair of 1887, (a year also of significance in the Ripper chronicles), Holmes' treatment of The Baker Street Irregulars, those streetwise but perceptive employees of the great detective, were treated with great affection by him.

Doyle's newspaper continued:

These comprise a series of arches, running under the Great Eastern Railway, and used by many of the railway men who are on and off duty at all hours of the night, and who live in the so-called Gardens.

This particular archway is a thoroughfare, connecting Royal Mint-Street with Chambers-Street, and the traffic through it, even at night-time, is considerable. This spot is much frequented by women of the unfortunate class, the darkness of the place shielding them from general observation.

The police, up to half-past nine o'clock this morning, had no clue as to the identity of the deceased, nor to the murderer. The only information they have was given by a railway employee, known among his mates as Jumbo. He says that on going through the arch at half-past one clock this morning, he saw a woman, whom he fully believed to the deceased, talking to a man.

However, it seemed nothing unusual, and he took no particular notice. The police are inclined to believe that the woman's throat was cut as she was standing, and that the wound on the head was caused when she fell to the ground.

It is certain that death overtook her before she could raise an alarm; the railway company's stables are on either side of the arch, and men are constantly at work there. No cries for help could have been given without their being heard.

The remains of the unfortunate woman were removed as speedily as possible to the Whitechapel mortuary, where they now await inquest.

Bloodstains were erased by the police, who cut a cross in the woodwork on the side of the arch to mark the exact spot where the body was found. Since daylight, large numbers of people have been visiting the scene, and to these the crosscut in the wood is the object of much interest.

Police are stationed at either end of the arch to regulate and keep the traffic moving. So far as can be ascertained, the fiend has committed another crime without leaving the slightest trace behind him, and the murder of Swallows Gardens will in all probability, swell the list of the undiscovered crimes of Whitechapel. There can be no doubt as to the Author.

Fig. 6. A drawing, showing the crime scene, which appeared in *The New York Herald*, the day after the murder of Francis Coles.

A Press Association representative who has visited the scene of the murder, writes of the police officials who have been summoned to investigate the terrible murder discovered this morning.

There is now practically no doubt that it is the handiwork of the terrible miscreant who has earned the name of Jack the Ripper. Ail the important details correspond, and the absence of the fiendish mutilation is only to be accounted for by the supposition that the murderer was interrupted before the completion of his full intentions.

The selection of the scene of the tragedy, the appearance of the victim, and the way in which her death was brought about, all correspond with the series of mysterious and as yet totally unexplained crimes, which was thought closed with the discovery in September 1889, of the trunk of a woman in Backchurch Lane, Pinshin Street.

All the Police Know.

So far as can be ascertained, the facts upon which the police are present able to base their enquiries are of a meagre character. It seems that the police constable, belonging to the Division, engaged in perambulating the district under his surveillance, was passing through the thoroughfare known as Swallows-Gardens, when he was horrified to discover the dead body of the woman still warm.

He shone his lantern upon the body and he at once saw that the unfortunate woman's throat had been cut almost completely round the front from ear to ear. The blood flowed profusely and formed a ghastly pool under and about the body. He at once communicated with Leman Street police station, and in a short space of time several officials were on the spot.

Dr Phillips, the Divisional Surgeon, who has had to do with most, not all, of the similar occurrences in and around the district, was quickly summoned. When he arrived, he was able to see what was only too apparent, that life was extinct, and that death had been almost instantaneous. Careful note had been made of the state of the condition of the body and its position when found; it was then removed by ambulance.

The woman apparently was only about 25 years age, her height being about 5 ft. 6ins., her hair and eyes brown. The knuckle of the third of the left hand showed an engagement ring. She wore black clothes, and to all appearances was in mourning.

A Startling Discovery

One of the most extraordinary discoveries which suggests a totally new clue, was the finding of the woman's hat on the body, besides the crape hat which she had evidently been wearing.

It must be said that this fact has caused no little surprise to the police, for it supports the suggestion that the crime might have been perpetrated by a woman, or, at any rate, a man in female attire.

The local police officials quickly recognised the gravity of the occurrence and saw that it was one of extraordinary character. Communications to this effect were telegraphed to the headquarters of Scotland Yard and at an early hour, Mr. MacNaghten, (Acting Chief Constable), with a large number of the most experienced detectives in the force, was soon in the locality.

He, accompanied by other officials, paid a visit the spot where the body had been found and made himself familiar with the surroundings. It must be admitted, however, that little came of this under the keen scrutiny of the detectives, to make them sanguine of an elucidation into the mystery surrounding the coming and going of the murderer.

The Very Spot of the Crime

Swallow-Gardens has nothing in its condition to bear out its name. It is little more than a passage passing through a railway arch, and so narrow that when a vehicle goes past, the pedestrian has to keep close to the wall to prevent contact with the wheels.

The railway arch has been divided by hoarding running up through it, forming on one side some sheds, used as old storehouses for bricks and railway debris, the other side being the narrow passage referred to.

It is very dark, even at best of times, the only light showing in being from the ends of the arch, Royal Mint-Street and Chamber-Street.

At the Royal Mint Street end are some goods offices of the Midland Railway, but nothing in the way of houses for some distance.

Chamber-Street is a narrow thoroughfare, one side of which is taken up by railway arches—of which the entrance to Swallow-gardens is one — and the other side has some small houses and a church school.

At the end of the street are more railway arches. almost impossible to give, in words, an adequate idea of the conglomeration of arches, courts, passages, and winding narrow streets, but even cursory examination demonstrates the ease with which the killer can disappear.

POLICE CONSTABLE PENNETT, WHO FOUND THE

Fig. 7. The constable who came across the murdered woman.
A drawing from an article in The New York Herald about the case.

Even a person unacquainted with the district could quickly disappear into some larger thoroughfares, without leaving a trace behind.

But how much easier it must be to a person who had carefully selected the spot for the perpetration of the murder. A quarter-past two is the time fixed for the time of the discovery, and it is said that not long before two after midnight, a woman was seen loitering about the archway. Whether this was the poor unfortunate creature who met such a tragic fate soon after, cannot, of course, be stated at present.

The victim's identity is, at the time of writing, shrouded in complete mystery, and towards the unravelling of this, the first knot, the detectives are now devoting every care.

At the hoarding of the archway, against which the body was found lying, the police have scratched a cross, and this is practically all that there is to gratify the morbid curiosity of the crowd gathered around the spot, discussing the case and its predecessors.

Later:

A Press Association representative states that it is now said that the body was first found by two carters in the employ of the Great Northern Railway Company, named Tim Sullivan and C. Clarke. It is also stated that the woman was seen about half-past one o'clock in the morning, talking to a man outside house 4, Chambers Street'.

What, then, did the enterprising and energetic Dr Doyle make of this article? Evidently, he regarded with some interest what had been suggested about Mr Druitt of Blackheath, although the author had entertained doubts about that theory. Then, of course there was the 'torso affair' so named after a murder of gruesome proportions had been committed subsequently and which bore some signs that the atrocity could be the work of Jack.

"The Pinchin Street Torso" victim was named as such because she was found headless and legless, under a railway arch on Pinchin Street, Whitechapel, on September 10, 1889, not that far from the 1891 atrocity.

Investigators believed that the victim was murdered at a different location, and the body then dismembered for disposal. The identity of the woman was a mystery, as the only clues were the facts that her arms and hands were "well-formed and showed no signs of manual labour." Still, the police came to the conclusion she was a factory worker.

As the body, missing both head and legs, was already heavily decomposed, and the stench was the first thing the constable noticed. Later investigations by Sergeants William Thick and Stephen White along with Sergeant George Godley revealed bloodstained clothing in Batty Street, but little was made of it. Immediately the constable present summoned assistance and proceeded to arrest three men (including Michael Keating and Richard Hawke) who were found sleeping under nearby arches. They were later cleared of the crime.

Conan Doyle returned to reading his copy of *The Portsmouth Evening News,* to now complete his knowledge of this new case. All along a small voice at the back of his skull had been telling him that Druitt, the lawyer and schoolteacher which he had learned about from both Macnaghten and his initial contact in The Crime Club, Arthur Griffith, was purported to be the correct Ripper suspect.

However, Doyle knew that he could most certainly not have fitted the profile since his body had been dragged from the River Thames in December, and quite obviously, this crime which he had just read about was certainly the hand of his old friend, Jack.

Conan Doyle read on:

Fig 8. Montague Druitt, a schoolteacher working at a boys' prep school in Blackheath, an area that Conan Doyle visited frequently since it was the home of his lover, Jean Leckie. Macnaghten was convinced that Druitt was the Ripper, but others were not so sure.

'An Arrest

About nine this morning a man of dejected appearance was arrested and taken to Leman Street police station, where he was charged on suspicion and detained pending inquiries.

The Deceased's Identity.

Telegraphing later, the Press Agency says the deceased has been identified as an unfortunate, well-known in the neighbourhood of Tower Hill as Catherine O'Neil.

Since ten o'clock communication has been in progress at the Leman-street Police-station between local police officers and those officers who have been brought from Scotland Yard to direct the operations of the plain-clothes staff, which is being increased.

The officers sent from Scotland-Yard include Detective-Inspectors Swanson and Moore, both of whom have had experience in the series of horrible murders which have occurred in the neighbourhood of Whitechapel. The object of the conference is to arrive if possible at some tangible clue to the perpetrator of the crime. It was suggested after one of the former "Ripper" murders that the perpetrator had probably escaped in one of the cattle boats lying in the Thames, but in this case the Thames police have ascertained that since the finding of the body no prison has left the shore to board the Spanish and Oporto cattle ships, and that the crews on board the vessels were all accounted for satisfactorily. It is, therefore, concluded that the criminal is now biding in the vicinity.

The Victim's Last Moments.

The Central News says :—

It is evident that the victim of this morning's tragedy could only have been murdered a few seconds before the policeman arrived. The warm blood was still gushing from the throat with each expiring breath. She opened her eyes once or twice, her lips moved slightly, but no sound came from them. She tried to move her arm, but in a few seconds all was still, and when Dr. Phillips, who had been summoned with all haste, arrived on the scene, the woman was dead. Taking all the circumstances into consideration, the police now have little doubt their minds that the crime was committed by the redoubtable Jack the Ripper. Evidently the murderer heard the sound of approaching footsteps, and this accounts for the victim not having been mutilated, as has been hitherto the case.

CLUE

Whitechapel, 11 a.m. —The railway man "Jumbo," who saw woman talking man in the archway known Swallow-gardens, or shortly after hail-past one o'clock this morning, has been closely questioned, and from the statement made him and by Constable H, the detectives now are convinced that it was the deceased whom "Jumbo" saw. His description of the woman, her height, and dress, all correspond with that of the deceased, and in the moments which elapsed between his seeing her alive and the policeman finding her in the throes of death, leave little doubt upon this subject. Naturally. "Jumbo" has been closely cross - examined in respect to the man's appearance, and fortunately, he appears to have taken rather more than a cursory glance at the man. He describes him as over the medium height, with somewhat the appearance of a foreigner. (The astute reader will note this was of great significance for Doyle).

He looked very much like a fireman. From other information which the police have received, and which tends to bear out this man's statement, a search was at once organised among the foreign vessels in the Thames. This is now being conducted by Inspector Regan, with a large staff, Spanish vessels in the river and in the docks being first singled out for examination, but the result will not be known for some time yet.

Fig. 9. (page 24). Conan Doyle when he was becoming well known as a crime writer A photo , taken for a *Strand Magazine* article about him, entitled 'A Day With Dr Conan Doyle'.

The medical examination, so far as it has gone, bears out the view that this is a Jack-the-Ripper murder. The cuts to the throat are not clean as on previous occasions, but the direction is the same.

Assistant-Commissioner Howard, Capt. Dean, Chief-Inspector Moore, and all the heads of Scotland Yard have now visited the scene, and the general opinion among the best experts is that the Police-Constable was within ten seconds of catching the Whitechapel fiend red - handed at his bloody work.'

Conan Doyle, who, when he died, left a huge collection of books on the subjects of crime analysis and crime detection, would certainly have been familiar with what was the first modern attempt in forensic science to describe the psychological profile of the Ripper.

In 1888, the first offender profile was assembled by detectives of the Metropolitan Police about the personality of Jack the Ripper, a serial killer who had murdered a series of prostitutes in the 1880s. Police surgeon

Thomas Bond was asked to give his opinion on the extent of the murderer's surgical skill and knowledge Bond's assessment was based on his own examination of the most extensively mutilated victim and the post-mortem notes from the four previous canonical murders.

In his notes to the police, following his detailed analysis of the corpse, or shall we describe it better as the remains of the killer's last victim Mary Kelly, dated November 10, 1888, he mentions the sexual nature of the murders, coupled with elements of misogyny and rage. Dr. Bond also attempted to reconstruct the murder and interpret the behaviour pattern of the offender, and soon thereafter, he came up with a profile, or signature personality traits of the offender to assist the police investigation. The profile explained that five murders out of seven in the area at the time the report was written had been committed by one person alone, who was both very physically strong, composed, and daring.

This unknown offender would be quiet and harmless in his outward appearance, probably middle-aged, and neatly dressed; most probably wearing a cloak to hide the bloody effects of his attacks out in the open. He would be a loner, without a solid occupation, eccentric, and very mentally unstable. He might possibly suffer from a condition then called 'Satyriasis', a sexual deviancy that is today referred to as hypersexuality or promiscuity. Bond also mentioned that he believed the offender had no anatomical knowledge and he could not have been a surgeon or a butcher. Bond's summary profile was thus:

'The murderer must have been a man of physical strength and great coolness and daring... subject to periodic attacks of homicidal and erotic mania. The characters of the mutilations indicate that the man may be in a condition sexually, that may be called Satyriasis.'

As a doctor in general medical practice, both in Birmingham and Southsea, it is quite likely that Conan Doyle would have previously come across this condition known as satyriasis. It is also possible that he may have acquired a copy of the most famous autobiographical account of this condition. In that century the condition was most commonly applicable to men, and for which there was apparently no obvious cure, apart from frequent doses of bromide, or when this did not work, through barbaric practices such as penile cauterisation. Doyle himself had also written a detail study of the symptoms of *tabes dorsalis*, a discreet reference to syphilis, and had even written a short story about it.

He used the subject of syphilis as the theme for 'The Third Generation.' In this rarely read tale, later reproduced in Doyle's *Round The Red Lamp*, a young aristocrat visits his GP with a skin condition diagnosed as a *strumous diathesis* – otherwise known as scrofula.

The name given to the condition by Doyle is really a euphemism for syphilis. The young man is told by his doctor that he must not even consider going through with his marriage, and that he has been cursed by a hereditary blight. References are made to his ancestor's 'hereditary blight.' The afflicted visitor then makes this impassioned plea:

'"But where is the justice of it, doctor?" cried the young man, springing from his chair and pacing up and down the consulting-room. "If I were heir to my grandfather's sins as well as to their results, I could understand it, but I am of my father's type. I love all that is gentle and beautiful— music and poetry and art. The coarse and animal is abhorrent to me. Ask any of my friends and they would tell you that. And now that this vile, loathsome thing—ach, I am polluted to the marrow, soaked in abomination! And why? Haven't I a right to ask why? Did I do it? Was it my fault? Could I help being born? And look at me now, blighted and blasted, just as life was at its sweetest. Talk about the sins of the father — how about the sins of the Creator?" He shook his two clinched hands in the air — the poor impotent atom with his pinpoint of brain caught in the whirl of the infinite.'

During the period when Doyle was practising as a doctor, the 1880s, there was a relatively new view of human sexuality gaining ascendance. Several 'authorities' on the subject regarded male sexuality as a biological imperative, which added fuel to many male writings on gender, and these in turn were countered by those who argued that 'civilisation' enabled humans to transcend animal instincts.

This view acquired a public voice through the Social Purity campaign against the sexual 'double standard', and for male as well as female continence outside marriage. Though the female Purity campaigners were sometimes mocked as 'puritans' who had failed to attract a spouse, the movement succeeded in raising public concern over brothels which, as we know, in the East End of London, had reached a record high at the time when the Ripper struck.

Fig. 10. Richard Von Krafft-Ebing, whose ground-breaking book on sexual dysfunction and sexual psychopathology led to the first criminal psychopath profile created by Scotland Yard.

It has been a long-held theory that Jack the Ripper may have contracted syphilis from a prostitute and that might have been precisely why he took his own form of barbaric vengeance on the unfortunate sex workers. His decision to remove the uterus of one victim has been interpreted as a direct attack on the "essence of being a woman" – and several experts believe he removed it, in order to mark his hatred of womankind.

I believe it is entirely likely that Doyle shared this view of the Ripper's profile. One thing about the killing spree which has attracted only scant notice, has been the possible use of the River Thames as a useful getaway route. In that period, the Thames River was where people got their drinking water. It also acted as a water-highway through England. Many people relied on it. What else was it used for? Many people threw their "trash" into the river witch made it unhealthy to drink and swim in.

In Charles Dickens' classic study of the great conduit, 'Our Mutual Friend,' in the midst of that vast overflow from London, two of the characters are depicted, earning their strictly illegal living by fishing dead bodies out of the murky waters:

'Allied to the bottom of the river rather than the surface, by reason of the slime and ooze with which it was covered, and its sodden state, this boat and the two figures in it obviously were doing something that they often did and were seeking what they often sought. Half savage as the man showed, with no covering on his matted head, with his brown arms bare to between the elbow and the shoulder, with the loose knot of a looser kerchief lying low on his bare breast in a wilderness of beard and whisker, with such dress as he wore seeming to be made out of the mud that begrimed his boat, still there was a business-like usage in his steady gaze.

'So, with every lithe action of the girl, with every turn of her wrist, perhaps most of all with her look of dread or horror; they were things of usage.'

In the late 1880s, the river would have been shrouded in virtual blackness at night and anyone who either worked on the river or might have given a large tip to a lighterman, would have escaped arrest, or even challenge by the Thames River Police.

The river police, who operated with both the Met. Police but also the City Police Force, had far fewer numbers.

They had at their disposal several small, low bottom boats and three steam launches. Doyle favoured the idea of the Ripper using The Thames as a dark tunnel where he could be entirely undetected and invisible from the riverbank, a view that was beautifully delineated in The Sign of Four,

Here, in the penultimate chapter of this Holmes story, one of the murderers, Jonathan Small, is chased by a steam launch down to Gravesend where Small attempts an escape by launching himself from the boat straight into a bank of mud.

According to Adrian Conan Doyle, the author's son, in a letter sent to Tom Cullen, a researcher Adrian recalled his father's view:

'I do remember that he considered it likely that the man (the Ripper) had a rough knowledge of surgery and probably clothed himself as a woman to approach his victims without arousing suspicion on their part.'

As was proved several times in the George Edalji case, Doyle understood much about psychological profiling and how it worked; unlike the police, it must be admitted. He would therefore have both read and thoroughly comprehended what Hans Gross, the Austrian magistrate .

Fig. 11. (Page 30). The Thames River Police, who were often required in the Ripper case to check boats and crew lists of foreign boats, a method which had been suggested by Conan Doyle. The illustration above is from The Strand, Vol 1, 1891, titled 'A Day With The River Police.'

The criminologist had much to say about this method of investigation, which in fact began with the first ever criminal profile, that of the Ripper himself. In Gross's *Psychological Criminal Investigation*, the ex-magistrate wrote this:

'If we stop with the phenomena of daily life and keep in mind the ever-cited fact that everybody recognizes at a glance the old hunter, the retired officer, the actor, the aristocratic lady, etc., we may go still further: the more trained observers can recognize the merchant, the official, the butcher, the shoemaker, the real tramp, the Greek, the sexual pervert, etc.

'Hence follows an important law - that if a fact is once recognized correctly in its coarser form, then the possibility must be granted that it is correct in its subtler manifestations. (A most Holmesian statement which might have had the sage of Bake Street nodding in agreement.)

'The boundary between what is coarse and what is not, may not be drawn at any particular point. It varies with the skill of the observer, with the character of the material before him, and with the excellence of his instruments, so that nobody can say where the possibility of progress in the matter ceases. Something must be granted in all questions appertaining to this subject of recognizable unit-characters.

'When he speaks of stupid and intelligent faces, he is a physiognomist; he sees that there are intellectual foreheads and microcephalic ones, and is thus a craniologist; he observes the expression of fear and of joy, and so observes the principles of imitation; he contemplates a fine and elegant hand in contrast with a fat and mean hand, and therefore assents to the effectiveness of chirognomy; he finds one hand-writing scholarly and fluid, another heavy, ornate and unpleasant; so he is dealing with the first principles of graphology;--all these observations and inferences are nowhere denied, and nobody can say where their attainable boundaries lie.'

Doyle was also convinced, mainly based on the evidence in the letters, that the killer was of foreign extraction, and that English was not his native tongue. I believe this to be also credible. So, did Doyle know the name of the Ripper? I think he did, but he was not going to disclose it.

It could well be that, among the papers and books sold, which formed that great collection of criminological works owned by Doyle, but auctioned after the writer's death in 1930, there might have been some clue into the final revelation of the man the world subsequently knew as 'Jack The Ripper'.

In conclusion, is it at all possible, to demonstrate that Conan Doyle had quietly and discreetly worked it all out? I believe he not only knew the identity of Jack the Ripper, but that he also arrived at this conclusion through the application of forensic methods, as demonstrated in his Sherlock Holmes stories.

The period of murders under consideration extends initially from August 31 to November the ninth, 1888. During that time, five prostitutes were murdered in the East End of London by someone that we still do not know the identity of. In my opinion, there was an additional murder which was the murder in Castle Alley near a railway arch. As we have already determined, from the extensive reports in Doyle's copy of *The Portsmouth Evening News*, from which, by inference, I deduced that Doyle gathered much of his data during this period, we might, like him, assume that the attacker wore female attire, and as the detectives under Macnaghten speculated, the murder bore the signs of an interrupted attack.

These murder victims were as follows:

Mary Ann Nichols, who was killed at Buck's Row in Whitechapel. on August the 31st. Then, Annie Chapman, also a person earning money from immoral earnings, who was killed in Hanbury Street, on September the eighth in that same year.

Next was a woman called Elizabeth Stride, who died on September the 30th at Berners St., Catherine Eddowes, who died at Mitre Square On September 30 of the same year and last, Mary Jane Kelly, who was gruesomely slaughtered at a place called Miller's court on November the ninth, 1888.

A look at the map of the area where the murders took place, clearly demonstrates that these murders were all connected. All of the victims had their heads almost completely severed and this kind of detail was reported in the newspaper which Doyle would have read.

And in addition to this, in five of these cases, the woman's abdomens were gouged, or opened. The very last murder, as we have seen, was reported in depth in the Portsmouth Evening News. And it was this bizarre nature and gruesome detail, which got into the newspapers of the period. No one seems to have taken much consideration of the totality of the Victorian news reports. However, as we have seen in previous chapters of this book, this totality of factual detail provides a very detailed and obvious series of links in a forensic chain.

Even long after the completion of these murders, police were unable to demonstrate who the murderer was, mainly, it seems from a distinct lack of forensic evidence, since forensic methods were very basic in the period that Conan Doyle created his character of Sherlock Holmes. Holmes was especially scathing about preserving a scene of evidence, and this is reflected in the discovery of the dead body in Lauriston Gardens in STUD, where he observes, despairingly, that the murder scene looked as if a herd of buffaloes had walked across the floor. Then there are other factors to consider which would have handicapped the enquiry. Fingerprinting did not get adopted by Scotland Yard officially in this country until 1902 which is very late, and only then, was it begun as a trial, to see if it actually worked conclusively.

Moreover, the card index filing system used by detectives at the Yard in that time was very primitive, to say the least, and police officers did not have the flexibility, or investigative connections, that the modern-day detective affords, especially since the advent of computer -driven software.

From our reading of the Sherlock Holmes stories, we know that Sherlock Holmes was an expert on handwriting analysis. Cyphers, footprints and distinctive marks on paper, plus the effects of a particular livelihood on the hand of a person who pursued that trade, all these and others were part of his expertise. In fact, his knowledge was as wide as was that of his maker, Conan Doyle, and it was also extremely precise.

It comes as no surprise, therefore, to imagine that Conan Doyle might well have solved the Ripper murders. He was most concerned, as he said in the interview in the magazine Titbits, that the police had not simply thought to ask people to look at the handwriting examples and see if they matched any of the letters that their relatives had produced.

In fact, in retrospect, it does not seem that the police actually compared newspaper reports at all. Yet, Conan Doyle, living as he was for most of that period in the mainly middle-class area of Portsmouth in Southsea, like many other residents of that bustling and busy tourist town, would have been able to take advantage of the *Portsmouth Evening News*' handling of the case. And as we have learned, this newspaper published very graphic and detailed accounts of the murders.

Therefore, Conan Doyle was in receipt of all of the evidence, and in some cases, even more detailed evidence, if we also take into account his membership of The Crime Club, about which he displayed a great deal of importance and significance, especially since a leading member of this august society was Major Arthur Griffiths, regarded by his fellow criminological enthusiasts as an expert reasoner in his field.

If we're looking at providing a solution regarding the handwriting of The Ripper, we must admit such analysis is very important. We know that Doyle would have analysed the message in the letter that was seen by him at the Black Museum. And we also know that he assumed, I think correctly, that the murderer was of foreign extraction, or had lived abroad, perhaps, for a long time. He also was of the opinion that the man who committed the crimes may have been of American origin. (This was the 'dear boss' letter which was sent to the Criminal Agency in September of 1888.)

The question as to whether Conan Doyle had an exact photo-fit description in his mind of Jack the Ripper is one that is it is not easy to

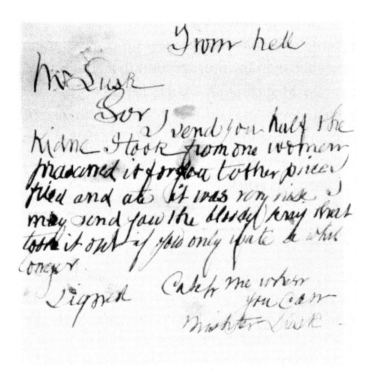

Fig. 12. Conan Doyle was intrigued by the handwriting of The
Ripper and two of the Holmes stories deal with handwriting,
and its analysis. In the 19th Century the art of graphology was
seen by forensics experts as a science, and in France, taken
more seriously by their leading criminologists.

determine. However, he inferred from his statement in the magazine article
from *Tit Bits* that the person he would be looking for was most likely to be a
personal foreign extraction.

This is referred to in several police documents which have survived, and
it would be unfair to assume, as some modern-day criminologists have
assumed, that such a theory was based purely on the xenophobia of the
English investigators.

Admittedly, there was a theory at one time that the Ripper could have
been a person of Jewish extraction. This idea, when the supporting

information was finally leaked to the press, caused a great deal of hostility within the Jewish Whitechapel community.

The person responsible for making this view official was undoubtedly Robert Anderson, who took over the murder hunt in its final stage in 1898, and who, in Blackwood's Magazine, in March 1910, Part Six, (a popular journal of its time which Doyle also had had dealings with), expressed his views about the possibility of the Ripper being a Jew in a decisive and, some readers thought, a balanced and well-reasoned manner.

The empirical nature of his article would certainly have appealed to the aspiring novelist and real-life crime investigator, as this extract from the piece clearly demonstrates:

'One did not need to be a Sherlock Holmes to discover that the criminal was a sexual maniac of a virulent type, that he was living in the immediate vicinity of the scenes of the murders. And, moreover, that he was not living absolutely alone.

'His people knew of his guilt, and they refused to give him up to justice. During my absence abroad, the police had made a house-to-house search for him, investigating the case of every man in the district whose circumstances were such that he could go and come and get rid of his blood stains in secret. And the conclusion we came to was that he and his people were low class Jews. For it is a remarkable fact that people of that class in the East End will not give up one of their number to Gentile justice and the results proved that our diagnosis was right on every point.

'For I may also say at once that these types of undiscovered murders are rare in London and the Jack the Ripper crimes are not within that category. And if the police here had powers such as we know the French police possess, the murder would have been brought to justice.

'Scotland Yard can now boast that not even the subordinate officers of the department will tell tales out of school. And it would ill become me to violate that unwritten rule of the service.

'The subject will no doubt come up again. And I will only add here that the Jack the Ripper letter, which is preserved in the Police Museum at New Scotland Yard, is the creation of an enterprising London journalist.

'I will only add this; that the individual whom we suspected was caged in an asylum. And that the only person who had ever had a good view of the murderer at once identified him correctly identified him. But when he learned that the suspect was a fellow Jew, he declined to swear to his original identifying statement'.

There was, perhaps understandably, an immediate reaction to Anderson's claims in this reported interview in *Blackwood's*, and in the Jewish Chronicle of the 4th of March 1910, a journalist attacked Anderson for his overt racist theory and explicit account of the Ripper being a Jew.

The journalist observed that this theory of Sir Robert Anderson was nonsensical and that it condemned a whole neighbourhood of immigrants by tarring them with the same brush.

What specific proof did Robert Anderson have to support this view? he asked. In fact, the only very detailed description of what the Ripper may have looked like comes from an eyewitness statement, made shortly after the last of the five so- called classic murders, ending with the murder of Jane Kelly, in the September of 1888.

In the statement made to the police the eyewitness has this description of him and this description comes from a document from a Metropolitan Police address, in Commercial Street, dated the 12th of November 1888. Here is the brief account:

'Description of the witness who saw the victim; a 'gentleman' describes him in vivid and clear detail.

'Age about 34 … height about 5ft 6ins., complexion pale, dark eyes and eyelashes. Slight moustache, cut off at each end and hair dark. Very surly looking, dressed in a long, dark coat, collar and cuffs trimmed and trim. The dark jacket under a light waistcoat, dark trousers, dark felt hat, turned down in the middle. Button boots, decorated with white buttons; he wore a very thick gold chain, a white linen colour, a black tie with horseshoe pin, of respectable appearance'.

That is the report given by detective, George Hutchinson, who was one of the detectives who gain access to the witness statements during the Ripper investigations.

The suggestion that the Ripper was of foreign extraction had been favoured by many people living in Whitechapel at the time of the Ripper murders. And this is supported by some of the phraseology used in the letters that the Ripper ostensibly sent either to the Central Press Agency or to the police directly. He was in no doubt that the person was a foreigner of some sort, who continued to use English phrases incorrectly in his letters.

He was in no doubt that the person was a foreigner of some sort, who continued to use English phrases incorrectly in his letters. And the vocabulary of several letters certainly supports the theory.

For example, in the letter dated 25 September 1888 and addressed to Sir Charles Warren, the author of the letter uses the phrase 'rip them (the women) til I get buckled'. Again, in the missive dated October 4th of that same year, he refers to his 'being an American' and says he has 'been living in London for ten months.'

Was Conan Doyle right about the Ripper being an American?

Fig. 13. Composite photo profile is an extraordinary match to the American psychopath, H. H. Holmes.

In 2006, Scotland Yard and the BBC together made a composite photo of Jack the Ripper based on detailed eyewitness accounts from 1888. The resulting photograph looks very much like H.H. Holmes, pictured here. Jeff Mudgett took the two photos to retired investigators, who agreed that

Holmes bore a striking resemblance to the suspected Jack the Ripper. In fact, both investigators said this was the closest match to a composite photo that they had ever seen.

While the resemblance is hard to deny, the photo evidence doesn't quite line up with the theory that Mudgett presents in his book *Bloodstains*. The principal problem is that Holmes just could not have been in Whitechapel at the time of the killings.

He argues that Holmes sent an assistant to commit the Ripper murders, so Holmes could not have been present for any eyewitnesses to identify.

Another letter from the Ripper, although sadly undated, and therefore admittedly less credible, describes any policeman who thwarts him as being a 'dead un,' Finally, in the letter dated for October 1888, which had been sent to England from Philadelphia, the writer tells police that he is 'now safe in New York,' and that he is soon going to Philadelphia to 'kill more whores.'

There is also, in several of the anonymous letters, a suggestion that the master psychopath did a great deal of travelling, using the national railway system, which by that stage of the great Brunel enterprise had succeeded in covering all of Britain with a comprehensive rail network, To Doyle, no doubt this would have given great credence to the theory that the Ripper could have used rail travel, to swiftly and easily move from one part of England to another, using the 'to be collected' facilities of nearly all main line stations to dispose of his blood- stained clothes, and that perhaps, therefore, he may have been some kind of commercial traveller.

Doyle opined that the phrases 'dear boss' and 'fix it up', are also phrases that a British person would not use, but that an American would.

We also now know that Conan Doyle visited Scotland Yard's Black Museum, on December the second, 1892, four years after the last of the Ripper murders took place in Whitechapel.

He would very probably have examined most carefully the reports given by the attending surgeons who investigated the state of the bodies, and he would be extremely interested in the perversity of the crimes, especially in connection with the knowledge that he had acquired from his reading of the forensic analysis of psychotic behaviour. The most comprehensive book on the subject, and which no doubt he possessed a copy of, was Krafft Ebing's classic study *Psychopathia Sexualis*.

Also, but perhaps to a lesser extent, he would have read the oedipal theories of his contemporary, Sigmund Freud, but also in the work of the Austrian judge, Hans Gross. It has always been assumed that Conan Doyle wrote nothing about the Ripper's crimes, or that they are not referred to even obliquely in his Sherlock Holmes stories, but this is not the case.

Fig. 14. The nightmarish slaying of Jim Browner's wife and her lover.

Although Doyle was intrigued by the nature of such criminological psychopathology, he was not so sure his readers always shared his fascination for the subject.

The most classic example is that which is given in 'The Cardboard Box'. Doyle wrote this story in the January of 1892, which is only four years after the last murder. And it is interesting that he decided that when it was republished, Doyle emphatically told his publishers of the collected edition of Holmes short crime stories that he would not allow the story to be included in what is known today as *The Memoirs of Sherlock Holmes*, because of the challenging and demonstrably savage nature of the crimes committed in the piece. As a frequent commentator on Doyle's fiction, I share the view of the veteran writer, Canadian Chris Redmond, who when compiling this trilogy on Holmes and crime, asked me if I had a theory as to why so many Doyle stories contain horrific or savage incidents, and I must only congratulate Mr Redmond regarding the accuracy of his observation.

This story, where the killer takes his adulterous wife and her lover out from the harbour in Liverpool in a rowing boat, then systematically beats out each of their brains with an oar before cutting an ear from each victim, prior to the disposal of their bodies overboard, is certainly one of the most specifically sexually motivated revenge and horror tales in the entire Sherlock Holmes corpus, with the exception of the story, *The Veiled Lodger*, where the wife of a violent circus performer is trapped by the wife's lover, Orlando, in a lion's cage, having had his skull pulverised and torn to ribbons by the object of his wife's affections his attacker using an improvised, nailed club.

In *The Cardboard Box*, the sister of the adulterous wife, is sent the ears through the post in a box and the police then ask Holmes to analyse the evidence, a task which he swiftly concludes.

It is interesting to compare this with the half of a kidney taken from one of the Ripper's victims, and which was sent to George Lusk, who was head of an organisation known as the Whitechapel Watch Committee. This committee had been set up to try and draw evidence together regarding the Ripper and his victims. The Central News Agency had also received a letter from a person describing himself as Jack the Ripper which said that he would 'Clip the lady's ears and send them to Scotland Yard.' This prediction was then borne out by effect.an called Susan Cushing receives two severed human ears, which had been packed in a box in salt. In the story of The Cardboard Box, it's again interesting to note Sherlock Holmes' own analysis of the parcel which contained the ears, its handwriting and the address provided. The analysis is very much on the lines of the modern graphologist.

There are interesting parallels between this story, and some of the Ripper crimes. One notable comparison is that the parcel sent to Miss Crushing did not contain a pair. By comparison, the cuts, which were inflicted by the Ripper on the ears of two of his victims, also turned out to be from different people. When Doyle wrote this grimmest of all the Holmes tales, I am convinced that he had in his mind the macabre details of the Ripper's victims' body parts sent to the police and newspapers.

I believe that when Conan Doyle analysed the Ripper murders, he would have approached it in a systematic fashion, just as his own detective had done so in the Holmes stories.

He would have been appalled by the chaos which ensued, especially after the Mitre Square slaughterhouse killing of Mary Kelly and the fact that many policemen and other people walked backwards and forwards through the small room where she had been so brutally and grotesquely savaged to death, her body then flayed and then dissected, creating a scene so horrific in the annals of Victorian crime, that no police constable would contemplate entering the room where a fire had been lit by the murderer, presumably to disgust even more the unfortunate attending officers.

Conan Doyle would have been interested in the fact that in the case of the Kelly murder, the room had unaccountably been locked. He would have wanted to know, for example, why this was thought necessary, and why it was also thought necessary to break the door down with a pickaxe. Did the boyfriend have a spare set of keys? Was he considered by police to have been a suspect?

Now, regarding fingerprints: Again, although fingerprint evidence and its collection was at this time in its infancy, we do know that such prints were occasionally collected and often analysed.

In another of the Holmes stories Doyle uses this theme. In the tale known as *The Norwood Builder*, a wax thumb print leads us to the solution of the criminal's identity. Doyle would also have been interested in the knives used by the murderer, as is evident in the Homes story of *Silver Blaze*, where a particular type of knife was used for the attempted maiming of the eponymous horse.

Conan Doyle was able to demonstrate these forensic skills in the real-life stories of persons who had been wrongly accused of crimes by the police, and especially in the case of George Edalji, where the type of knife used became important in the evidence provided by the author to the Home Secretary, regarding Edalji's undoubted innocence. Doyle thus was able to prove categorically that Edalji had been the target of a racist vendetta.

The timing of the Ripper killings also would have been of extreme importance to Doyle because of the small geographical area, in which the victims lived.

One curious factor Doyle may also have contemplated, is that no one in the police team appeared to look at the evidence of persons who had recently appeared in London as foreign nationals, and perhaps, crucially, who had used the River Thames to move from one area to another; and thus were able to simply disappear when they were in a tight spot; and therefore, were unlikely to be questioned near the scene of crime. On the river itself, of course, where there were far fewer River police, they would not have been likely to be questioned at all.

Then there is the question of trace evidence, such as, for example, tobacco ash which Holmes, as we know, frequently analysed at a scene of a crime, as in *The Resident Patient,* where he was able to determine where the victim's persecutors were standing, when the man they sought their revenge upon was hung by makeshift gallows. Elsewhere, tobacco ash seems to have been very prominent in several of the stories, as in *Yoxley Old Place.* In the Ripper evidence examined by police there is no specific detail regarding tobacco.

In fact, Conan Doyle's interest in the Jack the Ripper case can be traced back to the December of 1892 , when, as a member of the Crime Club, he determined to visit the famous Black Museum, then held at what is now Old Scotland Yard, but standing still today on the Thames Embankment, where it no longer serves its purpose as a headquarters to the Metropolitan Police Force.

The aspiring Conan Doyle, now gradually finding his feet in the literary world, travelled to London in the company of his brother-in-law, the writer E. W. Hornung, who shared Doyle's huge interest in real-life crime and criminology, and who was responsible for a series of amusing stories about a moralistically reverse Sherlock Holmes type of highly educated middle class, devious burglar and jewel thief known as Raffles, 'the amateur cracksman,' these amusing tales having been inspired by the character of Sherlock Holmes himself.

The crime hungry literary compatriots were also accompanied by another humorous writer, Jerome K. Jerome , author of the comic novel, Three Men in a Boat.

The Crime Club members met Dr Gilbert, who had been the attending surgeon in the case of Mary Kelly, a Whitechapel prostitute, whose savagely disembowelled and dissected corpse had been discovered in a small room which was part of a tenement building near to the Thames Embankment.

 The group, on this unusually ghoulish outing, were shown by the detectives a postcard and a letter which many police investigators believed were the work of the Ripper and which the Club members were allowed to handle, then analyse. These items were originally housed in the Black Museum and had been on regular public view there.

However, when Dr. Robert Anderson became the Assistant Commissioner of Police after the Ripper murders were thought to have been concluded, in 1890 he had them removed, much to the disappointment of some detectives, since Anderson did not share the general view that they were genuine.

Anderson was an Irish lawyer from Dublin who had been brought to London in 1867 as part of an intelligence branch to combat the threat of Fenian terrorism, a highly organised Irish home rule movement which had been seen as a pervasive threat to English democracy and whose activities form part of the appendices to the present volume.

When the branch was closed Anderson had remained behind at the Home Office advising in matters relating to political crime.

Conan Doyle and his friends were not the only people with a high public profile to attend this London tour; in fact it had been staged as something approaching a public relations event by the Commissioner and the party included a subsequent leading barrister Ingleby Oddie; the City of London police surgeon Dr Frederick Brown, who was something of an expert about the Ripper's victims, and several Scotland Yard Detectives, who had been involved in the Ripper investigations at the end of the previous decade.

Anderson, like Doyle, had every sympathy for the murdered women who had been described pejoratively by several of the newspapers of the time as 'drabs,' or 'fallen women,' and in his memoirs Anderson expressed his conviction that the Ripper might have attacked far fewer women if they had been prevented from plying their trade openly on the streets of Whitechapel during that blood-soaked period.

He wrote that, in his view, 'the measures I found in operation were, in my opinion, wholly indefensible and scandalous; for these wretched women were plying their trade under definite police protection. Let the police of that district, I urged, receive orders to arrest every known "street woman" found on the prowl after midnight, or else let us warn them that the Police will not protect them.'

Lastly, there is the question of a bloodied garment. How was it that the Ripper could so easily conceal the terrible and large bloodstains which would have accumulated on his clothes? Did he have a costume which he perhaps changed into near the scene of the crime? Did he have a confederate, who perhaps he was able to visit and change there in a private room - someone who maybe owed him a favour? One thing we can be certain of is that, regarding the last case, often referred to as the murder of 'clay pipe Alice,' the murderer was surely dressed as a woman, and Conan Doyle based his evidence about the Ripper as a cross dresser largely on the clay pipe Alice murder. Was the wearing of female clothes by The Ripper a fetish which made him feel both disarming, then sexually excited and controlling.

Finally, I've been intrigued by the psychopathology of the serial killer himself. And there's every suggestion that Doyle had not only identified the murderer's ambivalent sexually motivated behaviour, which I mentioned earlier, regarding the wearing of women's' clothes, but that he had also drawn specific conclusions about the use of the River Thames in regard to this analysis, for who would stop to apprehend a woman, getting into a lighterman's boat, when police officers were instructed to look for a man?

Undoubtedly Doyle had studied the leading authorities on psychotic and sexually motivated attacks on women by men who had, in their childhood, experienced trauma as a result of abusive parents. These cases and their causes had been dealt with in detail by the great German psychiatrist, Krafft-Ebing in his ground-breaking book on human sexuality, Psychopathia Sexualis.

Here it has to be confirmed that not only was Conan Doyle interested in the Ripper crimes, but that it is entirely likely that he had studied the reports, made by the police authorities, and probably had spoken to Macnaughton and other senior officers about it at some depth, since we have it on good authority that, as a fully active member of the Crime Club, the writer, along with other luminaries of the world of forensic crime and criminology had visited the scenes of some of the Ripper's victims.

Thus, by the time Conan Doyle got to the Black Museum and looked at the letters, some of which may well have been genuine and today are considered by most 'Ripperologists' to be the genuine item, he had pretty much made up in his mind and confirmed who the Ripper was. He may not have had a name and address, but he certainly had a very distinctive physical and psychological profile in mind.

It is only a pity that this profile was not shared or hinted at with the general public by the author. For if it had been, we would know so much more now about the identity of Jack the Ripper.

Here it has to be confirmed that not only was Conan Doyle fascinated by the Ripper crimes, but that it is entirely likely that he had studied detailed reports, made by the police authorities, and probably had spoken to McNaughton and other senior officers about them.

Thus, by the time he got to the Black Museum and looked at the letters some years later, he had pretty much made up in his mind and confirmed what kind of a man the Ripper was. He may not have had a name and address, but he certainly had a very distinctive profile. This, then, was a compulsive killer, who no doubt had suffered greatly from the effects of a venereal disease, most likely to have been syphilis. Either he had lived in America, where he had been brought up or where he'd worked and probably spent his childhood and his formative years,

It is only a pity that this profile was not shared with the general public by the author. For if it had been, we would know so much more now about the identity of Jack the Ripper.

Fig. 15. An illustration from the *Illustrated Police Gazette,* showing police, examining bloodstains at the Hanbury Street murder scene. In 1888, the year of nearly all of the Ripper atrocities, bloodstains were noted and reported in a manner as shown here; however, the science of microscopic blood analysis was still very limited.

EXTRACT FROM THE 1894 'TITBITS' INTERVIEW GIVEN BY CONAN DOYLE TO AN AMERICAN REPORTER REGARDING JACK THE RIPPER'S IDENTITY.

The Trail of Jack the Ripper

CONAN DOYLE: I am not in the least degree either a sharp or an observant man. I try to get inside the skin of a sharp man myself and see how things strike him. I remember going to Scotland Yard Museum and looking at the letter which was received from the Ripper.

Of course, it may have been a hoax, but there were reasons to think it genuine; and in any case it was well to find out who wrote it. It was written in red ink in a clerkly hand. I tried to think how Holmes might have deduced the writer of that letter. The most obvious point was that it had been written by someone who had been in America. It began 'Dear Boss', and contained the phrase 'fix it up' and several others which are not usual with Britishers. Then we have the quality of the paper, and a round, easy, clerkly hand. He was, therefore, a man accustomed to the use of a pen.

Having determined that much, we cannot avoid the inference that there must be somewhere letters which this man has written over his own name, or documents or accounts that could readily be traced to him. Oddly enough, the police did not, as far as l know, think of that, and so they failed to accomplish anything. Holmes' plan would have been to reproduce the letters in facsimile and on each plate indicate briefly the peculiarities of the handwriting. Then publish these facsimiles in the leading newspapers of Great Britain and America and in connection with them offer a reward to anyone who could show them a letter or any other specimen of the same handwriting. Such a course would have enlisted millions of people as detectives on the case.

THE UBIQUITOUS JACK THE RIPPER. PART THE FOURTH: IN CONCLUSION.

Regarding the identity of Jack the Ripper, it appears very clear to me that Conan Doyle was very preoccupied with the psychological profile of the killer. All along, Doyle had submitted the theory that the person responsible for at least some of the murders was a foreigner and nowhere greater was this confirmed, than in the case of the murder so well known to the young author from the considerable detail he had garnered from his readings of newspaper accounts of the Ripper murders, and which was known familiarly then as the 'Pinchin Street Murder'.

This victim was known as Emily Barker, and we know that she came from Northampton. Apparently, she had been leading a fairly wildlife. The last that was ever heard of her was that she had been found on a doorstep in London, half naked, by a passing missionary. She was put into his charge. But two days later, she escaped, and then her body was discovered. Or it would be better to say that the remains, mainly consisting of her torso, were discovered. A proper identification was subsequently confirmed by the clothes she had been wearing.

An inquest was held regarding the remains. On Tuesday the 24th of September 1889, only a year after the murder of Kelly, a verdict of wilful murder against persons unknown, was subsequently arrived at by the coroner's court.

Conan Doyle was very interested indeed in the ideas of a group of psychologists he referred to as the alienists and was keen on the concept of criminal profiling. As we know, the alienists' idea of the 'idee fixe,' as Doyle defined it, was also popular with the French criminologists, whose work he was much acquainted with, especially that of Lombroso and Bertillon; and it crops up in the Sherlock Holmes stories, most especially in the *Adventure of The Six Napoleons,* where it is suggested that the criminal who destroys the busts of Napoleon Bonaparte has an *idee fixe,* or fixed notion, a monomania, sometimes referred to as an extreme and irrational obsession.

This was at the time of the Holmes tales, a highly popular idea amongst the alienists. The name "alienist" in the late 19th Century became synonymous with that of "psychiatrist," a term we use today, but which then meant a medical doctor specializing in the treatment of mental illness, or ailment.

The word was most closely associated with the forerunners of the forensic psychiatrists. These were doctors with specific expertise in criminal psychology in the legal system, who were asked to assess insanity, competency etc., for those who stood trial for serious offences, like murder. As the field of clinical psychology evolved during the *fin de siecle*, psychologists specializing in profiling criminal behaviour and mentality, like Dr. Krafft Ebbing, were then often referred to as 'alienists.

The earliest alienists were biologically influenced, regarding their treatment of mental illness, like neurosis, but *especially* with the case of severe syndromes, such as schizophrenia, depression and sexual mania. It was Freud and his disciple, Jung, however, who together focused on the *psychology* of mental illness, rather than its neurological or physiological symptoms.

And, fascinatingly, it was also an alienist who got very close to understanding and, in my opinion, perhaps very close to solving the profile of Jack the Ripper, defining him as a 'homicidal maniac.'

Dr. Littleton Stewart Forbes Winslow, an eminent alienist, had taken an interest in the Ripper murders from the beginning of the murderer's campaign. But when he was alerted to the victim who had been identified as Emily Barker, he then began to ponder on the case and came to the conclusion that he would try and find a clue as to the identity of the murderer of this female victim, (who, incidentally, is *not often* regarded, amongst the host of Ripperologists of our own time, as being one of the Ripper's murder victims; although there are many people who, even to this day, 125 years later, dispute this definition, myself being one of them. Who decreed that the murders simply *ceased to exist* by the end of 1888? Surely, this is no more than an unverifiable conclusion based on an unverifiable assumption; especially since we know little about the murderer apart from his profile).

Fig.16. Dr Forbes Winslow, eminent barrister and psychiatrist, who gave evidence in many Important British murder trials. Winslow claimed he had stayed in lodgings with the man he believed was the Ripper, and gave convincing evidence about his encounter to an American reporter.

He decided that he would then try to trace the criminal, and he found an address of the lodgings where the murderer must have stayed on each of the nights of the murders. He then began to put together a kind of identikit and began to understand his ways of living and habits. He came to the conclusion that the man responsible for these murders was a homicidal maniac. This report about Winslow was given further credence in the newspaper known as the *New York Herald*, in the September of 1889. A copy of this was kept in the police archives at Scotland Yard, but finally lost, along with other vital Ripper archives in the 1970s, which was mainly put down to careless archiving techniques.

However, a facsimile photographic copy was subsequently obtained. And it makes for interesting reading, bearing in mind Doyle's independent conclusions. Below is a summary of what Winslow said to the reporter.

The report stated that Dr. Winslow had given an interview, saying that he had in his possession a pair of boots which actually belonged the Ripper, and he then produced these and showed the journalist, and then explained the following regarding their owner.

'Here are the boots,' he said. 'The tops of the boots are made of ordinary cloth material, but the soles are made of Indian rubber. You will notice that the tops have a number of bloodstains on them'. Listening intently to this Holmes - type account, the reporter then decided to put the boots on, and discovered that they were completely noiseless. The doctor then pointed out that he also had another pair of boots, this time a pair of walking boots, which are also very dirty. He also had the man's coat, and this too was heavily blood stained. Dr. Winslow then told the reporter what else he had discovered.

He said that on the morning of August the 30th of that year, a woman who he was talking to when at worship at St. Finsbury Church had been spoken to by a man. The man asked a woman to come down to a certain courtyard with him and offered her one pound if she would comply. This she refused, saying that she would require double the amount. The man said he would then double the amount but still the woman did not agree. She having refused, the man doubled the amount again. But she again declined to agree. Then he asked her where the courtyard led to. And then he left. She then explained what had happened to some neighbours, and several of the neighbours followed the stranger, though keeping a careful distance.

The man turned round and said, whilst raising his hat, that he did not care that they were following him but that he knew they were doing so. Then the woman said that she had seen this man at another house, and she had followed him for a while. She saw him going into a house and was struck by his odd manner. This was on the morning when the woman known as Mackenzie was murdered. That was July the 17th. She also saw him washing his hands in the yard of the house, and she said that she saw his face most clearly. This was at 4am in the morning.

'It so happens,' said Dr Winslow, 'that I decided to keep a tab on the man. He stayed in a house nearby. And he said also he had been waiting for a telegram in order to achieve the man's arrest.

It transpired that the suspected murderer had been living with a friend of Winslow's. And this man told the doctor that he had noticed the individual's odd behaviour.

At times he would sit down and write. as many as 60 sheets of manuscript, describing various women that he had encountered, which he described as being of a low type. He also told the other occupant of the house that he had a great loathing for these sorts of women.

In the latter part of the same week, when the body was found in Pinchin Street, it was discovered that the man had completely disappeared. But he left behind him several items of clothing. In addition to this, there was a bundle of manuscripts, which the doctor examined.

He maintained that the handwriting of the letters was the same as that of letters from the Ripper received by the Central News Agency; those received by Scotland Yard were done in exactly the same hand as those of the manuscript examined at the lodgings.

The man had declared his intention that he would be going abroad. In a few days prior to the discovery of the body, which happened to be September the 10th, he was last seen in the neighbourhood of Pinchin Street. The doctor was absolutely convinced that this man, who had emigrated to America, was none other than the Ripper, and he had been inspired by a fervid religious hatred of women, especially after he had then crossed to the USA.

Inspector Swanson, who had overall charge of the investigation. then interviewed Forbes Winslow. Then Dr Winslow explained to the police detective, that he thought he had been wrongly reported in the newspaper. But he was not explicit *as to how*. He also recalled that during the time mentioned, there was a person that had come to stay at the lodgings and that this man was on business from the Toronto Trust Society.

He had been renting a large sitting room in the house where the Winslows were staying…' Dr. Winslow told the reporter that the man had explained to him that he was here on business, and that he was writing about various religious subjects. (presumably an insurance firm? - KJ).

He also told the reporter that the man had many suits of clothes and eight or nine hats; that the man kept very late hours, and that when he returned to the lodgings, he was completely silent.

'In addition, he had a pair of India rubber boots, which he had put over his existing shoes to stop them causing possible sound. On August the ninth (this had been altered to the seventh in the documents that Swanson wrote - significantly perhaps, the date of one of the murders). At that time Mrs Callahan , the landlady, was in the country, and her sister kept house in her absence.

'She was expected home that evening.' said Dr. Winslow. She'd said to him:, 'We stayed up for her till 4am, and then when (our lodger), Mr Smith, returned, he'd stated, that 'he'd had enough'. He'd had his watch stolen.' However, the landlady added afterward that 'no such thefts had taken place'.

She also said that there were towels, hanging on his wash horse, and that he had washed them himself, but there were marks of blood on the bed. The detective in charge of the Ripper inquiry confirmed with Winslow that this took place two or three days after the murder on August the ninth.

Robert Anderson, the Assistant Commissioner of Police, who took charge of the Ripper investigations, just after the conclusion of what was regarded as the last of the 'Canonical' five murders, continued to affirm his belief in the suspect being of Jewish origin. Although he modified that view and his comments, perhaps because they were judged at the time racist by the Jewish community, he continued to stand by this theory in a series of comments, which were later published in *Blackwood's Magazine,* a popular magazine of the time which Doyle sometimes contributed.

This ended in June 1910. But the series of articles was not by then entirely completed.

Anderson based his remarks on the evidence given by a solicitor called George, Kebbell, who thought that his former client, a Mr. William Grant, a sailor, had been arrested in 1895 for attacking a prostitute with a knife in the East End.

This woman was so badly wounded that William Grant was sentenced to 10 years for the assault.

At his trial, the prosecutor said the crime bore a strange resemblance to the Jack the Ripper murders, adding that the police had turned their attention to the matter but without result. Kebbell, the solicitor, believed this man was not a Jew, but an Irishman, and was the author of the previous crimes.

These sorts of claims continued to appear sporadically, both in the British and American newspapers of the time. Detective Inspector Edmund Reid, the head of the Ripper enquiry between 1888 and 1891, who had been following the work of Swanson and others, decided that he did not believe any of them implicitly, although, in his opinion, some were certainly more convincing than others. However, the Dritt suspect was certainly not one of them.

In his article in *The Morning Advertiser*, (a newspaper for Hampton on Sea where Reid had later retired to), he added this:

'Some years ago, the late Major Griffiths, in his book, *Mysteries of Police and Crime*, tried to prove that Druitt was the Ripper, though his body was found floating in the Thames seven weeks after the last Whitechapel murder, on the last day of 1888.

'Considering that there were in all, nine murders, said to have been committed by the Ripper, I think it rather wonderful that the Druitt's body should have been found in the Thames before the first of the murders were actually committed.

'Now we have Sir Robert Anderson saying that Jack the Ripper was a Jew. That I challenge him to prove. And we have a solicitor stating that Jack the Ripper was an Irishman who had been educated for the medical profession, worked as a fireman on a cattle boat, and was arrested in the very act of mutilating a woman. That is news indeed.

'Then we come to a statement from Dr. Winslow, who professes to know all about the Ripper and who states that the last Whitechapel murder committed was that of Alice McKenzie, in July 1889. The doctor is a bit out in his statement. The last murder was actually Frances Coles in Swallow Gardens on the 13th of February 1891.

'Much has been said and written, which is not true about certain mutilations having characterised these murders. If Dr. Baxter Phillips, who held the post-mortems in cooperation with Dr. Percy Clark were still alive, he would confirm my statement. And if Dr. Clark, (*police surgeon - KJ*), who resides in Spitalfields, were still alive I know he would confirm what I say is true. The number of descriptions that have been given of Jack the Ripper are truly astonishing, but I challenge anyone to prove there was a tittle of evidence against man and woman or child in connection with those cases. In fact, there is no proof that it was a man who committed the murders, as no man has ever been seen in the company of the woman who were then found dead'.

Regarding the Pinchin Street torso, he said that, in in that case, the murder in no way resembled those in Dorset Street and Henry Street.

He concluded that as all the Ripper murders were similar in character, they were all the work of a homicidal maniac. The victims were, unfortunately, of the lowest type. It was his idea that the perpetrator was a man who had become insane, and added that probably he was a man of the lowest class.

One of the suppositions was that he was a medical student, or something of that sort. However, there was nothing of a professional character about those inflicted wounds. The bodies were simply slashed about from head to foot.

In one case, he said, there was exhibited a certain knowledge of butchery, or of killing animals. The Dorset Street murder was done inside a room so that he had plenty of time. But that the others were committed in a courtyard or a street.

When asked if he thought the murders were all the work of one man, he replied,' I'm not so certain of that. You see if you publish details of cases of that kind, and the evidence that the inquests then appeared in the newspapers, a weak-minded person would be induced to emulate the crime, which, incidentally, was evidently done with a butcher's knife, or a table knife. Because of this, it was thought that the deeds were perpetrated by a butcher, or someone acquainted with the killing or cleaning of animals. It does not necessarily need to have been a butcher because some people can do that work'.

He did, however, believe that one man was responsible for three of them though he would not say which one.

As to what happened to the Ripper, he said that he assumed that anything might have happened to him. 'He may have died or been shut up in a lunatic asylum. Each person involved in the murders since that time had held different views,' he concluded.

As we have seen, the body of the murdered woman Frances Coles was found in a railway arch but speculation regarding the truth about 'the five canonical Ripper murders' did not end there.

In fact, there were further developments. This case more than any other, which was examined by senior police detectives at The Yard at the time of the conclusion to the Ripper murders, proved to be for them the most convincing in the production of a suspect who may well have been capable of the other murders; however, against this man no charge could really be made *through lack of prime facia evidence.*

Chief Inspector Swanson and his team knew only too well that this suspect had motive and immense opportunity, yet it was the sheer lack of physical evidence, particularly primary and forensic evidence, which led to the abandonment of the case, much to their immense annoyance and frustration.

After some prolonged intensive teamwork, the detective team discovered that the nameless woman who had been discovered under the railway arch in early 1891, was indeed Frances Coles. This woman had a reputation as a drifter and was well known to locals. She had had an intermittent relationship with a man called James Sadler, and in fact, Sadler was subsequently one of those charged on suspicion of the murder of Coles.

For a short while this man, a violent drunk, with a fixation about a knife he carried permanently with him, was incarcerated for further police questioning. The senior detective put in charge of the case was an extremely seasoned and capable officer called Inspector Swanson. Swanson discovered the following facts about this man who was known to the Coles, and he subsequently gave a detailed statement to his interrogator.

Following his interview with Sadler, DCI Swansom went to Chatham where Sadler's wife was then living. Sadler's wife explained how Sadler had had a number of different jobs, but he did not often hold them down for long because of his constant drinking. At one time he had become a conductor, but this has only last 6-months. She told Swansom that he had evidently been working for short spells since then, in several warehouses, but that during the 11 years that she spent living with her husband, she did remember that he carried a knife, which she described as 'no ordinary pocketknife,' and that it had a brass decoration on the handle; and that he was most secretive about it.

He had left her in the August of the previous year and 7 months elapsed had then elapsed, before she heard from him again. The couple had met up near the railway station at Bethnal Green and they had then walked down the street together to the railway arch, where the murder had previously occurred.

She revealed that, following his being released from work at the London docks that day, several men had walked from the docks towards her, but she did not see Sadler with them. In fact, he appeared an hour later at the railway arch. They then together visited a local the pub and after that, he went on to quarrel with some people in the restaurant nearby.

Together they then proceeded towards Whitechapel church where she became afraid, and ran away from him. She then returned to Chatham where her mother was then living.

She explained that this was the last she saw of him, until the August of 1888. She told the officer that when drunk he was very irritable, but, when asked if he ever attacked her, she simply would not reply. She said to Swanson, in relation to the place where the murder had been committed, that Saddler had said: "it was miraculous that any person could do such a thing and get off with it."

The complete lack of any further forensic evidence regarding Sadler would have played a large part in his subsequent dismissal by police as a major suspect. However, it is clear, looking at the records which have survived, that as far as Chief Inspector Swanson was concerned, Sadler was a most important suspect. His profile matched all the evidence Scotland Yard had assembled by then.

In December 1891, for example, Swanson read a letter from a man who knew an old gentleman. This individual had been, for a short while, a lodger with the Sadlers. The old man had explained that when he was living with the couple as a lodger, Sadler not only often assaulted his wife but also treated her cruelly; and he repeatedly threatened to take her life; and that his wife was afraid to live with him. He himself locked his bedroom door at night for he thought that Saddler was 'highly dangerous.'

Then, on the 16th of May 1892, another report was obtained by Swanson at the Lambeth police court where Sadler had been charged with threatening to kill his wife. The magistrate heard evidence to the effect that the husband had threatened to cut his wife's throat on the 9th of May and that she was extremely afraid of him.

There are several reasons why I believe that Conan Doyle, along with Inspector Swanson and other senior detectives, would have been quite convinced by the evidence they'd collected regarding Sadler, but were frustrated, by being unable to proceed with the charge against him because of the lack of reliable and conclusive forensic evidence.

Sadler was clearly violent towards his wife and had threatened to cut her throat. He was frequently addicted to long drinking bouts and, moreover, he could, without inhibition, travel from one end of the East End to the other, without being intercepted; also he had no permanent abode, and for many years was not living with his wife.

Most important of all, however, was the fact that Sadler clearly possessed a dangerous knife to which he was much attached, and for which he nurtured a strange obsession. It is more than conceivable that, after the death of Frances Coles, this man simply moved on to pastures new and that might certainly have ended up somewhere in America; but sadly, the identity of this peripatetic killer in that vast continent still remains something of a mystery.

In his book of memoirs, *Scotland Yard and Its Secrets*, the author H. J. Allam, expressed his view about the Whitechapel murders of 1888.

'Despite the illusory operations of many, to Sherlock Holmes, there was no doubt in my own mind whatsoever as to the identity of the criminal. And if our London detectives possess the powers, and might have had recourse to the methods of foreign police forces practising at that time, (*the author here means more advanced data retrieval and forensic analysis techniques, like those much later employed by the FBI and the French surete - KJ*) he might then have been brought to justice, but the guilty sometimes escape through the workings of a system designed to protect the innocent person wrongly accused of crime. And many cases may be used to disparage your British detective, or rather to be hailed as a proof of the scrupulous fairness with which they discharge their duties.'

Sadly, however, this scrupulous attitude on behalf of certain police detectives did not always apply to some persons that were arrested and later put on trial and subsequently jailed for murders or mutilations, as was the case with Oscar Slater, and George Edalji. In the case of these accusations, the evidence was found by Conan Doyle to be faulty or not properly understood. And part of that can be explained by the clumsiness, or lack of coordination in collecting of evidence.

In our own period, things are much different. Since 1888, the collecting of evidence and the examination of forensic detail and its recording have become much more advanced and more enabled. But in Conan Doyle's period, such techniques were only in their infancy.

CONCLUSION

We shall probably now never know the true identity or the name of Jack the Ripper. But I do think that, because of Conan Doyle's research and that of others, like the psychiatrist Krafft - Ebing and not least, the imaginative and innovative German criminologist, Dr. Hans Gross, Doyle and others had learned much about the collecting and interpretation of both forensic and witness evidence; especially at scenes of crime; highly important also, as Hans Gross pointed out, were those factors which might be observed and interpreted, regarding the behaviour of criminals. Armed with this information, we now possess a much clearer and more empirically based profile of the sexual psychopath.

And that profile was very sharply delineated and made obvious to the creator of the earliest of all forensically trained consulting detectives, Mr. Sherlock Holmes of Baker Street.

Fig 17.Conam Doyle's famous criminal investigator was only too aware of
the importance of the accurate recording of scenes of crime evidence,
and no less so than evidence born from tobacco traces. Here is Holmes,
examining a cigar which has been left by one of three murderers at a
vengeance killing in RESI.

It should hardly surprise us then, that this most famous fictional figure
of Holmes remains, even until this day, the literary progenitor *per example* of
all subsequent forensic and criminal investigators, both in the worlds of
crime fact and fiction. * And it is this, I am certain, which is greatly

responsible for his almost mythological status and the great regard for him shown by his many followers.

*Many fans of the superbly conceived Dr Thorndyke stories by the scientifically trained author, Richard Austin Freeman, that appeared in newspapers in Britain during the period; (when, the Holmes stories were still being published in The Strand), will agree that the forensic methods used in these tales, along with their period settings, made them almost unique.

Fig. 18. Sherlock Holmes was the world's most original forensic Detective, who even had his own small a chemical laboratory. Illustration by Sidney Paget from *The Naval Treaty* in *The Strand*.

Fig. 19. Dr Joseph Bell, the Edinburgh Doctor of Medicine who taught Conan Doyle the science of patient diagnosis without the patent being required to give any indication as to his or her complaint. Bell's technique was based on the principles of observation and deduction, which qualities Conan Doyle subsequently bestowed on his immortal detective, and which Doyle also drew from the archetypical crime stories of Edgar Allan Poe.

SHERLOCK HOLMES' USE OF DRUGS.

SECTION 1. TOBACCO

Victorian epithet: 'Fill the bowl, you jolly sour, And burn all sorrow to a coal.'

It is an autumn night. Outside, the rain lashes against the windows with persistent fury and the dank streets are awash. Only a solitary gas lamp pierces the unremitting gloom. London huddles under the relentless fury of the storm.

But inside, behind the heavy velvet curtains of an upstairs room in Baker Street, a more tranquil scene unfolds before us. The room, though small and cluttered, welcomes us with its blazing fire and comfortable, upholstered chairs. A hiss of gas combines with the familiar smell of an oil lamp to produce a sense of domestic warmth. Portraits of Victorian celebrities hang from the ornate walls and before the fire is a luxuriant bearskin rug. And into that rug descend the slippered feet of a lean but impeccably dressed man. His keen eyes glitter in the soft gaslight. On his lap he has unfolded a medieval palimpsest which he is studying with such undeflected concentration, that he barely notices the acrid wreaths of blue tobacco smoke, spiralling upwards towards the ceiling.

For two hours he has been sitting here, motionless, like a spider at the centre of its web, pondering the intricacies of these arcane markings. And so, the comfortable room has become a dense fog-enveloped oven, more deadly perhaps than the great Grimpen Mire. Long since has his companion, Dr Watson, retired to the sanctuary of the upstairs bedroom where he is allowed to breathe freely, and where his visibility is permitted to extend beyond a yard…

A somewhat irreverent glimpse of the Baker Street ménage, you may feel. And to some extent I must agree. Yet, like all lampoons, the truth is somehow very near at hand, behind the obvious absurdity. It is quite true that scarcely a depiction of Sherlock Holmes appears before the public without some mention of his pipe, be it the meerschaum of apocryphal origin or the more accurate clay version. The smokescreens in the chambers of 221B are as much a part of the Holmesian totality as the pea-soup fogs, from whose depths the unkindly criminal springs on his victim.

Yet how accurate is our traditional view of that world? Would it disturb many of us to know that Holmes smoked as many cigarettes as he had recourse to his pipe tobacco? Would it shock us to consider for a moment that the habit may indeed have had its origins in a profound neurosis?

These are deep waters, my dear Watson. Yet let us set the record straight. Why not? To the man who cried "Give me data!" it would have seemed unnatural to do otherwise…

THE BEFORE BREAKFAST PIPE - THE HABIT

"Don't you smoke? Then you will excuse me if I light my pipe". ~ILLU.

"Tobacco smoke is the one element in which, by our European manners, men can sit silent together without embarrassment and where no man is bound to speak one word more than he has actually and veritably got to say…" - *Thomas Carlyle.*

If we have a distinct picture of Baker Street and its unforgettable sitting-room, that picture is surely incomplete without the acrid fumes of tobacco, the pipe-rack and the tobacco stuffed into the toe-end of a Persian slipper. And the image of Sherlock Holmes himself is quite without credence if we do not grant him the indulgence of a pipe. So all-pervasive is the tobacco aroma that curls its way around the tiny sitting-room at 221B that we must only assume Mrs Hudson to have been a long-suffering and intrepid woman. Apart from the clutter of papers and bric-a-brac on the mantlepiece and working surfaces, the walls and ceiling must have been stained to a dark brown and the daily debris of Holmes own "plugs and dottles" would surely be tolerated only by the strongest of stomach.

Perhaps the fire started by Moriarty's henchmen provided her with the perfect opportunity for a general cleansing and redecoration of these famous rooms. In our very first encounter with the detective, the compliant Watson is given an unequivocal warning:

"You don't mind the smell of strong tobacco, I hope?"

"I always smoke 'ship's' myself", I answered."

Fig, 21. The humble clay pipe, of which Sherlock Holmes was fond, and which Watson records in COPP, he frequently smoked when he was in a 'meditative mood.'

Fig. 22 . The American actor who first brought Holmes to the theatre, seen here holding a straight briar pipe, the correct canonical choice for Doyle's pipe-addicted sleuth. The meerschaum pipe, often seen in advertisements, etc., is an invention of Hollywood.

It was indeed fortunate that Watson was already a slave of the tobacco weed, or his patience would have been sorely tested.

What were the origins of Holmes' and Watson's addiction? And where did both men pick up the habit?

In Holmes' case, there was a compulsive need to smoke. Late on in his association with Watson, he attempted to justify this compulsion.

"You have not, I hope, learned to despise my pipe and my lamentable tobacco? It has to take the place of food these days".

"But why not eat?"

"Because the faculties become refined when you starve them".

Whilst the cocaine formed a means of escape from the dreary world of hum-drum criminality, the tobacco acted as a strop to Holmes' razor-sharp brain. It is a wonder that Holmes survived so long, considering the continual onslaught to his digestive and respiratory organs. It is well-known that cocaine acts as a stimulant to the mental processes. A combination of both cocaine and tobacco must have achieved considerable results, producing a rarefied mental state. If Holmes had a public-school education, then the practice of consuming "snouts" covertly behind the games hut is not an unlikely possibility. By the period of *A Study in Scarlet* he had progressed to the full complement of pipe, cigarettes and cigars. There is the possibility that, once contracted, the habit served to assist an already nervous sensibility, prone to neurotic fits of melancholia.

With Watson, we are on less speculative ground. As an army doctor, it is no wonder that he smoked. The services provided duty-free tobacco in large quantities, and we have his own word for it that he smoked "ship's", a rough, coarse cut tobacco popular amongst sailors of the period.

The frequency of tobacco consumption may be assessed by a careful reckoning of its many instances in the Canon. Holmes smokes cigarettes on no less than fourteen separate occasions. He has recourse to cigars twelve times, and the pipe features a staggering fifty-four times. In addition, he takes snuff, but this may have been a passing fancy. Mycroft, his brother, also indulged in snuff and it may be from him that the habit was contracted. These statistics mean nothing in themselves. But when we come to examine Holmes' consumption in detail, we realise that his recourse to the drug was both unremitting and dangerous.

In *The Man With The Twisted Lip*, for example, we begin the narrative by finding the detective in an eastern-style opium den in Upper Swandam Lane. Holmes remarks to Watson, with some amusement:

"I suppose that you imagine that I have added opium-smoking to cocaine injections and all the other little weaknesses . . . "

On the drive down to Kent, Holmes shakes himself and "(lights) up his pipe". In our very first encounter with the detective, the compliant Watson is given an unequivocal warning:

"You don't mind the smell of strong tobacco, I hope?"

What were the origins of Holmes' and Watson's addiction? And where did both men pick up the habit?

In Holmes' case, there was a compulsive need to smoke. Late on in his association with Watson, he attempted to justify this compulsion.

Fig. 23. Holmes was frequently subject to 'black moods,' and severe depression. Thus, he used drugs to establish for himself a c0ncentration and purpose. Here he is, on vacation in Cornwall, walking the moods on The Lizard Peninsula, a place of great isolation and where his friend, Watson, hopes Holmes will eventually overcome the effects of his addiction. Drawing by Sidney Paget, to accompany *The Devil's Foot* published in The Strand in 1910.

"You have not, I hope, learned to despise my pipe and my lamentable tobacco? It has to take the place of food these days".

"But why not eat?"

"Because the faculties become refined when you starve them".

Whilst the cocaine formed a means of escape from the dreary world of hum-drum criminality, the tobacco acted as a strop to Holmes' razor-sharp brain. It is a wonder that Holmes survived so long, considering the continual onslaught to his digestive and respiratory organs. It is well-known that cocaine acts as a stimulant to the mental processes. A combination of both cocaine and tobacco must have achieved considerable results, producing a rarefied mental state. Clearly, Holmes picked up the habit as a young man, for in *The Musgrave Ritual*, an early case, dating from his student days, we find him smoking cigarettes:

However, this is not an isolated case. In *The Hound Of The Baskervilles* he begins by smoking a number of cigarettes. On leaving the rooms at Baker Street, Watson is asked to instruct Bradley's, the tobacconist, to send up "a pound of the strongest shag tobacco". On returning, Watson imagines that "a fire had broken out", so dense with smoke is the sitting-room. The conversation that follows is not without its humorous side:

"Caught cold, Watson?" said he.

"No, it's this poisonous atmosphere".

"I suppose it is pretty thick, now that you mention it".

Holmes then admits to Watson he has "consumed an incredible amount of tobacco".

This pipe binge is equalled only, perhaps, by the example described for us in *The Golden Pince-Nez*. At Yoxley Old Place, near Chatham, Holmes and Watson meet Professor Coram who is a chain smoker of alarming rapidity. He offers Holmes an Egyptian cigarette one of many which he has supplied, tailor-made, from "Ionides of Alexandria". Watson soon observes that Holmes is smoking them with an extraordinary rapidity, to such an extent that the professor is led to observe, "why you are even a quicker smoker than myself". His reply is indicative of a lifelong passion for the weed:

"I am a connoisseur", said he, taking another cigarette from the box - his fourth - and lighting it from the stub of that which he had finished.

Of course, in this instance, it was Holmes' specific intention to litter the carpet with cigarette ash I order to trace the footprint of young Willoughby Smith's murderer. But note that he refers to the cigarettes in question as "excellent", proof positive of his position as a devotee.

The frequency of Holmes' recourse to the pipe is also indicated by Watson's references to a pipe in relation to specific mealtimes and parts of the day. In *The Hound* we find him pushing away his "untasted breakfast" and lighting "the unsavoury pipe which was the companion of his deepest meditations". In *The Engineer's Thumb* we find him lounging about in the sitting-room, "smoking his before-breakfast pipe". In *Charles Augustus Milverton*, we discover Holmes and Watson "smoking our morning pipe", after breakfast. In Wisteria Lodge Holmes speaks of a chaotic case "over an evening pipe" whilst in *The Cardboard Box* we find both partners chatting "over our cigars". Finally, in *The Three Garrideb*s, Holmes knocks out the ashes of his "after-breakfast pipe" and then slowly refills it. The conclusion we must inevitably draw from all this is that Holmes began at any time between the hours of 7 and 9 am, paused for breakfast, then resumed with two or possibly more. Maybe he then reverted to cigars or cigarettes, but he most certainly ended the day sharing a pipe with his roommate. The actual number of cigarettes consumed in a typical morning must have been considerable (twenty or thirty at least) since Watson carefully records in *The Norwood Builder* that "The carpet round his chair was littered with cigarette ends, and with the early editions of the morning papers". If Holmes found that "a concentrated atmosphere helps a concentration of thought", it helps to explain why he showed a reluctance to surrender the habit. Even well into his later years we find him still puffing away:

"A half-smoked, sodden cigar hung from the corner of his mouth, and as he sat down, he struck a match and relit it."

Clearly the warnings issued by the members of the medical profession (and we must remember that the good doctor was one) went unheeded by the detective. Yet by the 1880's the connection between heavy smoking and diseases of the respiratory system had been clearly established. A study, completed in 1859, demonstrated that of 68 patients in a hospital at Montpelier, France, who had cancer of the lips, tongue, tonsils and other parts of the mouth, all used tobacco and 66 of them smoked short-stemmed clay pipes.

The actor William Gillette, posing as Holmes, smoking a briar. The word was originally 'briere' from the French, who discovered that the root of this plant was durable and would not crack when subjected to heat.

Holmes' own attitude to Watson's own tobacco habits is interesting" since it provides us with a good insight into his personality. It is evident that he was not without some guilty feelings upon the subject - feelings which he projected onto the long-suffering doctor. Perhaps his rough treatment of Watson harked back to the early days when Watson had the effrontery to describe the detective as a "self-poisoner by cocaine and tobacco".

Ensconced in an Oxfordshire inn, Holmes remarks to Watson:

"Mrs Merrilow does not object to tobacco, Watson, if you wish to indulge your filthy habits".

Some commentators have detected a slight worsening of the relationship between the two men in later years. It is apt therefore, that Watson should apply this simile in *The Creeping Man*:

"As an institution I was like the . . . shag tobacco ..."

Mention of Watson's own tobacco consumption is much scantier. A pipe is referred to on seven occasions, a cigar only once and cigarettes twice. His consumption may well have been more moderate than that of Holmes, especially since he was a married man. Yet in *The Priory School* there is an indication that he occasionally chain-smoked:

"Holmes sat down on a boulder and rested his chin in his hands. I had smoked two cigarettes before he moved."

It comes as something of a surprise to the student of the Holmes stories that, although we are inundated with references to the consumption of tobacco in a variety of forms, there is specific mention of only three pipes smoked by Holmes. In *A Study in Scarlet*, the first of these stories, Holmes does not appear to smoke a pipe. He merely refers to his consumption of "strong tobacco:" later, he offers a cigarette to a visitor. (Watson, on the other hand, talks merely about "puffing at my pipe").

The Sign of Four, the second of the recorded cases (although not chronologically) is the first narrative to mention an "old briar-root pipe." Afterwards, reference is made only to a "pipe." We hear nothing further of the briar until we come to *The Man with The Twisted Lip* where it crops up again as "an old brier pipe." Thereafter the briar vanishes into obscurity.

The briar (brier) had been introduced into this country in 1859 and by Holmes' day had established an immense popularity. Its particularly hard properties make it ideal for a sturdy pipe. The root of the White Heath (*Erica Arborea*), a native of France and Corsica, is the origin of the briar.

Holmes demonstrated a particular predilection for the briar in *The Yellow Face,* where an amber-stemmed briar forms the basis of his deductions. The pipe in question had a long stem, but it was the amber which drew complimentary remarks from Holmes. Most briars of the period had their stems made from horn or vulcanite. Amber was expensive. For instance, an amber cigarette holder, advertised in the *Army and Navy Stores Catalogue* of 1907 which came complete in a silver case, cost as much as 32 shillings. Holmes, who made a study of pipes, remarked that "nothing has more individuality (than a pipe) save, perhaps, watches and boot-laces." Elsewhere, he observes:

"I wonder how many real amber mouthpieces there are in London. Some people think a fly in it is a sign. Why, it is quite a branch of the trade, the putting of sham flies into the sham amber."

The yellowish, translucent fossil resin, found chiefly along the southern shores of the Baltic, was much prized by collectors and manufacturers alike, but the entombed insects which it often contained were a sign of its authenticity. It was this aspect that the manufacturers of artificial amber mouthpieces strove to imitate.

We are not told the exact shape or even type of briar that Holmes owned but possibly it may have possessed an amber mouthpiece. Briars or briers - the more modern spelling is the anglicised form of the original French word - came in a bewildering variety of shapes and we must not assume that his own pipe was the curved variety so often depicted. In fact, the great majority of briars were straight pipes with short stems. Most of them had a silver band with a hallmark indented. The "dry-smoker" variety with a detachable bowl was very popular at this period. Briars with vulcanite or horn stems ranged in price between 2 shillings and 3 shillings. An amber-stemmed briar cost as much as 4 shillings.

The pipe which held Holmes' attention cost seven shillings and sixpence, which only indicates that it was in the luxury range. It is not surprising, therefore, that the pipe had been mended twice "with silver bands." Grosvenor mixture, selling at eightpence an ounce, was one of the more expensive mixtures.

Fig 25. In this drawing which appeared In The Strand Magazine in August 1914, where it served alongside an announcement, describing 'Conan Doyle's great new Sherlock Holmes serial, *The Valley of Fear*.. Holmes here, who is attempting a translation of the agent Porlock's cryptographic message, regarding Professor Moriarty's murderous plans, is smoking a short, straight briar with what looks like a vulcanite stem. The drawing is by Frank Wiles.

Fig. 26. Watson may well have used tobacco as a way of
lightening his mood and possibly also a tincture of
laudanum to relieve pain endured by him from a
shoulder shot through by a jezail bullet. Drawing
By Douglas Walters.

The second of the pipes to be specifically mentioned by Watson was
the "long cherrywood which was wont to replace his clay when he was in
a disputatious rather than a meditative mood." Like the briar, this makes
an exceptionally brief appearance, but its long-curved stem and
comparatively small bowl would undoubtedly have proved impractical on
expeditions. Cherrywood has long been a popular pipe wood, mainly due
to the fragrant, sweet smell of the cherrywood, but it is less durable than
the briar.

Of all the pipes in the canon, it is the clay pipe which receives most
attention. This was clearly Holmes' favourite counsellor and is variously

described as "the unsavoury pipe," the "old and oily clay pipe, "the "black clay pipe," "clay pipe," and "the oldest and foulest of his pipes."

Of all the various types popular in the Victorian period, the clay pipe cuts across class divisions. It had the advantage of being cheap and easily mass-produced. If broken, it was easily replaceable. It came in a variety of sizes and types and the designs which appeared on the bowls are today an important feature among collectors. The "churchwarden" variety, still popular today, was just one of many.

There was a period after the mid-century when the clay pipe waned in its popularity, owing to the 1859 report, already mentioned. It was thought then that the high incidence of lung disease was directly attributable to clay-pipe smoking. Now, of course, we know it to be the tar by-product of tobacco *per se*.

By the 1880's the manufacture of clay pipes had again risen and within the metropolis there were a vast number of firms producing them. Holmes no doubt obtained his pipe from either F A Albert of Devonshire Street or the much larger Triplex Pipe Manufacturing Company of Cecil Court, Charing Cross Road (1895). Both firms produced clay pipes of distinction in their day.

Holmes favoured a type of tobacco known as "shag". The pedigree of this particular type dates back to George 111 and is a preparation of tobacco rather than a specific leaf type. Any strong tobacco cut into fine shreds can be classed as "shag so Watson's description is hardly specific. "Golden Archer's a Virginia shag of the period, sold at 2s and 11 d per 1 lb, but judging by the "acrid fumes" produced by Holmes in an afternoon's sitting, one must imagine it to have been a deal stronger.

Watson appears to have switched from the coarse "ship's" tobacco some time before he met Miss Mary Morstan. For instance, in *The Crooked Man* Holmes remarks to him:

"Hum! You still smoke the Arcadia mixture of your bachelor days, then. There's no mistaking that fluffy ash upon your coat."

Arcadia, or Arcadia Mixture was mixture made by Surbrug's and was an American Cut Tobacco. Unlike the cheap shag of Holmes' liking, this was an expensive brand with a high leaf content,

Fig 27. Holmes in one of his many smoking reveries, seen here in *Shoscombe Old Place*. Illustration by Frank Wiles for The Strand Magazine, 1912.

It sold at 11 shillings and 3d per 1 lb. Watson evidently graduated to expensive tastes.

There is no record of Watson's own pipe, but I fancy that, as a military man, he would plump for a short-stemmed straight briar, reflecting his no-nonsense steady, reliable character. "The Bridge Player's Pipe" with a silver mounted vulcanite stem offered by Army and Navy at 2s and 6d fits just such a description.

The other two brand names which crop up in the Canon are Cavendish and Bird's-eye. Cavendish occurs in *Silver Blaze* where it figures alongside other oddments:

"We all filed into the front room and sat round the central table, while the Inspector unlocked a square tin box and laid a small heap of things before us. There was a box of vestas . . . an A D P briar-root pipe, a pouch of sealskin with half an ounce of long-cut Cavendish…"

The ADP pipe was an Alfred Dunhill Pipe and the vestas were unlike the vestas of our own period, being longer and more sulphurous. (Their manufacture involved a high incidence of disease among workers). Cavendish was a medium price pipe tobacco, which sold at 4s 6d per lb.

Bird's Eye, which features in Holmes' remarks in *The Sign Of Four*, was a popular type available in three qualities. The high grade sold at 4s 9d, the coarse cut at 5s 7d and the "First Quality" at 4s 9d. A number of manufactures produced it, Archer's, Franklyn's (Bristol), Wile's and Lambert & Butler's amongst them.

As we know, Holmes kept his tobacco in the toe-end of a Persian slipper. Such a custom indicates his high rate of consumption, for the tobacco, being exposed to air, would undoubtedly dry quickly. But he also owned more than one pouch. Sealskin pouches feature in more than one of the stories, but as to the make of Holmes' own pouch, there is insufficient evidence. Pouches were also available in rubber and leather at that period and have changed little in appearance over the years. A pouch could be picked up for under 2 shillings.

The pipe rack, which gains mention only once, would either have been wall-mounted or it may have stood upright on a shelf. These were invariably richly ornamented and were produced in oak, mahogany or alloys. A standard pipe rack, carrying seven pipes, cost as much as 5 shillings. The cigarette case which Holmes left behind at The Reichenbach Falls with a message to Watson attached to it was made of silver. These were often engraved with the owner's initials and could cost anything up to 50 shillings - an extravagant memento to leave on the edge of a precipice!

A visitor to 221B Baker Street would have discovered the cigars in the coal scuttle. This seemed a rather bizarre custom to Dr Watson who thought fit to mention it in *The Musgrave Ritual*, but in fact it was not an uncommon practice at the time. The modern coal scuttle with its bucket-like shape was but one of many that graced the hearth sides of late Victorian England and the type which Holmes most probably used, was a rectangular box affair, lined with a tight-shutting lid, japanned black and with brass mounts.

Holmes' choice in cigars is unstated, but one would imagine the Havana range to have served his liking. These were by no means cheap even then, a bundle of British made cheroots costing 17s and 6d (five in a bundle). The Indian cigars (which feature in Holmes' monograph on tobacco), were much cheaper (at 1s and 8d but considerably inferior. His taste in cigarettes was that of a "connoisseur," and he showed a liking for Professor Coram's Egyptian blend. The Alexandrian Variety, which he smoked in *The Golden Pince-Nez*, (Hadges Nessim), retailed at 2 shillings per 25 or 7s 9d per 100.

Fig. 28. One of Holmes' favourite pipes, the humble clay.
This is typical of the Victorian style of clay pipe Holmes used.

2. COCAINE, HOLMES' USE OF IT AND VICTORIAN VIEWS ABOUT THE DRUG.

Mike Jay, the author and cultural historian who co-curated The British archive collection relating to drugs, medicines and their history, has written an interesting article on the internet site of the Wellcome Collection's 'High Society' exhibition. In the article, he expressed his relief that we are now, in the 21st Century, starting 'to have a 'grown-up' conversation about current illegal drugs', and he also usefully examines how some of the drugs that we know of today came emerged into Victorian society:

'The 19th century was a crucial period of drug-taking development both in terms of potency and plurality. The Victorians took not just alcohol and opium but cannabis, coca, mescal and, with the invention of the hypodermic needle in the 1840s, morphine and heroin. The 19th century also saw the origins of drug control, and the medicalisation of addiction to these substances.

Sherlock Holmes, as a drug user, was experimenting with some of these substances when the pharmacopoeia of the western world was being substantially revised and expanded. Cocaine, its benefits and its possible disadvantages, was only just being understood by pharmacologists and the long-term effects of drugs like cocaine, heroin and morphine were far from clear.

According to Watson (YELL), Holmes only "turned to the drug as a protest against the monotony of existence." As we have already seen, his temperament often swung between severe melancholia and nervous hysteria.

Why cocaine? Well, the drug acts on the system fast. In five or ten minutes the effects are felt and they persist for at least twenty minutes afterwards. There are no violent withdrawal symptoms as there are with the alkaloids, and the user develops no severe physical addiction.

Holmes' depression could be banished in no time at all to be replaced by a delicious feeling of rarefied pleasure. And since Holmes perpetually abused his mental and physical constitution with "constant hard work," and would often work flat-out for a period of days without sleep, the cocaine would sustain him during these periods.

As I have demonstrated, there are clearly discernible changes in the user's general demeanour after long usage:

In YELL Holmes is described as "untiring and indefatigable" a clear indication of cocaine dependency. The insomnia referred to in TWIS is a classic symptom of cocaine use. So too is the extreme pallor of his face, a condition known as "*asthenopia*" and caused by excess adrenalin in the blood. Heightened sensory ability and the "minute and yet abstracted" gaze mentioned in IDEN also correspond to the classic picture of the cocaine addict.

As Jack Tracy and Jim Berkey have shown, in their classic book about Holmes and cocaine, [1] five of the cases in which cocaine figures or is given a passing mention span the period 1887-1889 and after 1887 there are marked signs of mental deterioration.

By December 1898 Watson reports: "For years I had weaned him from that drug mania which had threatened once to check his remarkable career." In the year that followed, 1896, very few cases of investigation are reported, indicating some kind of breakdown.

By March of the following year Holmes seems to have suffered another breakdown, caused partly by cocaine abuse but also overwork. For a year Holmes remained relatively inactive and was undoubtedly extremely ill. People who develop this degree of dependency on cocaine often lose weight (Holmes was ascetic-looking) and ultimately display signs of gradual mental deterioration. And in many of the cases which take place after 1897, there are clear signs of a diminution of Holmes' powers.

Psychologically, the cocaine addict may become defensive (Holmes was extremely sensitive to attack) and exhibit a paranoid tendency.

---

[1] 'Subcutaneously, My Dear Watson.'

Three years after Holmes and Watson met, a young doctor who worked in Dr Sigmund Freud's clinic in Vienna amazed eye specialists with his discovery of the anaesthetic powers of cocaine employed during eye operations. However, it was not Carl Koller himself but the zealous Dr Sigmund Freud who pioneered and publicised the drug, and he particularly recommended it in cases of depression and also offered it to morphine addicts.

Freud entered the Ophthalmological Department of Vienna in March 1885, having been appointed Lecturer in Neuropathology. Now in the August of 1885, his article on cocaine, suggesting the subcutaneous injection of the drug as a cure for morphine, appeared in the English medical journal, *The Lancet*. Since Watson was at that time in residence at Baker Street, we can assume that Holmes, with his interest in drugs, read the article, and then acted upon it. Morphine, with its unpleasant side effects and fast dependency and subsequent addiction, had already threatened his operational effectiveness as a detective and he was desperate for a release from Morpheus, the God of Dreams.

We may assume it was likely that sometime between April and December, 1887, Holmes may have travelled to Vienna and arranged for a consultation with Dr Freud. What the content of their conversation was we shall never now know, but it is conceivable that Freud tried to dissuade Holmes from using the drug. By December of the same year Freud had become extremely alarmed at the psychological dependence of the users of cocaine and had meanwhile turned to hypnotic suggestion as an alternative method of probing and ameliorating his patients' problems.

Six months later, Holmes, who had perhaps ignored Freud's advice, was already fulfilling and solving special cases with apparent ease. Among these were "The Adventure of the Paradol Chamber", "the curious goings on at the Amateur Mendicant Society", the death of Mrs Stewart of Lauder, the case of Bert Stevens, the "terrible murderer;" and "The Singular Adventures of the Grice Patersons In The Island of Uffa".

Although Watson had been married for about a year now, he nevertheless maintained links with his old companion. In *The Five Orange*

Pips (September 1887), we find him spending his evening at Baker Street "deep in one of Clark Russell's sea stories, until the howl of the gale from without seemed to blend with the text, and the splash of the rain to lengthen out into the long awash of the sea waves. My wife was on a visit to her aunt's, and for a few days I was a dweller once more in my old quarters at Baker Street."

One wonders what *precisely* were the marital arrangements, which allowed the doctor to accompany his companion at a moment's notice or to undertake, unannounced to his wife, a complete night's vigil (*The Red-Headed League*). Speculation has wandered far and wide about Watson's proclivity for the female sex (one suspects that there was about him something of the Victorian male chauvinist), but evidence of marital irregularities, is there none.

Three weeks before the bizarre tale of *The Red-Headed League* was brought to Baker Street by the corpulent Mr Jabez Wilson, the peculiar circumstances of Dr Percy Trevelyan and his lodger, Mr Blessington, were laid before the detective and his biographer. (RESI). On the arrival of the young doctor it is revealed by Watson that Dr. Trevelyan is the author of a "monograph upon obscure nervous lesions".

W.S. Baring-Gould, the Sherlockian writer and biographer, believed that "Watson planned shortly to resume an active role in medicine" and that "his knowledge of Dr Trevelyan's obscure monograph would indicate that he was 'boning up'." Perhaps Watson at this time thought of becoming a psychiatrist, since the work was on "nervous lesions."

Bearing in mind the recent breakdown that he had seen his companion through, it is small wonder that Watson should interest himself in nervous disorders that might apply to his friend.

One can imagine Watson's consternation, therefore, when, on confronting Mrs Hudson in his Kensington rooms in the November of that same year, he heard that Holmes was dying! Although Holmes had actually created an elaborate sham to entrap the malignant Sumatran planter, Culverton Smith, (he had already murdered a young man called Victor Savage - a crime which Holmes was investigating), and that he was found by Watson soon after to be physically healthy, there are clear indications of physical deterioration in the detective. ("This morning when I saw his bones sticking out of his face and his great bright eyes looking at me I could stand no more of it" observes Mrs Hudson).

OPIUM, AND THE CURIOUS CASE OF THE OPIUM DEN

'Isa Whitney, brother of the late Elias Whitney, D.D., Principal of the Theological College of St. George's, was much addicted to opium. The habit grew upon him, as I understand, from some foolish freak when he was at college; for having read De Quincey's description of his dreams and sensations, he had drenched his tobacco with laudanum, in an attempt to produce the same effects. He found, as so many more have done, that the practice is easier to attain than to get rid of, and for many years he continued to be a slave to the drug, an object of mingled horror and pity to his friends and relatives. I can see him now, with yellow, pasty face, drooping lids, and pin-point pupils, all huddled in a chair, the wreck and ruin of a noble man.'

So begins Watson's account of *The Adventure of The Man with The Twisted Lip.* The questions that Sherlock Holmes aficionados must consider are: was Isa Whitney a purely fictional invention, did Holmes smoke opium and was Sherlock Holmes actually addicted to opium?

Who exactly was Isa Whitney?

At first glance, it seems he was the brother of an ecclesiastical cleric. Was Whitney also a student of theology? Most likely. But why and how did he become so deeply influenced by the works of De Quincey?

De Quincey, who was well known to Conan Doyle, and who, similarly, lived for some years in Edinburgh, was in his formative years, greatly alienated from his solid, prosperous mercantile family by his sensitivity and precocity. At the age of 17, he ran away to Wales and then lived *incognito* in London (1802–03). There he formed a friendship with a young prostitute named Ann, who made a lasting impression on him.

Reconciled to his family in 1803, he entered Worcester College, Oxford, where he somewhat arrogantly conceived the ambition of becoming, in his words. 'the intellectual benefactor of mankind.' He became widely read in many subjects and eventually would write essays on such subjects as history, biography, economics, psychology, and German philosophy.

While he was still at college in 1804, he took his first dose of opium in the form of tincture of laudanum, to relieve the pain of facial neuralgia, following a near drowning episode. By 1813, he had become "a regular and confirmed opium-eater" (i.e., an opium addict), keeping a decanter of laudanum (tincture of opium, a mixture of pure opium and alcohol) by his elbow and steadily increasing the dose; he remained an addict for the rest of his life.

De Quincey was an early admirer of the Lakeland poets, and in 1807 became a close associate of its leading authors, Wordsworth and Coleridge. He rented Wordsworth's former home, Dove Cottage, on and off, from 1809 to 1833.

In 1817 De Quincey married Margaret Simpson, who had already borne him a son. Though he wrote extensively, he actually published almost nothing at all. His financial position as head of a large family then worsened, until the appearance of his book *Confessions* (1821), serialised in *London Magazine* made him famous. It was reprinted as a book in 1822. Sadly, he later revised the work, adding what can only be described as a great deal of discursive and pedantic flim – flam. De Quincey's rambling, and often self-congratulatory style, is something I find often intensely irritating, and the secret of his book's success is almost certainly due to the fact that no one in the Western world had, until then, bothered to make an accurate record of the drug and its side effects.

In the original version of the book, De Quincey, in the later stages of the drug, (and where his usage has significantly increased), begins to experience hallucinations. He compares his phantoms to the ghosts that children sometimes claim to see. He has some control over his hallucinations; for example, he can consciously think of a particular topic, and it will then manifest itself in the apparitions he sees in the darkness.

However, these conscious hallucinations often reappear in his dreams in more sinister forms. The tone of De Quincey's nightmares gradually becomes more depressing and melancholic; and this often affects his mood during the day as well, so that he feels 'suicidal despondency.' The opium also distorts the proportions of the things he sees and, seemingly, makes time pass more slowly. Insignificant events of his former existence now develop into ghastly spirit shapes.

In *The Man with the Twisted Lip*, Dr Watson stumbles accidentally on Sherlock Holmes, disguised as an old man, sitting in an East London opium den. However, he assures Watson that he does not indulge in opium-smoking, but he has bought some opium because he is conducting an undercover investigation. Other stories in the Sherlock Holmes canon do not suggest that he was addicted to opiates. But was he, one wonders, like De Quncey, also suffering weird hallucinations?

De Quincey explains that "The Pains of Opium" will be the memoir's most impressionistic and disorganized section; but it remains the most structurally rigid part of the text. De Quincey relates his thoughts in numbered lists, and clearly says, at the beginning of each new anecdote, and rather pedantically, what the anecdote is about, and what its broader significance is. Unlike in the early parts of the memoir, which read similarly to fiction, *The Pains of Opium* uses the rhetorical conventions of the classical essay.

De Quincey presents individual anecdotes as examples of broader changes in his lifestyle. He often dreamt of lakes and became worried this was a sign that his brain had 'dropsy,' This was a Victorian medical term which referred to the swelling of a body cavity due to internal fluid build-up. Basically, it is a medical term once used to describe a swelling on or in the cellular tissues.

In the May of 1818, De Quincey dreamt about '*The Malay*'. The dream was set in China, and in it, De Quincey is terrified of what he sees as an intimidating Chinese foreign culture.

A year later, he dreamt of visiting a child's grave and of seeing Ann sitting on a stone. The setting in the dream then changed to where he was walking with Ann through their old haunt, London's Oxford Street. The most recent of these dreams, from 1820, was a nightmare, in which De Quincey was surrounded by a chorus of loud music that evoked the "caves of hell" and "everlasting farewells." Shortly after this, De Quincey realized that he would die if he did not decrease his opium use, and he did so despite very painful symptoms he then suffered.

The opium den, with all its mystery, danger and intrigue, appeared in many Victorian novels, poems and contemporary newspapers, and, unsurprisingly, it rapidly then fuelled the public's imagination. Here are two examples, one of which was written some while after TWIS appeared in the Strand Magazine. Oscar Wilde in his novel, *The Picture of Dorian Gray* (1891) conveys a highly melodramatic picture.

"It is a wretched hole… so low that we are unable to stand upright. Lying pell-mell on a mattress placed on the ground are Chinamen, Lascars, and a few English blackguards who have imbibed a taste for opium."

Now compare this:

"There were opium dens where one could buy oblivion, dens of horror where the memory of old sins could be destroyed by the madness of sins that were new."

The above, very similar account, was reported in the French journal *Figaro*, describing an opium den in Whitechapel in 1868. The first of these is Wilde's classic account of a man who allows himself willingly to drift into decadence, and perversion. Wilde had written his novel as a response to an invitation both he and Conan Doyle had received from a American agent, who subsequently printed their work in *Lippincott's Magazine*. Intriguingly, Wilde chose to write about the gradual erosion of the self, experienced by his protagonist, through the use of drugs and a libidinous lifestyle, much like De Quincey.

The Sign of Four, Conan Doyle once admitted, is also a novel preoccupied with drugs and drug taking. The subject in fact takes up much of chapter two of the work.

Readers at the time would have regarded both the characters of Dorian Gray and that of Holmes as 'Bohemians', a widely used term which, during that period, had connotations of decadence, self – indulgence, 'art for art's sake' and a *'fin de siècle'* life weariness.

Wilde himself believed that he was witnessing the end of civilization, and that it was a period of decadence; much like the latter days of the Roman Empire. Apart from drugs, sex and art, what else was there to enjoy during those declining days of a decadent and a pernicious and corrupting Empire, which had grown 'glutinous' and terminally exploitative?

The public must have shuddered at these descriptions and imagined areas such as London's docklands, and the East End, to be opium-drenched, immoral, exotic and highly dangerous places.

In the 1800s, a small Chinese community had settled in the long established slum of Limehouse, in London's docklands, an area of back street pubs, brothels and opium dens. These dens catered mainly for seamen who had become addicted to the drug, when overseas. Despite the lurid accounts of opium dens in the press and fiction, in reality, there were very few 'dens' outside of London and the ports, where opium was landed alongside other cargo from all over the British Empire, but principally, from China and India.

The den visited by Holmes and Watson was situated in Upper Swandam Lane, in Rotherhithe. As a youth, I often cycled from my home in Lewisham to Rotherhithe, which was still then a place of gaunt red brick warehouses, interspersed with small public houses and residential buildings; and very much unlike today's bourgeois ambience, enjoyed mainly by the *nouveaux riche*. Here I discovered several likely contenders for the opium den of TWIS, with a basement and upper floor, at the back of which, doors opened to convey goods onto barges.

What puzzled me at the time when I first read Dr Watson's account, and what still intrigues me now, is Holmes' comment to his chronicler about his familiarity with the opium den:

"Had I been recognised in that den my life would not have been worth an hour's purchase; for I have used it before now for my own purposes, and the rascally Lascar who runs it has sworn to have vengeance upon me. There is a trap door at the back of that building, near the corner of Paul's Wharf, which could tell some strange tales of what has passed through it upon the moonless nights."

Exactly what does Holmes mean by telling Watson that he has used the place 'now for my own purposes'? Does it mean that he has used the den for recreational opium smoking? Or is he referring to some undercover work which in the past has necessitated him visiting the den in disguise? Both would imply that he stayed on the premises, smoking unspecified amounts of opium. *Even more curious* is the fact that in the June 1891 edition of the relatively new, illustrated Strand Magazine, an entire article appeared, graphically illustrated, entitled *A Night In An Opium Den*. The anonymous author describes in effusive detail the sordid den he visited in the Ratcliffe Highway. (see vol. 1 of *The Criminal World* in Appendices.)

Here, with the Ratcliffe Highway murders, we come full circle with De Quincey. As Nick Louras points out in his intriguing article about De Quincey and Doyle, (*The Baker Street Journal*, Vol 69, No 3): 'De Quincey wrote at length about the Ratcliffe Highway Murders which occurred in Wapping East London.'

The Ratcliffe Highway Murders are mentioned in *A Study In Scarlet* where they are compared to the Brixton Road murder.

Referred to also   in the newspaper report in STUD, Ratcliffe Highway is a road in the London borough of Stepney, subsequently renamed St. George's Street, mainly due to its notoriety. Holmes, it will be recalled, sent "a couple of messages" to "Sumner, shipping Agent," situated here in BLAC, and it was known as a lawless region of London's sprawling metropolis, where a number of murders took place in the early 19th century.

On December 7, 1811, a family known as the Marrs were found brutally murdered in their East End shop. In less than a fortnight, yet another massacre occurred. This time the victims were the landlord and his wife who were savagely done to death in a pub in Gravel Lane.

Four days later an Irish sailor was arrested on suspicion of both the murders. His name was Williams. At first, the evidence was hardly convincing. Fresh evidence, collected from witnesses who knew the publican, was only circumstantial, (for instance, a laundress, who washed William's linen, stated he had given her a shirt to wash which was torn and bloodstained.) While the inquiry was still in progress, Williams hanged himself in his cell at Coldbath Fields prison. Although Williams' and Marrs' pasts were connected, no real motive for the murders of the victims was ever satisfactorily established.

In the opening paragraphs of the Strand article, the name of De Quincey is mentioned twice. The author claims that his efforts to describe the effects of the drug are not as effective as those literary descriptions of Coleridge or De Quincey. The den hosts several Chinese operatives and, like the Swandam Lane establishment, it has a 'lascar' in charge of operations, – (slang for an East Indian sailor, army servant, or artillery trooper in Asia during the era of European colonialism).

The Ratcliffe Highway den also has an obligatory 'Malay' – a person from the east Sumatran peninsula. In the *Strand* account, the Chinaman in charge is described in grotesque and caricatured terms:

'The smile became even more rigid, when I explained that I was anxious to smoke a pipe of opium. The way in which he turned his face upon me was…for all the world like the turning on by a policeman of a bull's eye lantern. With a final grin which threatened to permanently distort his features, he bade us follow him…'

In a similar article to the Strand Magazine piece, published in *Tit-Bits* on 31st October 1891, an anonymous author describes a visit to an opium den near the East India Docks, 'within the sound of the big bell of St Paul's (cathedral)', where he then explains how:

'…we turn down a dreary side street, at the corners of which are loafing some rather ugly customers of the Lascar type, and then reach what appears to be a shop. Within lies the kitchen, with a tin pan on a fire of coke and coal, in which the opium is prepared; a staircase leads up to a pair of rooms where the customers wander through scenes which none but a De Quincey can portray.'

The close resemblance of the Ratcliffe Highway den to the one in Upper Swandam Lane poses for the discerning rea der of Dr. Watson's illuminating narrative this question: in writing up the events of TWIS, did Watson *simply reinvent the former location,* basing it upon these contemporary accounts?

If this was so, one is led to the conclusion that Watson *never actually visited an opium den at all, and that the opium den episode is simply a poetic elaboration;* a piece of sensationalism designed to intrigue and entertain his readers. We already know that Holmes injected himself with morphine, and no doubt this would also have been known by the editor of the Strand when the story appeared in its pages in the latter part of that same year.

If that assumption is correct, why the mention of opium at all?. Would it therefore be quite logical and inevitable to assume that he also was in the habit of smoking raw opium on a regular basis as a more recreational use of the drug?

If this were so, his 'undercover' operations in the opium den would then have seemed more convincing to the Malay or Lascar.

The links between De Quincey and Conan Doyle are intriguing. As both Nick Louras, (q.v.) and Michael Harrison in his *A Study In Surmise* suggest, Doyle had read De Quincey very closely, and the De Quincey *Confessions* book also comes up in a non - Holmes story entitled 'The Silver Hatchet'

Harrison also noted in his book, *A Study in Surmise,* that there was an 1888 edition of the De Quincey *Confessions* in Doyle's house at 1 Bush Villas, Southsea, where the author conceived many of the initial Holmes tales.

The use of opium as a powerful narcotic and as a substance which was frequently used in a criminal context, occurs elsewhere in the Sherlock Holmes Canon.

For example, the victim of the assumed attack in *Silver Blaze* – John Straker – has the remains of his supper analysed. However, '...an analysis has shown,' Holmes remarks, 'that the remains (of his supper,) left by the stable lad, contained an appreciable quantity of powdered opium, while the people of the house partook of the same dish on the same night without any ill effect.'

Holmes then conjectures: 'Powdered opium is usually by no means tasteless. The flavour is not disagreeable, but it is perceptible. Were it mixed with any ordinary dish, the eater would undoubtedly detect it, and would probably eat no more.'

Elsewhere, in the case of *Wisteria Lodge*, the victim has been drugged with opium to render her helpless. 'She bore upon her aquiline and emaciated face the traces of some recent tragedy. Her head hung listlessly upon her breast, but as she raised it and turned her dull eyes upon us, I saw that her pupils were dark dots in the centre of the broad grey iris. She was drugged with opium.'

Finally, the *Lion's Mane*, features the unwitting victim of an attack by a deadly jellyfish, *Cyanea Capilata*, where Holmes discovers at the end of the story, that a young school teacher was not in fact killed by a rival, but died of shock and neurotoxic damage, shortly after being stung by this monstrous jelly fish; before dying, he asks for opium to ease his terrible pain:

'He pushed himself up on one arm and swung his coat off his shoulders. 'For God's sake! oil, opium, morphia!' he cried. 'Anything to ease this infernal agony!' The Inspector and I cried out at the sight.'

There was certainly nothing remarkable or unusual about Holmes' taking opium, in the form of its derivative, morphine, or indeed about it, being administered by a doctor, to one's patients.

In a letter written to the *British Medical Journal* in September 1879, Conan Doyle comments on his research into the effects of a somewhat similar drug, *gelsemium*, which, we learn, he has self-administered in order to describe its effects on his physical and mental state.: 'The system may learn to tolerate gelsemium, as it may opium,' Doyle thoughtfully concludes.

As we have seen, recreational opium smoking was very popular among the 'Bohemian' set. In fact, opium and other narcotic drugs played an important part overall and at many levels in Victorian life. Shocking though it might seem to us in the 21st century, in Victorian times it was entirely possible to walk into a pharmacist's and buy, without prescription, laudanum, cocaine; and even arsenic, as long as the recipient of such drugs signed for them. Opium preparations were sold quite freely in towns and country markets, where they were often obtainable from market stalls, run by 'quack' doctors. Indeed, the consumption of opium was just as popular in the country as it was in urban areas.

The most popular preparation was of course, laudanum, an alcoholic herbal mixture containing 10% opium. Called the 'aspirin of the nineteenth century,' laudanum was a popular painkiller and relaxant, recommended for all sorts of ailments including coughs, rheumatism, 'women's troubles' and also, perhaps most disturbingly, as a soporific for babies and young children. As we know, Samuel Taylor Coleridge became addicted to laudanum after he took it on a regular basis to quell the pain of his rheumatism. As twenty or twenty-five drops of laudanum could be bought for just a penny, it was also very affordable. Laudanum addicts would enjoy highs of euphoria, followed by deep lows of depression, along with slurred speech and restlessness. Withdrawal symptoms included aches and cramps, nausea, vomiting and diarrhoea, but even so, it was not until the early 20th century that it was recognised as addictive.

Many notable Victorians are known to have used laudanum as an effective painkiller. Authors, poets and writers such as Charles Dickens, Elizabeth Barrett Browning, Elizabeth Gaskell and George Eliot were users of laudanum. Anne Bronte is believed to have modelled the character of Lord Lowborough in 'The Tenant of Wildfell Hall' on her brother Branwell, who was a laudanum addict. The poet Percy Bysshe Shelley suffered terrible laudanum-induced hallucinations and Robert Clive, 'Clive of India', used laudanum to ease gallstone pain and depression.

Many of the opium-based preparations were targeted at women. Marketed as 'women's friends'. These were widely prescribed by doctors for problems with menstruation and childbirth, and even for fashionable female maladies of the day, such as 'the vapours', which included hysteria, depression and fainting fits. In the Sherlock Holmes Canon, there are numerous examples of people experiencing fainting fits. Watson incorrectly assumes that brandy is the antidote to such fits (see the fainting fit by Ryder, the hotel attendant, in BLUE), but as Doyle would have known, laudanum would have sufficed, though he does not actually use it.

Children were given opiates. To keep them quiet, babies were often spoon-fed Godfrey's Cordial (also known as Mother's Friend), consisting of opium, water and treacle, and recommended for colic, hiccups and coughs. Overuse of this dangerous concoction is known to have resulted in the severe illness or death of many children. People were censorious about the working class taking it, which they regarded as a misuse of the drug whereas the middle-class users of the narcotic were often above reproach.

But what of Holmes? I believe that he was a regular user of opium; that as a typical 'Decadent' of his time he indulged in a number of substances which heightened consciousness. He abhorred the dull routine of everyday existence and, like the 1890s poets, who similarly used the notorious French drink absinthe [2] to escape from the *ennui* of their urban existence, Holmes the self - poisoner by tobacco, the morphine and cocaine user, also smoked opium but when Watson came to write up the Neville St Clair case, Holmes instructed his companion and amanuensis to slightly bend the truth.

ALCOHOL

Sherlock Holmes, a connoisseur of French wines, was fond of good alcohol, but he never indulged too much in drinking. His favourites were burgundies, especially Montrachet and Meursault. In *The Sign of Four*, he drinks red burgundy for lunch, and in *The Gloria Scott* he drinks port after

---

[2] It was believed by Richard Ellman, Oscar Wilde's biographer, that absinthe may have had a part in determining the author's death.

dinner. In *The Adventure of the Dying Detective* Holmes refreshes himself

Fig. 30. The seemingly indomitable aesthete, Oscar Wilde,
seen by some as a challenge to the society which chose to
pillory him for his homosexual lifestyle.

with a glass of claret. In *His Last Bow*, he tries a bottle of Imperial Tokay. Holmes, who was also fond of whisky and soda, had a gasogene in his sitting room for making soda water. He drank brandy for medicinal purposes. Occasionally, he also drank a glass of beer. An expert on wines, spirits, and beer, Holmes used his knowledge of the habits of imbibers to solve one of his most difficult cases, *The Adventure of Abbey Grange*.

A BIBLIOGRAPHY OF SHERLOCK HOLMES AND DRUGS:

BOOKS ON THE MORPHINE PHENOMENON
Foxcroft, Louise. *The Making of Addiction: The 'Use and Abuse' of Opium in Nineteenth-Century Britain*. Burlington, VT: Ashgate Publishing Company, 2007.

Gootenberg, Paul. *Andean Cocaine: The Making of a Global Drug.* Chapel Hill, NC.: University of North Carolina Press, 2008.

Grinspoon, Lester and James B. Bakalar. *Cocaine: A Drug and Its Social Evolution.* New York: Basic Books. Place, 1985.

LITERARY AND CULTURAL REFERENCES

Guy, Partricia. *Bacchus at Baker Street. Sherlock Holmes & Victorian Drinking Lore* Lincoln: iUniverse, 2007.

Pearce, D.H. *Sherlock Holmes, Conan Doyle and Cocaine,* Journal of the History of the Neurosciences: Basic and Clinical Perspectives, 3(4), 1994, 227-232.

Shreffler, Philip A., ed. *Sherlock Holmes by Gas-lamp: Highlights from the First Four Decades of the Baker Street Journal.* New York: Fordham University Press, 1989.

Lastly, I have included for those wishing to learn more regarding the use of morphine, this extract from: *The nature of gunshot wounds of the abdomen, and their treatment: based on a review of the case of the late James Fisk Jr. in its medico-legal aspects,* by Eugene Peugnet, New York, 1874. The book is an early study of morphine as a treatment of a severe gunshot wound.

THE PHYSIOLOGICAL AND TOXICAL ACTIONS OF MORPHINE.

This is the most active alkaloid of opium, and in its pure state one grain of it is equal to six grains of the latter. When taken into the stomach, it passes directly into the circulation by *endosmose,* thus passing through the delicate mucous membrane of the stomach and the walls of the capillaries into the blood; but if, as previously mentioned, the capillary circulation is arrested, or partially so, this absorption or *endosmosis* is either prevented or delayed.

When introduced by hypodermic injection, it comes in direct contact with the walls of the capillaries, for in the cellular tissue there is no intervening mucous membrane, and the *endosmose* takes place much more rapidly. Perchance the injection may have been thrown into a vein; then the action of the agent is much more rapid. Therefore the same rule of *endosmose* does not apply to this mode of administration as to that by the stomach. It has been found by some experimenters and observers that morphine itself, by its peculiarly irritating action, delays *endosmose* in the stomach.

There are, in general, two classes of individuals in which the action of morphine or opium manifests itself differently:

1, Those who are readily affected by its hypnotic action, and who suffer little or no inconvenience from its excitant effect upon the brain or its depressant action on the pneumogastric nerve; and 2, Those who are distressed by its deliriant or depressant effects, or both, to such a degree, that its hypnotic notion is altogether counteracted until it has passed away.

I. On the Brain. — Its primary action is that of a stimulant or excitant ; its secondary one that of a hypnotic and sedative, even to anaesthesia. When the drug is once absorbed, its specific and individual effects are determined by the nervous peculiarities of the individual. When these two effects on the nervous system are evenly balanced, the drug then has no very marked action, but at the furthest only an irritating or exciting one, which in large doses may cause active delirium.

II. On the Spinal Cord — It has a marked sedative action. In cases of hypodermic injections this sedation is so rapidly induced at times on and in peculiar idiosyncrasies, that it gives rise to that alarming condition known as spasmodic cramp of the respiratory muscles. In these cases the chest becomes fixed, the respiratory movements are arrested in the lungs, the latter becoming contracted through the action of the pneumogastric on the bronchial tubes, down to their most minute ramifications.

The circulation through the lungs is then arrested; the heart, no longer able to propel the blood through them, its right ventricle becomes distended and the pulse rapidly sinks, which is intensely painful in these cases .

The action of morphine on its sentient fibres manifests itself through the brain, whilst that on its motor fibres through the spinal cord. When the sedative action manifests itself on the spinal cord, causing a gradual diminution of the respiratory efforts, the conducting power of its sentient fibres being diminished by anaesthesia, this nerve fails to communicate to the brain, the *besom de respirer*, which would, by reflex action through the *medulla oblongata* and spinal cord, make itself manifest by giving the necessary impulse to its motor branches, and to the other spinal nerves controlling the respiration, if the spinal cord itself were not under the sedative or paralyzing action of the drug.

In certain idiosyncrasies, and in dogs, morphine gives rise to nausea, and even purging ; this is also due to a peculiar action on this nerve.

III. On the Sympathetic system

The stimulating action of morphine on the nerve of organic life has been already alluded to. The action of the heart, which is essentially controlled by it, remains unimpaired in all its vigour, until the physiological and physical impediments to the flow of blood through the lungs mechanically arrests the action of the heart, as an obstructed pipe will stop the working of a ram. Whilst treating of the absorption of morphine, I stated that a contraction of the capillaries first manifested itself. But it is susceptible of proof that the prolonged toxic action of the drug will
ultimately cause a dilatation, with consequent stasis of the blood. This is due to the final sedative action of the drug on the sympathetic nervous system, causing a partial paralysis of the vaso-motor nerves.

A fine illustration of this is seen in those extreme cases of poisoning in which the surface of the body has a peculiar bluish appearance, owing to the dilatation of the integumentary capillaries, and the consequent stasis in them of the non- oxidized or carbonized blood. The dilatation is also observable in the blood-vessels of the eye.

IV. On the Pupils. —

Contraction of the pupils is an early manifestation of the effects of opium. It is due to the stimulating action of the drug on the brain, thence transmitted through the *motores oculorum*, or third pair, and the fifth pair of nerves; but this influence is counteracted by the action of the fibres from the sympathetic nerve, which prevents a complete contraction. Hence, when the pupils are pretty well contracted they still respond to light; but when, towards the last, the stimulus to the sympathetic is overcome by the sedative action of the drug, the contraction becomes complete, the pupil is then insensible. In a fatal issue the pupils will, towards the last, dilate; this is perfectly natural, for the sedative action of opium is usually more pronounced, and first manifests itself on the cerebro-spinal axis. Therefore, the *motores oculorum* lose their power of contracting the pupil, and the sympathetic, as yet unimpaired in its action, favours the dilatation.

BOOKS ON PHYSIOLOGY

Dalton, *Treatise on Human Physiology*. 5th ed.

Flint, *Physiology of Man, Nervous System*. 1872.

    " *Alimentation, Digestion and Absorption*. 1873.

    " *Blood, Circulation, and Respiration*. 1874.

PHYSIOLOGICAL AND TOXICAL ACTIONS OP MORPHINE.

Stille, *Therapeutics and Materia Medica*. 3d ed., 1868.

Gubler, *Commentaires Therapeutiques*. Paris, 1873.

Harley, *The old Vegetable Neurotics*. London, 1869.

Eulenberg, *Die Hypodermatisch Injection der Arzneimittel*. Berlin, 1867.

" *Handbuch der Toxicologie*. Berlin, 1862.

Christison, Robert, *On Poisons*. London, 4th ed.

Wiseman, *Chirurgical Treatises*. London, 1686.

Benjamin Bell. Surgery. Vol. v., 3d ed., Edinburgh, 1789.

John Hunter, Treatise on the Blood, Inflammations, and Gunshot

Wounds. Vol. ii., p. 206, Am. ed., 1796.

John Bell, Nature and Cure of Wounds. Vol. ii., 1st Am. ed., 1807.

FREUDIAN HOLMES: (PSYCHOANALYSIS AND SHERLOCK HOLMES)

Fig. 31. Freud in older years. Master of the psychoanalytical
method. Freud, and Havelock-Ellis, had a profound effect on what
Krafft-Ebing described as the study of 'perverse sexuality 'and ritualised
pathological behaviour. Without them, criminal profiling would
Probably not exist in its present form.

In 1932, T, S. Blakeney wrote that "the psychoanalyst has yet to plumb
the depths of his (Holmes') subconscious mind," and that what was needed
was a "deep investigation of the man's personality." [1]

Since that time, however, the denizens of Baker Street's 'Higher
Criticism' have not been idle. Contributions to this branch of Holmes
studies have come not only from established Sherlockian writers but also
(refreshingly) from professional psychiatrists.

Sadly, the work of Freud and his followers is now held by some largely in contempt by the modern school, who tend to see the father of psychiatry more as a myth maker or philosopher than as a scientist. Whatever one's own prejudices in the matter, it remains true that Freud's methods are still useful, and especially so in the field of literary analysis, as long as one also accepts that any conclusions reached must, of necessity, remain contentious.

Perhaps it should not be forgotten that some of Freud's most illuminating work was in the field of art and literary interpretation. His essays on Leonardo da Vinci and the 'Moses' of Michelangelo were particularly revealing, whilst his monograph *Gradiva and Dreams*, in which he analysed the dreams of a character in Jensen's novel of the same title, showed the psychoanalytical technique at its most incisive.

All the papers and longer studies of the psychoanalytical approach to the Holmes Saga published over the last forty years have something worthwhile to offer. Whilst some point the way, others (such as Rosenberg's study (*Naked Is the Best Disguise*) make out a strong case for Holmes's manic - depressive behaviour and obsessional traits. There is no doubt (in my opinion) that the circumstances of Conan Doyle's own upbringing (graphically outlined in Owen Dudley Edwards' *The Quest for Sherlock Holmes*) contributed to the personality of Sherlock Holmes. and that the characters of Holmes and Watson represent some form of duality in Doyle's subconsciousness. The overriding femininity of Watson and the sometimes hard, emotionless, asexual quality of Holmes suggest an unreconciled oedipal conflict that is very hard to ignore.

There is also what I shall describe as the *mythopoeic* aspect to the stories, which has not yet been fully investigated. By this I mean those aspects of a narrative, whether it be a poem, a novel, or even an autobiographical piece of writing which links those things that we perceive, as of the real world, with those of the imagined or the unseen.

II. THE SETTING OF THE STORIES: BAKER STREET (THE PSYCHIATRIST'S CONSULTING ROOM?)

To those aficionados who devote a considerable part of their spare time and energy to the study of Sherlock Holmes, the setting of the stories holds a special affection. As the late, great Vincent Starrett remarked: "For every reader there is, no doubt, a different picture of that famous living room, and probably it is not subject to change. "2

The rooms at Baker Street are central to our understanding of the Sherlockian myth, They mark the commencement of each excursion into the Victorian hinterland of nefarious dealings, and, when the trap has been sprung, and the criminal placed safely behind bars, it is to 221B, this inner sanctum of clutter and cosiness that the reader adjourns to hear the exposition of the case and its problems.

Starrett's words hold the key to this inner suite of rooms: 'It is not subject to change.' Each one of us retains a picture of the place, freshly imprinted on the retina, as fresh as the day that we first encountered that memorable description by Dr. Watson. 3

The Baker Street flat is immutable and immortal; and the fact that it is so, places the stories in a mythological realm altogether divorced from the mainstream of detective fiction.

Jung, Freud's errant disciple, would surely have recognized that personalized picture for what it is: an archetype. As a primordial mental image, it offers succour to us all. What better antidote to the uncompromising grind of reality than the flaming hearth, the hiss of the gas-jet, and that sense of inner security offered to the reader as the detective rationalizes the improbable and the irrational? There is a passage in *The Five Orange Pips* which entirely demonstrates this quality of *angst*-relief:

'All day the wind had screamed and the rain had beaten against the windows, so that even here, in the heart of great hand-made London we were forced to raise our minds for the instant from the routine of life, and to recognise the presence of these great elemental forces which shriek at mankind through the bars of his civilization, like untamed beasts in a cage. As evening drew in the storm grew louder and louder, and the wind cried and sobbed like a child in the chimney. Sherlock Holmes sat moodily at one side of the fireplace, cross - indexing his records of crime, whilst I at the other was deep in one of Clark Russell's fine sea stories, until the howl of the gale from without seemed to blend with the text, and the splash of the rain to lengthen out into the long swash of the sea waves.' 4

Those "great elemental forces," of course, are not merely the rain and tempest. They also represent the intrusion of the unreasoning *id*, that "untamed" beast which the conscious mind denies itself to reappear in dreams. And no matter how hard those forces batter at the door of the conscious mind, the comfortable living room wherein our thoughts are secure, we shall not submit to its wicked way.

Within this secure setting, with its ordered Victorian clutter, lie the impedimenta of two lives. If Holmes once referred to the mind as an attic wherein are stored all manner of things remarkable, memorable, even irrelevant, then the living room at 221B is the living embodiment of the mind of Sherlock Holmes: eccentric, singular, eclectic. 5 If the room were empty, then we should expect Holmes and Watson to enter it at any moment, for without them, that room has no intrinsic sense of durability or comfort. It is, truly a time capsule.

Once ensconced with a client in the intimate atmosphere of that 'large airy comfortable room,', Holmes places his fingertips together, and he listens. And he rarely interrupts. 6 Here we have the parallel of the patient and consultant with client and detective. From what has been written about Freud, we know that he, like Holmes, was gentle with his clients.7 He only broke in on their spoken thoughts to check significant detail. This was also central to the psychoanalytic method. Freud soon dispensed with hypnotic suggestion. What replaced it was the simple setting of talker and listener, in that quiet room in Vienna.

Nothing takes place in a psychoanalytic treatment but an interchange of words between the patient and the analyst. The patient talks, tells of his past experiences and present impressions, complains, confesses to his wishes and his emotional impulses. The Doctor listens, tries to direct the patient's processes of thoughts, exhorts, draws his attention in certain directions, gives him explanations and observes the reactions of understanding or rejection which he in this way provokes in him." [8]

This could almost be a commentary on the Holmesian method. Indeed, an analysis of the first part of *The Speckled Band*, for example, confirms one's suspicions. Observe, if you will, Helen Stoner's account of her upbringing, Holmes' demands for 'precise details,' his interruption regarding the whistle and metallic sound, and his observations that "there are a thousand details which l should desire to know before I decide upon our course of action." [9]

There is, of course, one essential difference between the Freudian and Holmesian methods. Although both recognized the significance of detail, the Freudian mode of analysis deals with the nature of experience and sublimated emotion. *The Holmesian method is concerned with the world of external phenomena,* with the bits and pieces of everyday existence (a method first demonstrated by Dr. Joseph Bell). Nevertheless, both Freud and Holmes perform their apparently 'magical' acts by a process of imaginative induction (and not deduction, as Holmes erroneously states).

The living room at Baker Street provides us with a window through which we may glimpse this process.

III. SHERLOCK HOLMES; THE NEUROTIC.

In the course of his career, Freud defined six clinical examples of the main forms of neurosis; (1) hysterical illnesses; (2) anxiety states and vulnerable personalities; (3) obsessive, compulsive disorders and the obsessional personalities who endure them; (4) neurotic depression; (5) hypersensitive and paranoid attitudes; (6) disorders related to sexual immaturity.' These are distinct from the psychosis, in which the individual's relationship to his surrounding environment becomes disjointed and incapable of interpretation by him.

Freud believed that anxiety (a universal experience) was the prime cause of all these manifestations of human behaviour and that it was inevitable. Prolonged anxiety naturally leads to disturbances of the individual's physiology and mental well - being, despite the need to repress such an emotion.

To what extent, if any, was Sherlock Holmes a neurotic? The evidence is interesting although open to question. One of Watson's earliest impressions of his colleague suggests the swing between compulsive activity and prolonged inactivity, typical of the manic-depressive.

'Nothing could exceed his energy when the working fit was on him; but now and again a reaction would seize him, and for days on end he would lie upon the sofa in the sitting room, hardly uttering a word or moving a muscle from morning to night.' 10

That this condition was not merely an isolated one becomes obvious when we read in *The Musgrave Ritual*:

'The outbursts of passionate energy were followed by reactions of lethargy, during which he would lie about with his violin and his books, hardly moving, save from the sofa to the table.'

Watson reiterates the symptoms of manic depression when he observes that his friend

'... could be bright, eager and in excellent spirits, a mood which in his case alternated with fits of the blackest depression.' 11

Watson, whose medical grounding obviously did not exclude a firm grasp of basic psychology, went on to observe:

'In his singular character the dual nature alternately asserted itself, and his extreme exactness and astuteness represented, as I have often thought, the reaction against the poetic and contemplative mood which occasionally predominated in him. The swing of his nature took him from extreme languor to devouring energy. 12

There is no doubt at all that Holmes lived for his work, or, as he saw it, his art. 'My life is spent in one long effort to escape from the commonplaces of existence,' he once observed," 13 and elsewhere: "My mind rebels at stagnation." 14

Holmes was a compulsive person, a 'man of habits," as Watson recorded, "narrow and concentrated habits." 15 Although an untidy man to live with, he had, "a horror of destroying documents" 16 and was eccentric, both in his addiction to music and to odd hours,' 17 and in his habit of secreting his tobacco and cigars in unusual places" 18 (which indicates an unreasoning fear that they might be stolen). 'Naturally reclusive,' 19 he had few friends and 'lived in an atmosphere of seclusion.' 20

Holmes had repressed his emotions to a dangerous degree. As Watson pointed out early in his career, 'All emotions were abhorrent to his cold, precise but admirably balanced mind.' 21 His inability to admit feelings as a real phenomenon led him to rationalize them as unwanted and unnecessary. 'The emotional qualities are antagonistic to clear reasoning,' he pointed out," 22, and elsewhere; 'l use my head, not my heart.' 23 Because of this self - administered repression, he was unable to sustain a meaningful relationship with a woman ('I should never marry myself, lest I bias my judgment.' 24). Even his friendship with Watson was kept frequently at arm's length and operated on a master-servant basis, In this way, Holmes was able to use Watson as a bulwark for his insecure feelings.

Naturally, the dam had to burst, sooner or later. The instinctual drive which Freud termed the libido cannot be forever blocked. Although Holmes had banished his feelings from the conscious mind, they undoubtedly re-emerged under the pressure of work.

He experienced two major breakdowns in his career, 25 and it is entirely possible that the period termed the Great Hiatus 26 marked a steep descent into paranoia, 27 from which he did not emerge entirely unscathed. His addiction to cocaine and morphine did nothing to help this fragmentation of his personality; rather, they impeded his progress toward self - illumination.

Freud saw obsessional neurosis as a displacement neurosis. That is, it was a regression of the libido to an earlier stage of the infant's sadistic-anal organization, a stage in which the patient could not directly experience the love of his parents without the attendant feelings of aggression and destruction. In other words, the obsessional neurotic is the victim of conflicting feelings which cannot be reconciled. So, every person he meets and with whom he may desire to establish a sexual or even a platonic relationship becomes identified in some way with his father and mother." 28

If Holmes *was* a compulsive neurotic, as the evidence would suggest, then he was almost certainly in the grip of a resistance which would constantly reassert itself despite his attempts to break its grip.

One of the ways in which this re - emergence persisted was in Holmes's symbolic ritualisation of conceptual thought. He placed considerable store by the process of deduction, yet a detailed analysis of several stories reveals an inductive process at work.

Holmes does not reduce the means of data at his disposal to a single cause. In fact, his usual method is to induce one cause and effect from another. This is a linear process which chooses to ignore certain data and to recognize other data. Holmes chooses to ignore his intuitive feelings about a case. Yet on many occasions it is his feelings which lead him to make the important link 29. On those occasions upon which he chooses to ignore his instinctive feelings, disaster often strikes. 30

Beneath this complex pattern of emotion, repression, and displacement, Freud perceived the Oedipus complex at work - that threat to the child of its primary desire for an exclusive possession of the mother and the inevitable resulting punishment by the father for this powerful desire. Failure to resolve this conflict led to the development of the neurotic state. Exactly what kind of relationship Holmes had with his mother it is impossible to speculate. It is, however, entirely possible that he may have endured a painful paternal rejection at an early age. The fact that Holmes never once mentioned the existence of his parents to Watson, his sole confidant, is extremely significant.

IV. THE OEDIPAL HOLMES

In his illuminating essay, *Sir Arthur Conan Doyle: To See and To Be Seen,* 31 Dr. Andre Gabriel suggests that Holmes was an oral personality and that his obvious dread of female-kind was based on a deep-seated fear of his own castration. He goes on to observe that it is the phallic/masculine females such as Irene Adler to whom Holmes is particularly attracted.

In a concluding paragraph, Dr. Gabriel concludes that Holmes is the "materialization of Sir Arthur Conan Doyle's fantasies and that, through the character, Doyle was able to liberate his non-sexual voyeurism, thus establishing a renewed loyalty with his errant father.

Students of Sherlock Holmes grant him a reality all his own - a delightful falsehood. Of course, the truth is something altogether different. Throughout his literary career, Holmes dogged Doyle and the author saw him as something akin to a parasitical life form which he was unable to throw off. Like Christ, Holmes was destroyed by him, only to resurrect himself later in invincible form.

This peculiar persistence suggests a profound meaning in Doyle's imagination. Holmes was that most worrying of literary creations-a flesh-and-blood character who was originally destined to be merely a cipher, operating in the literary creator's lesser work. Destiny, however, and the British reading public decreed otherwise.

As we have seen, there is what can only be described an unresolved oedipal conflict in the personality of Holmes. This should hardly surprise us, for Doyle's early background provided a family situation of considerable tension in which the father earned his son's eventual disrespect.

The story of Charles Doyle's remarkable artistic talent and his ultimate tragic incarceration in a Scottish madhouse named Sunningdale need not be given much space here. As a young man, Arthur Conan Doyle was left in the unenviable position of part wage-earner with his sisters and spiritual guide to the other members of his impoverished family and some of his in-laws. And, although his own autobiography, *Memories & Adventures*, would lead us to believe that he held his father in considerable respect, there are clues in his fictional work which tell us that his subconscious mind held other, more violent, inclinations. In *The Stark Munro Letters*, (1894), the narrator (thinly disguised, but clearly Doyle himself) recalls his father's urging him to find regular employment, since the character is in the grip of a terminal illness:

'Of course, I could only answer that I was willing to anything. But that interview has given me a heavy ever-present gloom of my soul, which I am conscious of and it has for a moment gone out of my thoughts. I had enough to make up for before, when I had to face the world without money or interest, But now to think of my mother and my sisters and little Paul, all leaning upon me when I cannot stand myself. It is a nightmare...'

The nightmare that dogged young Doyle in these years enable him to strengthen the bond with his mother, whom he once described as 'the quaintest of housewives and a woman of letters, a 'high-bred spirited lady;' as a basis for some of his fictional characters. Doyle's mother was a reverse image of his father, that rather wistful and melancholy neurotic who bears no actual resemblance to the man 'of moral courage' described by the author in *Memories and Adventures*. And it is significant that it was to his mother that Doyle initially wrote when he announced the imminent murder of his creation, Sherlock Holmes, prior to the writing of *The Final Problem*.

The theme of innocence seduced is one which frequently haunts the Holmes stories, and it is hardly surprising, therefore, that revenge also features so largely in the sixty plots that make up the Canon. From the fertile brain of Sir Arthur Conan Doyle was summoned an avenging angel: asexual, moral, a character of extreme logic but also, as is often portrayed in fiction of the *fin de siecle*, of intense spirituality. It does appear that Sherlock Holmes sought out the image of Doyle's father and slew him repeatedly, in these often bizarre, and frequently disturbing stories.

There is a passage in Freud's *Introductory Lectures on Psychology*, 32 which best explains the compulsive relationship between Sherlock Holmes and Conan Doyle. Freud comments:

'Do you recall the outcome of our dream-analyses; how the wishes that construct dreams are so often of a perverse, incestuous nature or reveal an unsuspected hostility to those who are nearest and dearest to the dreamer? At that time... we gave no explanation of the origin of these evil impulses. Now you can find it for yourselves. They are allocations of the libido which date from early infancy and have long since been abandoned as far as conscious life is concerned, but which prove still to be present at night-time and to be capable of functioning in a certain sense ... Everyone, not only neurotics, experience these perverse, incestuous and murderous dreams...' 33

More than any other form of literature, the crime story provides a catharsis for those unresolved feelings and emotions about our parents, which we carry with us from childhood, in the shape of memories, fantasy, and dreams. To writer and reader alike, there is, in convincing crime fiction, a freedom to kill and be killed, to crucify and resurrect characters in these tales, until at the stories' reasoned conclusions, the phantoms that beset us are finally laid to rest.

The Sherlock Holmes Saga is no exception, and these often perverse, dark, and cruel accounts of dysfunctional characters, mutilations, incestuous fathers, and predatory males, are none the less memorable and remarkable for that.

NOTES

1. T. S. Blakeney, *Sherlock Holmes: Fact or Fiction?* (London: John Murray, 1932). p. vi.

2. Vincent Starrett, *The Private Life of Sherlock Holmes*: (London: Allen and Unwin, 1961), p. 42.

3. *A Study in Scarlet*, Ch. 2.

4, Ibid.

5. Ibid.

6. *The Speckled Band.*

7. Ibid.

8. Sigmund Freud, *Introductory Lectures on Psychoanalysis.'* (Harmondsworth: Penguin, 1976), p. 41.

9. See D. Stafford-Clark, *What Freud Really Said.* (Harmondsworth: Penguin, 1979), p. 118.

10. *A Study in Scarlet, Ch. 2.*

11. *The Sign of Four, Ch. 3*

12. *The Red-Headed League.*

13. Ibid.

14. *The Sign of Four, Ch. 1.*

15. *The Creeping Man.*

16. *The Musgrave Ritual.*

17. *The Dying Detective.*

18. *The Musgrave Ritual.*

19. *The Greek Interpreter.*

20. *The Mazarin Stone.*

21. *A Scandal in Bohemia.*

22. *The Sign of Four, Ch. 2.*

23. *The Illustrious Client.*

24. *The Sign of Four, Ch. 12.*

25. *Recorded in The Reigate Squire.*

26. *See The Final Problem and The Empty House.*

27. Some have argued that Professor Moriarty was an invented or mythological being, a manifestation of Holmes' own irrational fears.

28. Freud made it clear that this process of displacement was also at work in the sexual perversions.

29. *The Abbey Grange.*

30. *The Hound of the Baskervilles, The Five Orange Pips.*

31. *Bulletin of the Menninger Clinic,* Vol. 4-6, No. 6 (November 1982), pp. 530-39.

32. Sec Michael Baker, *The Doyle Diaries,* (New York. 1978).

33. Freud, ibid,p. 381

THE MADMAN OF DARTMOOR

Fig.32. Charles Altamont Doyle, seen here with his
diminutive son, Arthur Conan, in happier times in Edinburgh .

SELDEN
Selden,
The Notting Hill murderer
Was seldom to be seen
Here on the dark, fog-bound Moor,
Though one man had seen him
Walking as if in a dream
Of the dreadful crimes
That still assailed and haunted him.

Here, where the seven black crows
Crouch, gathered in a line,
Their ragged voices
Mocking him,
Spitting at him
Cursed names
From long ago.

Like that of the damned rapist,
The cruel and wicked Hugo
Who, one cold Michaelmas night,
When the moon shone upon the moor
In an unearthly silver light,
And good folk were told not to stray
From the moorland path
That by Hound Tor did lay,
For fear the Devil might steal their Souls
And they would suffer for eternity
Behind these stark and riven granite walls.

Aye, they had seen him,
Selden,
Staring out from the rocks,
Crying, sometimes moaning,
His mournful eyes hollow, lost,
Like a thing possessed.
For the madman Selden
There never could be rest
For his loved
He'd left dying;
For those he'd maimed and brained,
For those he'd stabbed and cleft.

On the night Selden died
There was only one sound.
It was not
The booming of a bittern,
Nor the shrieking of a pony
As it foundered, then drowned
Beneath the morass of the great
Grimpen Mire
Where, t'is said,
The dead do live forever
With their tongues as black as liver
And their lungs half expired.
No, this was a dread, unearthly sound,
As if the dead they all had risen
From the churchyards on the Moor
And joined with that devil dog
They had seen, so oft before
At the eerie breaking of the dawn
When all lay soft and moist,
And uncannily grey.

They say that Death had come for him
To rip from him his heart,
To serve his master pale and grim,
Carrying his sharpened scythe
Along these Grimspound paths.

And others are heard to say
Here in Princeton prison,
That, though on that day of reckoning,
Each soul will duly have arisen,
There is one that shall be missing,
And he shall have no blessing,

For Selden often walks here
On such a night as this,
When the harrowing wind doth cruelly bite
And the rank bog of Grinpen
Doth smell of rot and piss.

You may see his white face
Set hard as fractured bone,
Or glimpse his sad reflection
On a shattered sarsen stone.

For you know
What good folk do say on the Moor,
And you know that it be true,
That the Devil Dog shall rule his own;
And on rank, mist - drenched nights like this,
When the east wind doth shriek and moan,
Selden shall march forever in their midst,
With that dammed, dead, demented crew.

There are few more fascinating, but annoying murder cases so obliquely referenced in passing in the Sherlock Holmes stories, as that of Selden, the Dartmoor convict, who had escaped from Princeton prison. As we know, in *The Hound of The Baskervilles*, Selden died when he was pursued by the Hound, and then fell to his death from a rocky outcrop on The Moor.

The facts we learn from the narrative are these. Selden was a man who narrowly escaped the death sentence, after he had attacked and killed members of his family in Notting Hill. He was related to Barrymore's wife. In fact we learn later in the story that he was the brother-in-law of Mrs Barrymore. She then helped him to remain free, whilst he hid from the prison authorities on the Moor, by supplying him with food and some of Sir Henry's clothes. He is also described as the infamous 'Notting Hill murderer', and was sent to prison, rather than be hanged, because he was in fact found to be insane.

Several of the prisoners who were found guilty of murder but had been declared to be insane in the 1880s, were sentenced thus, because they were regarded as not responsible for their actions, but this had to be verified by a doctor, and it had to be proved in a substantial manner in order that it might convince a jury. Many people who appealed to the magistrate and the jury for this type of commuted sentence during the second half of the 19th Century were no doubt 'mad', but were, nevertheless found to be guilty and subsequently executed.

There were only two notable and famous murders in the Notting Hill District at that time, the first being that of Percy Lefroy Mapleton. Percy was eventually executed in 1889, and interestingly, he was represented in court by the barrister who thought he'd shared lodgings with the real Jack the Ripper.

The barrister's name was Stewart Forbes Winslow. On first examination, it might appear that Percy does not really figure as being a possible parallel for Selden, for he certainly did not wipe out his family.. But he did shoot and murder a man on a train on the Brighton railway link. And this callous and vicious act was done because he had fallen into debt as a result of his doomed infatuation with an actress, called May Gordon.

Because he was so utterly besotted and obsessed by this attractive looking actress, Percy impersonated a playwright in order to gain entrance to the theatrical world.

His family, who by then had despaired of him and his eccentric and obsessional behaviour, decided to send him to Australia, and subsequently, he was provided with letters of introduction to the Bishop
of Melbourne. However, having completed the long sea voyage, where his bizarre behaviour had several times attracted the attention of the captain and his crew, he then spent all his money on theatres and concerts. He sold his clothes and then slept in parks and boats, until his family were able eventually to provide him with the fare back to England.

Fig. 33. Percy in the dock, listening to evidence. An artist's impression , which appeared in *The Illustrated Police Gazette* in July, 1888.

His father had died, but had left the value of his estate to Percy's sisters. Percy then went to live with his friends, who were situated in Croydon, where they ran a school.

Still smitten with the actress, May Gordon, now unemployed, unemployable and now having no money, he decided to carry out a robbery on a Brighton express train. On the 27th of June, 1881, armed with a gun and a razor, he arrived at London Bridge, and then took the train to Brighton.

The first person he encountered in the carriage was Mr. Frederick Gold, a retired baker, who lived in Sussex. When the train sped along, and eventually entered a tunnel, Percy closed his eyes momentarily, then took out from his overcoat pocket a large, heavy, Webley revolver and after demanding that the wealthy stranger should give him money and receiving a sharp denial to his request, shot at the gentleman sitting opposite him. There was a brief struggle. Then, as he declared in his statement, 'pursued by fresh demons', he opened the carriage door and pushed Mr Gold to his death.

When the high speed LBSCR commuter train finally arrived in Preston Park Station, the ticket collector found Percy drenched in blood, hysterical, and wanting to be seen by a doctor. He declared he'd been attacked by a rough looking man who'd been in the same compartment. However, a gold watch chain had been half hidden in his shoe. And so, being suspected of theft, he was taken to the police station in Brighton, where he gave his name. He repeated several times that he'd been attacked on the train by a stranger and demanded hysterically and loudly that he must see a doctor.

On Friday, the first of July 1881, a celebrity trial took place, at London's Old Bailey. Percy was subsequently found guilty of murdering Mr Gold and the Queen's Counsel proved that the crime was premeditated.

 Although Percy claimed his innocence to the last, and even wrote his autobiography, confessing to the murder, which he had asked was not to be published, but only read by his wife, he was nevertheless hanged for his murder. After his death by hanging, which was declared to be instantaneous, he was buried in a grave in the precincts of the prison. A waxwork figure of Percy was displayed for many years, in the Chamber of Horrors at Madame Tussauds, in London, where no doubt, Conan Doyle duly noted the case. Clearly, Percy had been of unsound mind when he shot his victim, but though expert witness testimony was offered to the jury by a senior psychiatrist to this effect, clearly it was not enough to change their minds, nor, indeed, that of the presiding judge.

The other significant and highly published murder inspired by what might be described as an act of madness during the 1880s, which did, in fact, take place at Notting Hill, was of two people who set fire to a building in order to destroy the family, who were its inhabitants. This was fuelled by lack of money, and it was indeed known of and referred to by the national and provincial newspapers as 'the Notting Hill Murder Case' which is where, no doubt, Conan Doyle got the title of the Selden case from..

The defendants in this case were Maria Wright and also, Elizabeth Clark, and the trial took place in the August of 1881.

However, a much more likely contender, in my view, for the 'Selden' case was reported in 'The Leighton Buzzard Observer for the 16th of March, 1886, which now follows:

TERIBBLE MURDER BY MADMAN.

'A domestic tragedy of most painful and shocking character occurred at Quardon, a picturesque village three miles from Derby, at an early hour Thursday morning. The facts are as follows ;—William Wagstaffe, a farm labourer in the employ of Mr. Kidger, has for some time past had a son at home suffering from brain fever, and has sat up at night with the youth. The worry and fatigue consequent upon these vigils would seem to have affected his mind.

'During Wednesday, his cousin, Mary Ann Morrell, a married woman, whose home is in Derby, was sent for to assist in tending the youth, in the evening, after the usual family prayers. Wagstaffe (who seemed to be in his customary health and spirits), his wife, and five children retired to rest in one large room, the youngest, an infant, occupying the same bed as the parents. Mrs. Morrell and an elder daughter. Lizzie, aged twenty, sat to nurse the invalid. About two o'clock on Thursday morning Wagstaffe got up and went into the sick room. The young man was then raving, and his father asked him to be quiet like a good boy, and not to disturb his mother. Wagstaffe then sought his own bed.

'About half-past four Mrs. Wagstsffe was rudely awakened by her husband striking her violently, and seemingly attempting to force her out bed, Snatching up the child, she jumped out of bed and ran into the next room, crying, "For God's take let somebody come to me, father! He's going crazy." Mrs. Morrell attempted to quiet her, and went into the room to Wagstaffe, who was sitting up in bed with his hands clenched, and a frenzied look his eyes. Seized with terror, the woman rushed back to the sick room, and Wagstaffe followed. Dashing past the three affrighted women, the madman sprang like cat on his son, and, kneeling on his chest, attempted strangle him.

'Mrs. Wagstatfe and her daughter ran downstairs, but Mrs. Morrell stayed and endeavoured to pull the man away from his son and off the bed. The last thing Lizzie Wagstaffe saw was her father turning from her brother and seizing Mrs. Morrell by the throat. The son was quite conscious, and cognisant of much of what subsequently transpired. Mrs. Wagstaffe and her daughter, hearing cries of "Murder!" from above stairs, called their neighbour Shipley, who, in the urgency of the case, came to the house in his shirt and endeavoured to force the door of the room, but, failing, went out for further assistance. When he returned with two other men, named Cooper and Payne, he found that the son had come downstairs and was lying unconscious the floor. Going upstairs, a horrible sight met their view. Mrs. Morrell was lying dead, and most terrible injuries were at once apparent. Wagstaffe appeared to have broken a leg from a chair, and to have battered the poor woman's head with it. In his fearful frenzy, too, he seems to have seized her by the jaws and torn open her mouth, the right jawbone being broken. Other injuries lead to the surmise that he threw her onto the ground and placed his foot her throat, and it is thought that death actually occurred from suffocation by this means.

'When taken into custody by Police Constable Allen, Wagstaffe coolly remarked, "You were here to find snares (alluding to some snares his son had set in the garden), but why weren't you here to prevent someone doing this?" The prisoner was taken to Derby in a cab, and there brought before the J.P., Mr Whiston at the county police office. After the arrest he developed further symptoms of derangement, but afterwards became calmer. The magistrate remanded him until next Friday.

The son, it may be added, lies in a very precarious condition, owing to the rough treatment he received in his weak state, and fears are entertained as to his recovery. Naturally, the tragedy had caused much local excitement.

Mr. Coroner Whiston opened an inquest on Thursday night last the body of Mary Ann Morrell, wife of Samuel Morrell, Percy Street, Derby, whose death occurred stated above. Elizabeth Wagstaffe, daughter of W, Wagstaffe, and now in custody, identified the body. Mrs, Morrell was forty-three years of age. As the coroner only desired to call evidence of identification in order that the body might prepared for a post-mortem examination, the inquiry was adjourned. The five children who slept in the room with their parents were not injured.

By the end of the 1880's, the number of hanging sentences given out to men like Selden, who were described as 'mad,' began to shrink rapidly, and madness 'experts' were required, like Winslow, to give evidence under oath in the preparation of reports on the accused.

The 19th century saw fundamental changes in society's response to the mentally ill with the creation of purpose-lit asylums throughout the country. Some of these were run on fairly benign principles.

The Victorians were ambivalent in their reaction to the mentally disturbed. Whilst they sought to segregate the insane from the rest of the population, they were also horrified by the prospect of the wrongful confinement of sane people. The trial of Daniel McNaughton in 1843 for the assassination of Sir Robert Peel's Private Secretary, and the subsequent legislation, provoked general public debate about the nature of madness.

Fig.34. Images like this, in late Victorian ladies magazines, reaffirmed the popular notion of the frequency of women liable to fainting.

The view of the Victorian mental asylum that persists today has the reputation of a place of misery where the inmates were locked up and left to the mercy of their keepers. However, when the first large asylums were built in the early 1800s, they were part of a new, and more humane attitude towards mental illness, so an inmate like Selden, if he had survived his attack by the Baskerville hound, and been rearrested, would not have been that cruel as it might have been in the early 1800s.

In fact, benign private asylums, like that portrayed in the novel *Dracula* by Conan Doyle's friend, Bram Stoker, often possessed a position of esteem. In 1843, the talented schizophrenic artist Richard Dadd, believed his father had become controlled by evil spirits, and then stabbed him to death, prior to escaping to France, where he was then arrested by detectives and, after sentence, incarcerated in Bedlam for the rest of his natural life, where he proceeded to produce some of his finest work.

The Middlesex County Lunatic Asylum at Hanwell, for example, on the outskirts of London, was one of the first of the new non-private lunatic asylums, and it set many of the standards for mental health care in the Victorian age.

Charles Altamont Doyle, Arthur Conan Doyle's father, was much afflicted by madness and was an alcoholic who produced no less than ten children with Mary Doyle, Arthur's mother. The Doyle family lived a precarious existence in a poorer part of Edinburgh, but it was the burden of Doyle's father, who endured frequent alcohol related periods of work, punctuated by long spells of employment, which finally drove Mary Doyle to despair. Therefore, it is hardly a surprise to find references to types of irregular behaviour, psychotic episodes or extreme mental states induced by alcoholism, depicted in the Holmes stories. Charles Doyle, most probably an epileptic, whom Conan Doyle depicts in his *Memories And Adventures* as also something of an impractical dreamer, was eventually incarcerated in a succession of asylums from where he periodically but successfully escaped. As the authors of the internet site. *The Victorian Web* astutely observe about this shadow figure:

'The strange dislocations of scale and subject-matter that appear in his paintings and sketchbook have led some commentators to re-frame the unfortunate Doyle as another example of the classic 'mad artist' – a new Victorian anti-hero to compare (and compete) with Richard Dadd and 'Mad' John Martin. With little practical evidence beyond the fact of his incarceration, Chris Frith and Eve Johnstone present one of his paintings as a typical example of schizophrenic art (p.66), and this is a characteristic view. Labelled as idle, a drunk, and/or a madman, Doyle is too often treated as a freak: in Baker's terms, a 'strange and curious case', rather than an artist in his own right. His work deserves closer investigation'.

In several of the Sherlock Holmes stories there are references to people who faint or who are sometimes referred to as 'neurasthenic.' Perhaps the clearest example of one suffering this condition is the character of Percy Phelps in The Adventure of the Naval Treaty, where a young man who works for the Foreign Office in London has an important government treaty stolen from his desk when he momentarily leaves his room. Doyle describes his mental condition as one of 'brain fever.'

In Victorian literature, people who experienced a severe emotional shock sometimes became ill with "brain fever," this being characterized by a high fever with delirium, lasting for weeks. In reality, "Brain fever" is a most inexact and obsolete term which might describe for example, any inflammation of the brain, e.g. encephalitis. In fictional terms, some so-called 'brain fevers' could act like the fictional ailment that killed, Heathcliffe's lover, Catherine Earnshaw, in *Wuthering Heights*.

In *The Naval Treaty*, Percy, a civil servant who appears to being in the grip of 'brain fever,' following the theft of an important military treaty at the Foreign Office, describes to Sherlock Holmes his descent into what seems to be a mixture of hysteria and 'madness,' in the following manner:

'I was ruined; shamefully, hopelessly ruined. I don't know what I did. I fancy I must have made a scene. I have a dim recollection of a group of officials who crowded round me endeavouring to soothe me. One of them drove down with me to Waterloo and saw me into the Woking train. I believe that he would have come all the way had it not been that Dr. Ferrier, who lives near me, was going down by that very train. The doctor most kindly took charge of me, and it was well he did so, for I had a fit in the station, and before we reached home I was practically a raving maniac.

'You can imagine the state of things here when they were roused from their beds by the doctor's ringing, and found me in this condition. Poor Annie here and my mother were broken-hearted. Dr. Ferrier had just heard enough from the detective at the station to be able to give an idea of what had happened, and his story did not mend matters. It was evident to all that I was in for a long illness, so Joseph was bundled out of this cheery bedroom, and it was turned into a sickroom for me. Here I have lain, Mr. Holmes, for over nine weeks, unconscious, and raving with brain fever. If it had not been for Miss Harrison here and for the doctor's care I should not be speaking to you now.'

Unlike some writers of the period, Doyle is usually quite specific about the type of abnormal psychiatric features of the characters who inhabit his Holmes tales, and his complex characters who suffer psychological abnormalities, are not often, like other writers, portrayed in terms of caricature.

Doyle may have also drawn some inspiration from other doctors, such as William Gowers, who wrote the standard work on Victorian neurology, the *Bible of Neurology*. (Conan Doyle himself had specialised in neuro-degenerative disease as a doctoral student, and he and Gowers had a mutual friend in the author, Rudyard Kipling.)

Gowers often taught his students to begin their diagnosis from the moment a patient walked through the door, as seen in a record of one of his clinical demonstrations, later published as *A Clinical Lecture on Silver and Syphilis:*

"Did you notice him as he came into the room? If you did not then you should have done so. One of the habits to be acquired and never omitted is to observe a patient as he enters the room; to note his aspect and his gait. If you did so, you would have seen that he seemed lame, and you may have been struck by that which must strike you now – an unusual tint of his face."

To the follower of Mr Holmes, this is uncannily familiar and very like the methods used by Dr Joseph Bell whose technique with patients inspired the now famous 'observation and deduction' method employed by Sherlock Holmes. And finally, what of the pre-disposition of characters in the Holmes stories - not all of them female by the way, to fainting? The most obvious female example is perhaps that of Mary Morstan n SIGN but the most significant male example, apart from Watson himself who faints when he sees the figure of Holmes standing before him in EMPT, is that of Dr Thorneycroft Huxtable of *The Priory School*, who ends up prostrate and lying unconscious on the 221B bearskin rug.

In 1899 an author called Gwynn published an article in *The Cornhill Magazine* called "The Decay of Sensibility." He defined "sensibility" as the rapturous, exaggerated joy the characters felt, their "copious tears," hysterics, and fainting fits. His idea in this article was that women were often fainting in real life because their favourite heroines in fiction also did so, and he credited the Brontë sisters with putting a stop to fainting. He wrote, "It was only when woman herself took up the pen and began basely to open men's eyes to a sense of the ludicrous in this particular situation (fainting) that all these tender susceptibilities shrivelled like a maidenhair fern exposed to an east wind, and man began to revise his position."

Gwynn thought that, as female writers gained power and popularity, they also had the motivation to put a stop to womankind's hysterical antics.

Many doctors then believed that what were seen to be fits of hysteria by women were the result of uterine irregularity, defined as 'woman's or Eve's curse.' In Holmes' day, hysteria was considered a diagnosable physical illness in women, and it was assumed that the basis for this diagnosis was the belief that most women were predisposed to mental disturbance; in the early twentieth century, this option of extreme behaviour then shifted and was considered an observable and easily definable mental illness.

Many influential psychiatrists such as Sigmund Freud and Jean-Martin Charcot dedicated considerable research to hysteria patients. Charcot studied women in an asylum in France and used hypnosis as treatment. Another French psychologist, Janet, who studied five of hysteria's symptoms (he defined these as anaesthesia, amnesia, abulia, motor control diseases, and character change) proposed that hysteria symptoms occurred due to a lapse in consciousness. Both Charcot and Janet inspired Freud's work on hysteria, but nowadays few psychiatrists share that view.

HALF MAN, HALF BEAST;
THE PSYCHOPATHOLOGY OF DR. GRIMESBY ROYLOTT

"At Waterloo we were fortunate in catching a train for Leatherhead...."

– Dr. Watson (SPEC)

Sherlock Holmes was already twenty-nine years old when he was first required to use the South Western Railway.

Watson had known Holmes and had shared rooms at Baker Street with him for two years, during which time, he developed a keen "pleasure in following…(Holmes') professional investigations, and in admiring the rapid deductions with which he unravelled the problems which were submitted to him.

On 6 April 1883, the good doctor was awoken at 7:15 A.M. to find Sherlock Holmes "standing, fully dressed" by his bed.

His client, a young woman of thirty, her hair "shot with premature grey," was waiting in the sitting room below.

Holmes quickly and adroitly observes:

"You have come in by train this morning, I see."

"You know me then?"

"No, but I observe the second half of a return ticket in the palm of your left glove. You must have started early, and yet you had a good drive in a dog-cart, along heavy roads, before you reached the station."

The young woman was Helen Stoner. Until two years ago, she and her sister had been living with their stepfather, Dr. Grimesby Roylott, on the family estate near Leatherhead.

"The family," she observes, "was at one time the richest in the county, with Berkshire in the north, and Hampshire in the west."

The reason for Miss Stoner's "pitiable state of agitation" soon becomes clear as she relates her story. The uncanny death of her sister, the sadistic behaviour of her sinister stepfather, and the inexplicable mystery of the Speckled Band have brought her hotfoot, via the South Western Railway to Baker Street.

Curiously, it was also in April when, four years later, Holmes and Watson travelled down to Reigate via the old South Eastern Railway *(The Adventure of the Reigate Squires)*. 'My old friend Colonel Hayter, who had come under my professional care in Afghanistan, had now taken a house near Reigate, in Surrey, and had frequently asked me to come down to him on a visit,' Watson confides in his reader.

It was the year of the Golden Jubilee of Queen Victoria's accession to the throne, and the same year in which the grotesque affair of *The Speckled Band* had occurred. The weather and the jubilation of the British people were both memorable features of that year, a year which signified the slow and some Victorians would have said, wearisome, termination of a decade. For Holmes, it had been a busy and exhausting time. When the decade commenced, the events of Lauriston Gardens launched him on a career which was to be quite unparalleled in his depth and range as a consulting detective. We have no record where exactly Colonel Hayter's house of *The Reigate Squire* events stood in Reigate, but the visitor of today will find little that has changed since the construction and development of Reigate as a commuter railway town.

The windmill that fronts Reigate Heath is still there; so too is the 12th century parish church and the ancient Reigate Priory, built in Tudor times, but looking decidedly 18th century, in its outward appearance. Intriguingly, Reigate town, set in the Vale of Holmesdale, was the home of George Eliot and the once popular Gothic novelist, Harrison Ainsworth, who wrote his last twelve novels here. His was a handsome, portico building and the perfect setting for the disturbing Gothic story of *The Speckled Band,* with its dark overtones of incest and murder.

In 1883, the London and South Western Railway Station was situated in the centre of Leatherhead. In those days there were two railway stations. The main competitor of the LSWR was the London, Brighton, and South Coast, but it was the South Western Railway, a competitor, which made Guildford and Leatherhead, towns of prominence.

In 1846 this competitor obtained powers to open a line just north of Guildford station, leading to Farnham, and by 1881, two years before the Stoke Moran affair, the South Western obtained powers to run a line from Surbiton to Leatherhead.

It is therefore, when we examine the words of Miss Stoner that we encounter a problem here with the railway timetables. She states most clearly that: "I started from home before six, reached Leatherhead at twenty-past, and came in by the first train to Waterloo." As Holmes no doubt might have observed, this would have been singularly impossible.

As has been pointed out before, (Roger T. Clapp, 'The Curious Problem of The Railway Timetable, in *The Seventh Cab*, Boston, 1947,) Miss Stoner's earliest train to Waterloo left at 7:22 and then arrived at Waterloo at 8:11. An earlier train, leaving at 7:13, and by arriving at London Bridge, still would not have conveyed her to Baker Street before 8:00A.M.

Even four years later, the earliest train from Leatherhead left at 7:53. We can therefore only assume that Watson's record of that memorable day must have been somewhat inaccurate and that the time he took between waking and dressing was considerably longer than he assumed.

Whatever the origin of Watson's error, the old South Western had the edge over the rival LBSCR. Its average journey from Leatherhead was a mere 47 minutes, as opposed to the LBSCR's 65 minutes. (*Bradshaw*). The train passed through Wimbledon and Epsom, the latter a picturesque village in those days, some 21 miles from Waterloo.

In 1883, the town of Leatherhead still stood very much in a rural setting. However, even then, the wealthier classes found it a convenient and tranquil environment in which to build their resplendent villas.

Thorne's Handbook (1858), that intrepid and reliable Victorian railway guide, hints at this encroachment some 25 years before. Over that intervening period, the population of the town rose from 2,455 to 4,694. The ever-romantic prose of *Thorne's Handbook* remarks:

'The town stands on the right bank of the Mole, at the foot of the beautiful Vale of Mickelham, which extends hence to Dorking. The ground rises somewhat steeply from the Mole, many of the houses being built on a series of irregular terraces. The shops are mostly collected about the crossing of the Guildford and Dorking roads, and in the centre stands a steep-roofed clock and engine house. Several of the houses are old, and some picturesque; but the picturesqueness of the place as a whole, formerly very marked, has been almost improved away of late years. The town of Leatherhead stands on a hill and is centred about crossroads. Its 18th century bridge, with 14 arches, spans the River Mole.'

There are still some fine 16th century buildings left standing here, but the town is predominantly a rather red-brick affair. That masterful Sherlockian, the late Michael Harrison, in his nostalgic book, *In The Footsteps of Sherlock Holmes*, recalls several old shops that still survived until the year 1958 – Leavey's, the tailors, which used to make liveries to supply the staff of the surrounding wealthy houses, and Riddington's, the baker-cum-coffee shop where, in the 1880's, elegant ladies exchanged the latest gossip about their neighbours. Glimpses of the Victorian Leatherhead - if one has a mind to look for it - exist along Gimcrack Hill where decaying mansions still hold their own; however, in the town centre itself, mock-Tudor restaurants now mingle with their genuine ancestors in a bewildering confusion.

The once great houses of this neighbourhood which rank alongside 'Stoke Moran' are still there even now: Eastwick Park, Horsley Towers, Clandon Park, and others – although many are now owned by schools or companies rather than wealthy individuals.

Three years after the murder case of *The Speckled Band* came the long-awaited 'Leatherhead to Guildford Railway'. Then the population doubled and doubled again, making the word "commuter" a reality.

The identity of Stoke Moran itself remains a problem. There are, of course, clues for the eager pilgrim, most of which can be gleaned, thankfully, from Miss Stoner's comments.

We learn that the house was two hundred years old and that the building "was of grey, lichen-blotched stone, with a high central portion, and two curving wings, like the claws of a crab, thrown out on each side." How very Gothic and somewhat disturbing that seems.

Even though the estate had fallen on hard times, there were still a few acres of ground left. A.J. Ginger, recalling Victorian Leatherhead, paints an enduring but melancholy picture for us: '...the wheelwright, the waggon and carriage builder, the saddler, the slaughterer, the leather currier.... All these trades could be found operating in Leatherhead town.... The sound of the hammer ringing on the anvil... could be heard all over Leatherhead town every day."

The location of Stoke Moran ultimately may be deduced both from Miss Stoner's remarks and Watson's description.

It took her twenty minutes in a dog cart to the station and Watson mentions a drive of "four or five miles through the lovely Surrey lanes." The most obvious choice of house would be in Stoke d'Abernon, a village just five miles north-east from Leatherhead station. Stoke d'Abernon manor house is situated just off the present A245.

Watson mentions in his narrative, "the deep tones of the parish clock" striking during that long vigil, and this is most convenient, for Stoke d'Abernon church stands close by, on the banks of the River Mole. Although much restored, the 13th century building has ancient stained glass and a Jacobean pulpit. Certainly the setting of Doyle's tale is perfect, if the house is not. Set in resplendent grounds, the manor house lies not far off the road and behind it the church rises from the riverbank. The atmosphere and mood are ideal and with a little imagination, one can picture the sadistic Roylott, striding about these grounds, his "bile-shot eyes" full of malevolence and spite.

Stoke d'Abernon house dates mainly from the 17th century, but is remarkably different from the grey gabled place of Watson's description. There was an earlier house here as far back as the 16th century. Before that, a Roman villa with a bath house stood where the lawns front the terrace. But neither of the residents of this manor house resemble the Morans of Watson's record. Canon F.P. Philips, a grandson of the Due d'Orleans, lived here for seventy years and was the rector of the church and his successor was also a priest. Neither seemed to me to fulfil the Doylean profile of men possessed of a psychopathic fury.

The alternative to Stoke d'Abernon manor house is the nearby Slyfield Manor. This is a large 17th century building which can be seen from the road but does not have the qualifications of Stoke d'Abernon.

The answer, I would suggest, is that Watson had good reason to disguise the true identity of Stoke Moran.

The Crown Inn, which Miss Stoner claimed lay opposite the house, and where she hired her dog-cart, has long since disappeared, but the old

Station Inn at which Homes hired a trap was most probably the Swan or The Bull coaching inn. Both of these lay within an easy distance of the station and are therefore, suitable candidates.

Despite the changes that Leatherhead itself has undergone, the village of Stoke d'Abernon has altered little since the 1880s. The narrow road that connects it with the town is a lonely, winding route and it is easy enough to picture the heavily veiled figure of Helen Stoner, driving in her dog-cart along the muddy road (there was no tarmacadam in those days), her mind burdened by the memory of her sister's death and that sinister low whistle which preceded it.

The owner of Stoke Moran, Dr. Roylott, was a man of both considerable strength and singularity of purpose, like many of Conan Doyle's male characters, including both Professor Challenger of 'The Lost World' and Sherlock Holmes himself. Roylott, the plotting and scheming father, is the key to this whole case. He is ruthless, a psychopath of the first order, and he appears to live a life of unremitting violence , shown to all those who dare to challenge him.

In India, we learn, he beat his Indian butler to death, and thought, outrageously, he just might be exonerated.

Throughout the Holmes stories walk a procession of intimidated and exploited women, possessing, however, both the practicality and immense moral strength and spirituality of Doyle's own mother: Helen

Fig. 35. Roylott's attack on the village blacksmith.

Stoner of *The Speckled Band*, Violet Hunter of *The Copper Beeches*, Violet Smith of *The Solitary Cyclist,* and several others, including Kitty Winter of the vitriol throwing renown, or the woman who pumped several bullets into the odious Charles Augustus Milverton; each is willing to confront the powers of darkness. and each possesses considerable warmth and reason for our admiration. Their foes are invariably lecherous, scheming, cold, and mercenary opponents. They exist only to be eventually destroyed, and about each, is a suggestion of the nightmare world of the madness of his younger years, when he was often confronted by a deranged and alcoholic father, a period which Conan Doyle had so clearly suppressed. It is no coincidence that these phallic, aggressive males often bear an extraordinary resemblance to each other. Dark, sensual, and thin faced; each carries within him a suggestion of sexual perversion, and a stench of incest. Compare, for instance, these vivid descriptions of the odious Dr. Grimesby Roylott, of *The Speckled Band* with the sexually perverse predator, Baron Gruner of *The Illustrious Client*:

'A large face scarred with a thousand wrinkles, burned yellow with the sun, and marked with every evil passion, was turned from one to the other of us, while his deep, bile-shot eyes, and his high thin, fleshless nose, gave him the resemblance to a fiery old bird of prey.' (SPEC).

Fig. 36. Holmes beats the phallic attacker back to the lair of its unsuspecting master.

'His face was swarthy, almost Oriental, with large, dark, languorous eyes which might easily hold an irresistible fascination for women. His hair and moustache were raven black, the latter short, pointed, and carefully waxed. His features were regular and pleasing, save only his straight thin-lipped mouth. If ever I saw a murderer's mouth, it was there - a cruel, hard gash in the face, compressed, inexorable and terrible...' (ILLU).

The theme of innocence seduced is one which truly haunts the Holmes stories, and it is hardly surprising therefore, that revenge also features so largely in the sixty plots that make up the Holmes Canon. From the fertile brain of Arthur Conan Doyle was summoned an avenging angel: asexual, moral, a character of extreme logic but also of intense spirituality.

Sherlock Holmes sought out the image of Doyle's father and slew him repeatedly in these often bizarre, and frequently disturbing stories. There is a passage in Freud's 'Introductory Lectures on Psychology,' which best explains the compulsive relationship between Sherlock Holmes and Conan Doyle.

Freud comments:

'Do you recall the outcome of our dream-analyses; how the wishes that construct dreams are so often of a perverse incestuous nature, or reveal an unsuspected hostility to those who are nearest and dearest to the dreamer? At that time... we gave no explanation of the origin of these evil impulses. Now you can find it for yourselves. They are allocations of the libido which date from early infancy and have long since been abandoned as far as conscious life is concerned, but which prove still to be present at night-time and to be capable of functioning in a certain sense ... Everyone, not only neurotics, experience these perverse, incestuous and murderous dreams...'

More than any other form of literature, the crime story provides a catharsis for those unresolved feelings and emotions about our parents, which we carry with us from childhood in the shape of memories, fantasy, and dreams. To writer and reader alike, there is, in all good crime fiction, a freedom to kill and be killed, to crucify and resurrect in these tales, until at their reasoned conclusions, the phantoms that beset us are finally laid to rest. The Sherlock Holmes Saga is no exception, and these often perverse, often dark, and cruel accounts of dysfunctional characters, mutilations, incestuous fathers, and predatory males, are none the less memorable and remarkable for that.

The Speckled Band is undoubtedly one of the most popular of the Sherlock Holmes stories and was Doyle's favourite Holmes story. Yet its popularity has rarely been explained. As a detective puzzle. it is a little ingenious, but perhaps unlikely. Could an assassin really train a snake to climb up and down a bell rope, squeeze through a ventilator and bite its victim?

Could it rehearse this scenario without being at least noticed by its intended victim?

These are deep waters, Watson.

It is perhaps better to regard this tale as a mythic, rather than a realistic, story. After all, its interest lies in the peculiar nature of the relationship between Dr Grimesby Roylott and his daughters and in the even more bizarre nature of his murder plan. The power of such a story depends largely on this mythic level where an appeal is made to our innermost fears. That is surely what gives the story of *The Speckled Band* its disturbing ad enduring power.

What do we know of the characters of the story and how do they fit into a possibly mythic structure?

In traditional terms we have Sherlock Holmes himself, who is the classical prototype of the hero. In this story he is also Holmes the dragon slayer (or Holmes the serpent/ worm slayer —a worm was identified with a dragon in Northern European pagan sagas). Holmes is also the defender of womanhood, and here, in this tale, also the preserver of female virginity. In *The Speckled Band*, as in a number of Aryan and Scandinavian ancient sagas, Holmes rescues the defenceless and innocent and protects them from the evil intentions of the dark, all-destroying father figure — Roylott.

How well does Dr Roylott fit into the picture of the dark destroyer, and what archetypal qualities does he exhibit? To begin with, Roylott is a psychopath of the first order. The son of an aristocratic pauper squire, he obtained a medical degree and emigrated to Calcutta, where he established for himself a large practice. Whilst there, he married Mrs Stoner, the young widow, formerly the wife of a major general in the Bengal Artillery.

The family subsequently emigrated to England and lived in the ancestral home on the western borders of Surrey. Both the gypsies and the wild animals who wander around the overgrown property surrounding Stoke Moran are aspects of the exoticism within this story. They are depicted as vague threats, thus giving the place a strange, sinister, and disturbing ambience.

Roylott's wife died in a railway accident at Crewe, although she left a considerable annuity for her two daughters, Helen and Julia. Roylott has indulged in numerous brawls with local people, including the blacksmith, whom he hurled into a stream in a fit of anger. While in Calcutta, he beat his native butler to death and narrowly escaped capital punishment. The character profile that emerges is of a deeply disturbed individual, prone to unreasoning rages.

There is also evidence in the story that Roylott abuses his two daughters. On her first visit to Baker Street, Miss Stoner is described in the following terms: 'She raised her veil as she spoke, and we could see that she was indeed in a pitiable state of agitation, her face all drawn and grey, with restless, frightened eyes, like those of some hunted animal. Her features and figure were those of a woman of thirty, but her hair was shot with premature grey, and her expression was weary and haggard.'

The key word here is 'hunted'. In fact, Miss Stoner shows all the classic symptoms of a daughter who is being sexually abused by a father who exhibits sadistic tendencies towards her. Later on, Holmes questions Miss Stoner further:

'You are screening your stepfather.'
'Why, what do you mean?' For answer, Holmes pushed back the frill of black lace which fringed the hand that lay upon our visitor's knee. Five little livid spots, the marks of four fingers and a thumb, were printed upon the white wrist.
'You have been cruelly used,' said Holmes. The lady coloured deeply, and covered over her injured wrist. 'He is a hard man,' she said, 'and perhaps he hardly knows his own strength. '

Note that Miss Stoner is anxious to conceal Roylott's cruelty towards her and that she tries to excuse his actions. Her own guilt as a victim of sexual assault is here evident.

Roylott's physical appearance corresponds to what Wilhelm Reich (the errant pupil of Freud, who wrote extensively about the sexual characteristics of neurotic character types) referred to as the 'phallic personality'. 'A large face, seared with a thousand wrinkles, burned yellow with the sun, and marked with every evil.' Here is confirmation of what we also find in the criminologist Cesare Lombroso's observation of criminal types - the notion that the evil intentions of the criminal are writ large in his face. Grimesby Roylott - the first name has echoes of filth, and 'filthy lucre' while the last name carries with it suggestions of a former nobility gone to seed- is the Gothic villain and abuser personified. He gets his sexual kicks from beating, bruising and attempting to kill his two daughters to gain access to their incomes.

Commenting on the Gothic qualities that this tale possesses, Raijosta, in his internet essay, 'Analytical Analysis of "The Speckled Band" by Arthur Conan Doyle,' (February 24, 2013) comments: 'Gothic tropes like oppression of women, and murder, which are set in a dark, decaying estate in the possession of an heirless male introduce the element of the uncanny in this story.

This was a familiar technique of Gothic authors during this time. As Ed Cameron says, in his essay *Ironic Escapism in the Symbolic Spread of Gothic Materialist Meaning,*

'Along with these arguments in favour of understanding the Gothic sublime as at least, a latent form of the uncanny, lies the supposition that the late eighteenth century fostered a favourable environment for the literary development of the uncanny.'

Fig. 37. Roylott with the curious snake headgear illuminated by Holmes' candle.

The entire piece is essentially about darkness: hidden and murderous objectives, darker deeds, and above all, Roylott's barely sublimated and incestuous desires for his clearly virginal daughters. *The Speckled Band* is thus a paradigm of the Late Gothic genre.

Roylott is also most representative of patriarchal values in Victorian society. He is a survivor of the rigours and climatic challenges of British colonial India where he has identified himself as a killer of one of its Indian servants and where imperial ideology has allowed him to escape justice. As in another case, *The Copper Beeches*, where a young governess is offered a post in the house of Mr Rucastle, and is offered her post only on the condition that she cuts her hair, the case becomes increasingly threatening and sinister, containing the Gothic themes of dispossession, greed, potential incest and madness, and Roylott is the stereotypical example of the criminologist Lombroso's idea of 'the criminal type,' where he argued the idea of 'the born criminal.' Such 'types,' Lombroso argued, were atavistic reversions where criminals exhibited remarkably similar anatomical and behavioural features.

Equipped with a cane, Holmes waits in the darkness until he hears the serpent advancing. When the serpent is struck, it returns to its master, and then deals him a fatal blow. Despite all his attempts to destroy the feminine principle, thus blotting out women entirely from his wretched life, Roylott is himself killed and emasculated by his own rapacious desires.

As Holmes and Watson listen in the dark, they hear 'the most horrible cry'. 'It swelled up louder and louder, a hoarse yell of pain and fear and anger all mingled in the one dreadful shriek.'

When Holmes and Watson enter Roylott's chamber, they find him sitting on a wooden chair. He is dressed in a grey dressing-gown, but his 'bare ankles' protrude from beneath, indicating that he is perhaps naked beneath the gown. Night after night he has stood on the edge of that chair and peered through the ventilator grille. This is a powerful image of a middle-aged voyeur who projects his own phallus like a lance of death into the chamber beyond. And there, round his forehead lies the snake.

'In an instant his strange head-gear began to move, and there reared itself from among his hair the squat diamond-shaped head and puffed neck of a loathsome serpent.'

It is interesting that Roylott here resembles the ouroboros, the serpent eating its own tail. In this symbol we see that male and female energy have been united. There is also an echo here of the serpent's head as the Jewel in the Lotus, a symbol which is perpetuated in many world mythologies. According to this imagery, the divine male serpent acquired a 'blood-red jewel' in his head. So, in the death of Roylott, we see the final union of the male and female energies. The great solar phallus has at last been grounded in the darkness of the abyss.

Fig. 38. A stunning piece of art work from an America newspaper, The San Francisco Call, 1905, by W. Francis, showing the terrifying figure of Roylott, feeling the force of the phallic backlash of the swamp adder.

BIBLIOGRAPHY OF WORKS CONSULTED FOR THIS STUDY

Jones, Kelvin I. - The Chthonic Sepent, in *The Speckled Band*, ed. by Chris & Barbara Roden, Calabash Press, 1997.

Rosenberg, Samuel - *Naked is The Best Disguise: The Death and Resurrection of Sherlock Holmes*, Penguin Books.

Fig. 39. The phallically predisposed and aggressive Dr Grimesby Roylott.

THE BAKER STREET BOYS

Fig, 40. An unusual interpretation of the Irregulars, listening intently
to a very chubby Sherlock Holmes. Published in *The Wilson Advance*,
an American syndicated newspaper, 18th April, 1895.

*'As (Holmes) spoke, there came a swift pattering of naked feet upon the stairs,
a clatter of high voices, and in rushed a dozen dirty and ragged little street arabs.
There was some show of discipline among them, despite their tumultuous entry, for*

they instantly drew up in line and stood facing us with expectant faces. One of their number, taller and older than the others, stood forward with an air of lounging superiority which was very funny in such a disreputable little scarecrow.'
   -The Sign of Four.

One important advantage Holmes gained over his official rivals, the detective force at Scotland Yard, was the inexpensive employment of the gang of street children, introduced to us in STUD as 'the Baker Street Irregulars'. The beggar children, or 'street arabs', as Watson calls them, were to be found everywhere.

The police could do little about these children, apparently, partly because they were a source of great amusement to the general middle-class public, partly because the police really did not know who they were since they carried with them no accurate proof of identity; but also because they were extremely agile and evasive, and therefore, when they were arrested, they often escaped police custody. For those who were arrested, and then appeared in the magistrates court, the only place open to many of them was the workhouse or the relatively new 'Ragged Schools,' and most of these schools quibbled or even occasionally refused to take responsibility for them.

They didn't stop these youths from committing crimes, either. Henry Mayhew thought that 'however well- intentioned such instructions offered to them were, from the mere fact of bringing together so many boys of a vicious nature (is) productive of far more injury than benefit to the community. If some boys are rescued… many are lost to them.' (Letter to The Morning Chronicle, 29th March, 1850.)

 Like many gangs of their kind, the Irregulars of Baker Street lingered during the daytime in the streets of the capital, where they usually slept rough, cavorted, stole goods from the costermongers, made a mischief of themselves by mobbing and often picking the pockets of affluent looking passers – by, or were then often sexually abused by child offenders and foreign sailors.

If the 'street arabs' were often viewed as beyond all redemption and consequently untameable in their anarchic and wild behaviour, then the girls of this abandoned class were without doubt or exception, seen by most as far worse. Mary Carpenter, who researched the plight of juvenile miscreants like the 'Irregulars', observed:

'...the tenderness of the woman's nature renders her more completely diseased in her whole nature when thus perverted by evil and when a woman is thrown aside, the virtuous restraints of society are enlisted on the side of evil and she is far more dangerous to society than the other sex.' (*Our Convicts*, London 1864.)

In the dangerous day to day world of the Irregulars, girls - especially if they were attractive - were often used as look- outs or decoys for the juvenile gangs and the garrotters employed girls of this sort to lure wealthy men into the narrow side alleys of London where two male criminals would then beat him into submission, using a lead weighted cosh, tie a rope round the neck of their male victim, then rob him of all his belongings, sometimes leaving him stark naked.

Of the character of Nancy in Dickens' famous novel about Victorian gangs of juvenile delinquents, he wrote, in his 1841 preface to his novel, Oliver Twist,

'The girl is a prostitute, though I endeavoured, while I painted the truth in all its fallen and degraded aspects, to banish from the lips of the lowest character I introduced, any expression that could possibly offend... in the case of the girl, in particular, I kept this intention constantly in view...'

In a frank interview with a young girl, Henry Mayhew reported her as saying this regarding her time as a juvenile prostitute:

'At the age of ten, I was apprenticed a maid of all work in Duke Street, London. My master beat me and my mistress knocked me downstairs so I ran away and stayed in lodging houses.. I went to Brighton...begging but couldn't get much, not enough to pay for lodgings...I was constantly insulted in the lodging houses and in the streets...I couldn't be virtuous...no girl could be circumstanced as I was...I hated being wicked, but I was tricked and cheated...'

In the world of juvenile gangs like the Baker Street boys, gangs of urchins could take goods from a badly loaded cart worth as much as their fathers earned in as week. To be caught doing this was therefore worth the risk and so these young girls were seen as valuable commodities. These girl 'irregulars' could not only act as lookouts but were also able to convey stolen goods from one place to another where there was less chance of them being stopped and searched by the beat constable.

Girls, unlike boys, were also frequent customers of pawn shops, chandlers and marine shops where stolen goods could easily be turned into hard cash. Many of the more intelligent girls soon became respected accomplices of certain boy gangs since they then quickly earned a reputation. As they grew older, these prostitute-thieves got most of their income from robberies of those people they came into contact with, stealing money, watches and clothes.

Boys like Wiggins, the favoured leader of the 'irregulars;, who are portrayed so endearingly by Conan Doyle in *The Sign of Four,* often had dire tales to tell about their troubled past lives. W. A. Miles, of the Prison Discipline Society, gives us an insight which is typical of its kind. A Shropshire lad, at the age of 14, ran away to London to seek his fortune. When his luck ran out, he joined a gang of boys like the 'Irregulars' whose headquarters was an old prison van which had been abandoned under the arches of the Adelphi theatre. Here a man called Larry bought from the gang silk handkerchiefs they had stolen from passers-by. He showed so much ability with his technique of thieving that he became known to two men who found him useful. He worked with the gang but was then arrested and served a short spell in prison. Another youth, George Nutt, went on to say:

'When I was between 12 and 13, I became acquainted with bad women. I was introduced to them by my (gang member) friends. When I was 12, I went shoplifting in the Old Kent Road. We stole a pair of scaled but I was arrested and sent to Horsemonger Gaol. After my release we stole things in Chelmsford and for that I spent 12 months in the House of Correction. This time when I came out I then got into burglary...'

Because of the enterprising nature of the Irregulars, it is quite conceivable that they may have at some point received some form of education at the so called 'Ragged Schools.' These were schools which sprang up around 1840 and were not part of an organised group. William Locke, one of the four founding fathers of the much later Ragged Schools Union, did his best to encourage children who had renounced dishonesty.

The ages of the children received in these school were between 4 and 16. But half of these were under 10, and this is the most likely scenario with the irregulars that they would have received some, possibly minimal, education in this way. Huge numbers were by this time being sent to the colonies, where they were eventually able to gain an honest living, instead of remaining dishonestly at home.

William Locke reported in the middle century that many of the boys who had frequently been in prison and who at first had behaved in a disorderly and insulting way, through honest and kind treatment, had 'almost invariably been brought in subjection and obedience,' and many of the very worst of these boys had turned out to be 'better men'.

As Sherlock Holmes and his rivals also must have known, these boys who had been found guilty of committing multiple offences of theft and often would be sentenced to short terms of imprisonment, on the ship hulks, either at Chatham Dock and at Dungeness or in the River Thames, where they would be made to work as skivvies, much demeaned by acting as virtual slaves to some of the staff or prisoners.

One boy, Charles Thomas. who had been sentenced to work on a prison hulk for the crime of larceny, had later been appointed as an assistant on the hospital ship moored at Chatham, and treated boys occasionally, as his work demanded, when he went on board, He explained to a member of the Commons Select Committee in 1835:

'There was sometimes up to 40 or 50 boys in the hospital. I have known boys to take an old copper button and apply it very hot to the skin. And then apply rum and soap to the sore made by the very hot button. And then they would then wrap it up or two or three days, then show the wound to the doctor, and then come to the hospital in a state piteous to behold. It would look very like a sore. Sometimes the settling of these cases would give more trouble than any others. I have known cases in which they have broken their arms to get into hospital. They would hold their arms on a form and let the edge of the table drop on it. They would get other boys to do this for them. The excuse was that they had tumbled down a ladder. I have had patients come into the hospital on the Hulk who have declared that they had not tasted meat for three weeks. They had been obliged to give their portions to the 'nobs' and had fed themselves on gruel and pairings of potatoes. They had committed these acts to get into hospital in order to have a more regular diet.'

Sometimes they were transported to Australia, if the judge was able to confirm the fact that they had committed multiple crimes of theft. And they often dreaded this intervention. Often, though, they simply died of lack of medical attention, or were reduced to the piteous state of starving to death, or of dying from hypothermia, as is described in two of Dickens' novels. However, they are most affectionately remembered in *The Sign of Four* but also in Dickens' work as part of the of the gang of youths who were led by Sykes, the psychopathic killer in the novel, 'Oliver Twist'.

Aided by the newly emerging forensic methods and his own ingenious street hard working and enterprising junior detective force, Holmes had all the advantages over his competitors in the field. The 'Baker Street Irregulars' were at the top of their game and, faced with an often bleak and forbidding future, they would have provided Holmes with the very welcome 'street cred' information he often had to rely upon.

Young lads like those in the Wiggins gang also played a prominent role in the day-to-day affairs of professional beggars. A beggar would often use a young boy to claim the interest of passers by the sheer ragged nature of his clothes and his downtrodden looks. And having had his attention once drawn attention to the boy, the latter would then talk to the sympathetic onlooker and introduce him to the beggar himself, and the stranger would thus gain further information about the man's lowly circumstances. The professional beggars often used young boys to help remove a rival from a much sought after 'patch'.

Holmes was quick to perceive the potential in the rapid wit and street knowledge of these street urchins. Unhampered by the demands of an elementary education, they were available at all hours, and could be relied upon to offer their services under the most unlikely of conditions. The workhouse didn't want them, the reformatories rejected them, but Mr. Sherlock Holmes of Baker Street paid them by the hour.

The Irregulars appear in several of the stories (namely CROO, SIGN, STUD, HOUN and LADY) and appeared to be an indispensable part of the detective's data gathering. Apart from finding the missing boat, Aurora in SIGN, they appear to have achieved a great deal else for Holmes. Wiggins ('the scarecrow') was clearly the leader of the pack but that Holmes used others in an individual capacity is certain. Simpson and Cartwright were employed separately on two occasions. Holmes' wages of a shilling a day provided a handsome remuneration. However, it was also sadly the case that in Victorian London, these boys could earn even greater sums by offering sexual favours to men as male prostitutes.

The 'Telegraph Boy Scandal,' in which many prominent homosexuals were involved, points to the unrestricted abuse of young children who were left to roam the streets of Victorian London.

For many years, the General Post Office in London had employed young men of under sixteen years of age to deliver telegrams to private individuals within the city and beyond into the suburbs of London.

In the July of the year 1889, a police constable was investigating a theft from the Central Telegraph Office and, during his investigation stumbled across the fact that one of the employees, a 15-year-old Telegraph boy, called Charles Thomas Swanscow, was found to have a large sum of money for which he had no satisfactory explanation. When questioned closely, he said that he had obtained a sum of money by 'acting on behalf' of male clients in a house in Cleveland St at number 19 and, moreover, had earned quite a considerable sum of money amounting to 14 shillings.

When asked precisely how he had obtained this sum, he explained and then confessed to the policeman, that he had earned this money as 'ill-gotten gains'. When questioned as to what that actually meant, he explained that he had been in attendance at a male brothel, which happened to be situated locally within the city at number 19, Cleveland St. Another boy was found to have been working with him. who was a boy of 18 years, one Charles Henry Truelove. He had also been working for Hammond in the brothel there, when the police conducted their raid. The boys revealed to the officer that there were some 'very upper-class looking people' who re attending the house in Cleveland Street. And some of those they suspected, they told police, were connected with the aristocracy, including possibly a member of the Royal Family.

The case was then handed over to senior Scotland Yard detectives who raided the brothel where they then found that Hammond had narrowly escaped custody by being informed by another visitor and had subsequently sought refuge at his relative's house in Gravesend, Kent. Armed with this knowledge and also the knowledge that two other boys have been implicated in the business of the brothel the process of interrogation and the arrests were taken charge of by Inspector Fred Abberline of the New Scotland Yard team. He was one of the most successful police officers of his generation at the Yard. However, by the time that Abberline and his team arrived at the brothel, Hammond had long gone and Abberline and his detectives were only able to arrest two other participants who had been on loan to the male homosexuals at the brothel. They were subsequently arrested.

Fig . 41. The unfortunate Prince Albert Victor; "Eddy" to the family, also known as the Duke of Clarence, he was the oldest child of the future King Edward VII and Queen Alexandra. He was engaged to Princess May of Teck, but died of pneumonia before they were married. Police witness evidence demonstrated he had been involved in the Cleveland Street male brothel.

On the way to the police station, one of these called Newlove named Lord Arthur Somerset and Henry FitzRoy, Earl of Euston, as well as an army colonel by the name of Jervois, as visitors to Cleveland Street.

Lord Somerset had certainly been seen there and he was the head of the Prince of Wales's stables. And although he was subsequently interviewed at length by police, no further action was taken against him.

An arrest warrant was then issued in the name of George Veck, an acquaintance of Hammond's, who had pretended to be a clergyman. Veck had worked at the Telegraph Office, and had been sacked for "improper conduct" with the messenger boys. A seventeen-year-old youth found in Veck's London lodgings told police that Veck had gone to Portsmouth. The police subsequently arrested Veck at Waterloo railway station.

On 16 December 1889, a new trial commenced in London, when Newlove's and Somerset's solicitor, Arthur Newton, was charged with obstruction of justice. It was claimed by the police that he conspired to prevent Hammond and the two boys from testifying by offering them passage and money to go escape arrest and go abroad. Newton was then defended by Charles Russell, and the prosecutor was Sir Richard Webster, the Attorney General. Newton pleaded guilty to only one of the six charges against him, claiming he had helped Hammond to escape only to protect his clients, who weren't then charged, from possible blackmail. The Attorney General accepted Newton's pleas and didn't present any evidence on the other five charges.

However, on 20 May, the presiding judge sentenced Newton to six weeks in prison, then widely thought by the legal profession to be rather harsh. A petition which had been signed by 250 London law firms was then sent to the Home Secretary, Henry Matthews, protesting at Newton's treatment.

All those subsequent leads which were investigated by police failed to produce much more evidence against the suspects and the aristocratic gentlemen, like Somerset and his companions, had by then disappeared, as it were, into thin air. So also unresolved was the mystery of the Prince of Wales son's presence there, Albert Victor Eddy. He had been seen by some of the suspects as present in the brothel, but had apparently escaped before the police began their interviews and were able to complete their investigation.

As a result of this, and partly because of the furore which arose in the newspapers of the time, the Cleveland St Scandal ended as thoroughly confused as it began, with no real proof or hope by detectives that the Prince Albert Eddy could ever be prosecuted, even if they had the evidence to do so, which is unlikely, since most of the evidence against him was simply circumstantial. And circumstantial evidence, as Sherlock Holmes would have known, is highly unsatisfactory, without some empirical evidence also being produced. with which to back it up.

Somerset himself escaped to France and thence travelled to Europe and America, and he was never brought to the courts in person to account for his offences, apart from the inconvenience of paying high legal fees to his solicitor. The fact that the two leading boys involved in the conspiracy also were given short prison sentences was yet another unsatisfactory component of the issue. The whole affair of the Cleveland Street Scandal certainly does demonstrate how very vulnerable and open to corruption young boys were, particularly on the street, even when pursuing an apparently legitimate lifestyle or occupation.

Part of the problem experienced by homosexuals of the Holmes period was that society refused to believe in its existence and often so, as a consequence the more promiscuous homosexuals used young boys as their confidantes but also as their pimps.

Before 1892, when the taxonomic term 'homosexuality' first appeared in English in a translation of Krafft-Ebing's *Psychopathia Sexualis*, there was no homosexuality, only sexual inversion. The ground-breaking book by the German psychiatrist *Psychopathia Sexualis* was a freely available text. However, in Britain there was a marked resistance in this period among the medical community to regard homosexuality as a subject fit for scientific enquiry. And as Sean Brady points out in his study of the period: (*Masculinity and Male Homosexuality in Britain, 1861-1913*):

'Nearly all developments in early sexology were continental achievements. The significant exception was, of course, the work of the English sexologist, Havelock Ellis.

But Ellis' work was suppressed by the English authorities throughout this period; his ideas did not receive significant attention in Britain until the early 1920s.

The 'Irregulars' appear in several of the stories (namely CROO, SIGN, STUD, HOUN and LADY) and appeared to be an indispensable part of the detective's data- gathering. Apart from finding the missing *Aurora* in SIGN, they appear to have achieved a great deal else for Holmes. Wiggins ('the scarecrow') was clearly the leader of the pack but that Holmes used others in an individual capacity is certain. Simpson and Cartwright were employed separately on two occasions. Holmes' wages of a shilling a day provided a handsome remuneration. But what did they do for the rest of their time? Were they used just on an ad hoc basis or had Holmes other uses for them?

In later years we do not hear so much about the Irregulars. Perhaps they were disbanded and absorbed into the system of elementary education. Or perhaps Holmes found fewer occasions when he could use them.

With such men as Mercer (CREE), Shinwell Johnson (ILLU) and Langdale Pike (3GAB) at large, the 'Irregulars' may have seemed dangerous bait for hardened criminals. But I have a hunch that at least one of them, Wiggins, was to provide a continued service to the detective in his later years.

Most commentators give the date of MAZA in which we encounter Billy the pageboy, as 1903. This being the case, and assuming that 'Billy' Wiggins was roughly eleven or twelve in SIGN (1887), it would make him all of 28 years old, which is highly unlikely. But if the assumption of 1903 is incorrect, and the case belongs to an earlier year, it would indeed be possible that Wiggins was the page boy. That he had been pageboy for some years is evident from Watson's remark to him: 'You don't change, either'.

From the very outset of his career in STUD, it is clear that Holmes was dogged by a sharp social conscience, regarding boys of this class in what was an uncaring age.

His remarks about the boarding schools (NAVA), often quoted, show his concern with the welfare of young people from the lower classes and may even be evidence of his own impoverished upbringing. The Irregulars' enlistment shows one aspect of this concern and he probably provided them with more charity and assistance than we are aware of.

FOOTNOTE

I have included here the following comment about Albert Victor, the young son of Edward V11, and his possible involvement in the case of the Telegraph Boy Scandal, as a reflection of the way in which the 'Royals' were always, and are even today, some might claim, a 'protected' class of their own, and, seemingly, accountable to few. The comments below were by the editor of *'The Stauntons'*, by A. Ayers, in the *Notable British Trials* series of the same title:

'Prince Albert Victor died in 1892, but society gossip about his sex life continued. Sixty years after the scandal, the official biographer of King George V, Harold Nicolson, was told by Lord Goddard, who was a twelve-year-old schoolboy at the time of the scandal, that Prince Albert Victor "had been involved in a male brothel scene, and that a solicitor had to commit perjury to clear him. The solicitor was struck off the rolls for his offence, but was thereafter reinstated. In fact, none of the lawyers involved in the case was convicted of perjury or struck off at the time, indeed most had very distinguished careers. However, Arthur Newton (*involved in the case - kj*) was struck off for 12 months for professional misconduct in 1910 after falsifying letters from another of his clients—the notorious murderer Crippen.

In 1913, he was struck off indefinitely and sentenced to three years' imprisonment for obtaining money by false pretences. Newton may have invented and spread the rumours about Prince Albert Victor in an attempt to protect his clients from prosecution, by forcing a cover-up. State papers on the case in the Public Record Office, and released to the public in the 1970s, provide no information on the prince's involvement, other than Newton's threat to implicate him.

Hamilton Cuffe wrote to the Director of Public Prosecutions, Sir Augustus Stephenson, "I am told that Newton has boasted that if we go on, a very distinguished person will be involved. I don't mean to say that I for one instant credit it—but in such circumstances as this one never knows what may be said, be concocted or be true.

The Dramatis Personae of the Cleveland Street affair (with grateful acknowledgements)is an very useful internet site, from which the notes below have been included (www.clevelandstreetscandal.com):

Henry Horace Newlove 16 yrs old. Telegraph Boy - GPO 'Recruiter' for Hammond.

Charles Thomas Swinscow 15 yrs. Telegraph Boy - First boy arrested for 'theft.'

George Alma Wright 17 yrs. Telegraph Boy - 'Performed' with Newlove for voyeurs.

Charles Ernest Thickbroom, 17 yrs. Telegraph Boy.

William Meech Perkins 16 yrs. Telegraph Boy - ID's Lord Alfred Somerset as a 'client.'

Algernon Edward Allies. 19 yrs. Houseboy - The Marlborough Club, used by Lord Somerset.

George Barber 17 yrs. George Veck's 'Private Secretary' and boyfriend.

John Saul. 37 yrs. Infamous London rent boy - Possibly aka Jack Saul.

Charles Hammond 35 yrs Brothel keeper of 19 Cleveland Street, London.

George Daniel Veck, aka, Rev George Veck. aka Rev George Barber.
 Ex General Post Office (GPO) employee, sacked for indecency with telegraph boys. Lived at 19 Cleveland Street. Kept a coffee house in Gravesend, Kent. Has an 18 year old 'son' that travels with him.

PC Luke Hanks. Police officer attached to the General Post Office.

Mr Phillips. Senior postal official who questioned Swinscow with Hanks.

Mr C H Raikes. The Postmaster General.

Mr James Monro, Metropolitan Police Commissioner.

Frederick Abberline; 46 yrs Police Chief Inspector, infamous for the 'Jack the Ripper' investigations in 1888, London's Whitechapel district

PC Richard Sladden. Police officer who carried out observations on the Cleveland Street brothel, following Swinscow's arrest.

Arthur Newton. Lord Arthur Somerset's solicitor. Later to defend Oscar Wilde at his trial in 1895 and notorious murderer Dr Crippen.

Prince Albert Victor, the Duke of Clarence. 25 yrs/ Rumoured to be a 'Brothel Client' - Went on a seven month tour of British India in Sept 1889 to avoid the press & trials.

Colonel Jervois of the2nd Life Guards. 'Brothel Client' - Winchester Army Barracks

Lord Arthur Somerset aka Mr Brow 37 yrs 'Brothel Client' - Named in Allies letters as 'Mr Brown'

Henry James Fitzroy 39 yrs,. Accused of being a 'Brothel Client' - Earl of Euston.

Sir Augustus Stephsns, Director of Public Prosecutions (DPP).

Hon Hamilton Cuffe Assistant DPP - Six years later he would prosecute Oscar Wilde at his trial in 1895 as the Director of Public Prosecutions.

Ernest Parke, Journalist - North London Press.

APPENDICES

Introduction by John H. Watson to the Sherlock Holmes monograph on: The Use of Disguise and The Art of Deception

by Sherlock Holmes and Dr. Hans Gross, Examining Magistrate.

'It was not merely that Holmes changed his costume. His expression, his manner, his very soul seemed to vary with every fresh part that he assumed. The stage lost a fine actor, even as science lost an acute reasoner, when he became a specialist in crime.

- Myself, Dr. John Watson, there, writing about my friend, Mr Sherlock Holmes, private consulting detective of Baker Street, when chronicling the case of the American adventuress, and contralto singer, Miss Irene Adler, in my account of the case, published in The Strand Magazine, in 1891.

In these now famous but once obscure series of monographs which Sherlock Holmes, we may assume, based on his notes and analyses from many real-life cases which he solved, demonstrate to me beyond doubt, that my former friend and colleague of past years truly did possess an innate talent, and almost uncanny ability to become other people, which I have never seen rivalled in others – and this view of him also applies to some leading professional actors some of whom I have had the pleasure to know during the last twenty or so years of association with Holmes and others on many unique cases.

Naturally, Mr Holmes has his own view upon the matter. He prefers to attribute his success to three basic principles which lie at the heart of his investigative method: and those are, observation, interpretation and deduction. However, regarding this so called 'empirical' interpretation of his abilities, I would not entirely agree, for there is more to it than just plain observation and the application of logic. Holmes certainly possesses a unique and cherished talent, both to imitate and to represent the presence of other people whom he has known, often but a short while. It is an ability he possesses, not only to echo their movements, but also their individual mannerisms, even including, in some instances, the timbre of that person's voice, or of his specific accent, or choice of words.

This remarkable ability to quickly and efficiently imitate their moves, sentiments or particular foibles thus enables my colleague to see rapidly and lucidly through others' disguises.

With regard to the latter skill, I especially well recall that Holmes seemed to be in his element, when able to retrieve and confirm the true identity of Hugh Boone, the beggar, who turned out, to be, once his se was revealed by Holmes, to be the missing businessman of The Cedars in Lee, Kent.

I was therefore much delighted to be asked to provide a preface to this second edition of the volume, since I regard it as perhaps his most worthy, and most wide ranging of small works; and since it is also the result of a period of close and diligent collaboration with that other master of European criminology, Dr Hans Gross, who also provides throughout the work, references to parallel European examples. But perhaps I do not need labour the point that these two maestros of crime, and criminal investigation, have collaborated widely in the past.

This assertion of mine is based on a close reading, not just of the criminology journals here in England, but also of the criminology journals in France, Germany, Switzerland and Sweden.

However, I should also not forget to mention that the labours of these two pioneering sons of justice have just recently received much praise from M. Villon, currently head of the Criminal Investigation department of the Paris Prefecture; but also that these two men have received commendations from M. Bertillon, now one of the world's most renowned but contentious criminologists; and Cesare Lombroso, that other unparalleled criminologist and sociologist, whose career has always, like that of my colleague, Mr Holmes, often courted initial disagreement both in his precepts and sometimes his methods.

I might remind readers of this short but fascinating work that, to quote Sherlock Holmes himself,

"You know my methods, Watson. Apply them."

John H. Watson, M.D.

Sherlock Holmes' monograph upon the art of disguise and deception, with comments and contributions, by Dr Hans Gross.

Section 1. Disguising the face, by Sherlock Holmes.

Criminals have constantly recourse to disguises. With what cleverness and persistence they keep on disguising themselves, and yet it is not superfluous to urge attention to the matter; for indeed there is nothing which malefactors will not try to simulate, nothing they will not try to dissimulate. Frequently. the medical man alone can decide whether or not there is dissimulation, and it will be the business of the detective to place no faith in pretended infirmities and maladies, and to call in regularly the advice of the doctor.

But there are numerous cases where it is impossible to fall back on the medical expert. It may be the nature of the affair excludes medical assistance or, it may be, an important decision must be arrived at before being able to call in the aid of the physician. I therefore mention some of the disguises which a criminal assumes for the purpose of altering his appearance from the description given in the warrant of arrest. As a general rule, it is often the case that a novice who commits a crime afterwards disguises himself; while the expert criminal disguises himself before the commission of the offence.

The former therefore tries to escape in disguise; the latter, on the contrary, is in his natural appearance, and consequently he finds himself much more favourably situated than the former. If the criminal is captured or even placed under observation, the disguise is easily detected, and the individual is generally quickly convicted of having committed the offence.

Suppose then that a novice at the game commits a piece of roguery; he has no beard and wears his hair cut short; he is pursued on this description but travels, disguised in a red beard and a long-haired wig. This disguise will be quickly detected and he will be compelled to dispense with it. The scoundrel does exactly the opposite: when committing the fraud he dons the red beard and the long-haired wig; he is so described in the warrant; he is pursued, but immediately after the offence, he throws away his beard and wig and the most minute search can no longer discover him.

When an arrest warrant, containing a description of the 'man wanted,' is studied, a point of view is to assume everything which appears unnatural should be considered as suspicious and unauthentic; it matters little whether this unnatural appearance is artificial, designed only to disguise the individual, or whether it is genuine. In both cases, the fugitive will get rid of it if he can.

If, for example, the arrest warrant mentions 'an unkempt black beard', either it was false, or it has been shaved off after the crime, and before the flight; if it is said 'he wears blue spectacles,' either they have been put on specially for the crime and then removed, or the criminal is really in the habit of wearing blue spectacles, and has got rid of them during his flight, however accustomed he is to wear them. Even special signs incorporated with his person will not be of much value. Thus, the criminal may, at the moment of the offence, assume a very high-toned or falsetto voice; or if the timbre of his voice is naturally high, he will pretend, often with difficulty, to possess a deep-toned bass voice. He will also thus disguise his walk, carriage, mannerisms, costume, even his height.

For instance, a swindler had managed to cash with a banker a number of false coupon, cleverly forged; but the description the banker gave of the man, which was immediately published, was not true in one single particular; the beard, the spectacles, the hair, the dress, the voice, the corpulence, the height; all were false.

The strangest part was that the man was described as being below middle height, although he was notably tall. As a matter of fact, on his visit he wore a long great-coat; the banker's desk, about the height of an ordinary bank counter, was boarded up in front; hence the man could easily cover the short distance between the door and the desk and back again with his knees bent; thus in the bank, he produced the impression of a short man.

Swindlers also pretend to special characteristics, club foot, stiffened arm, or a deformed hand; and if this is mentioned in the description, generally in big black type, the inexperienced constable or detective sees only this peculiarity and pays no attention to people who do not walk lame, who have no stiff arm or withered hand. It is the same with birthmarks, warts, etc.

A well-known railway pick-pocket, at the moment of effecting a big theft, put on his cheek a large mole with carpenter's glue mixed with grated leather. A cash-keeper, who had committed serious defalcations, had a large natural wart by the side of his eye. This wart was specially mentioned in the warrant of arrest; but the fugitive had, immediately after the offence, shaved it clean off and placed spectacles on his nose. The small cut made by the operation was horizontal, i.e., from the eye towards the ear, and afterwards when a very fine, straight reddish scar was produced, it looked exactly like a mark caused by the pressure of the arm of the spectacles.

The criminologist, Waddell (Lyon), p. 523, notes that the bruised roots of the *Lal-Chitra* (Plumbago), when applied to the skin, causes desiccation and quotes a case reported in 1898 of a false charge having been made at Murshedabad, Bengal, in which the alleged injuries of the complainant were shown by the Civil Surgeon to have been artificially produced by the application of this irritant.

I can perfectly attest, from my long and varied experience, that the art of beautifying has in these days attained great perfection; warts, burns, red stains, scars, freckles, etc., are removed without any difficulty; even discolorations of the skin can be removed without leaving any roughness, thanks to the process invented by Dr I. Paschki of Vienna. The skin covering the portions affected is tattooed with special colours. It remains reddish for two or three days, but at the end of a week assumes a normal tint. We can readily understand that criminals often display a lively interest in these processes of beautification.

An infallible method of making faded scars visible was discovered nearly a century ago by the criminologist, Devergie. The places on which scars, especially burns, are supposed to have existed, are lightly beaten with the palm of the hand until the spot becomes red. The old scar will appear white and in its original shape. In all this type of business, face massage now plays a great part.

The changes in physiognomy produced by changes of complexion are well-known; and whoever is acquainted with the excellent composition of the pigments usually employed, will not be surprised at criminals making such frequent use of them.

It is especially easy to transform a dark rough complexion into one of a delicate rose tint; it is more difficult to turn the blonde into a brunette, especially when the illusion has to be effective at close quarters. A deep rouge tint can in some cases be remarkably well imitated with a solution of permanganate of potash. This colour takes well, lasts a long time, and resists washing.

An artificial paleness generally goes along with a sickly appearance; the person affecting it walks slowly, painfully, and doubled up; his neck is carefully wrapped up with a shawl and he coughs incessantly. Women are special adepts at this kind of imitation.

The criminal is assisted in his task if he comes to know the description given of himself, and then that is easy enough. In important cases it appears in all the newspapers, in other cases it is inserted in the police journals and circulars, which in their very nature and to attain their object, cannot remain hidden to the authorities, but must be brought to the knowledge of dealers in second hand goods and antiquities, pawn-brokers, and the like, to acquaint them with the nature of the missing articles.

But among such people, the person wanted can but so easily learn the contents of the warrant. Sometimes, he applies to the police either directly or through the intermediary of a comrade, who, on the pretext of giving information, obtains a sight of the warrant for the arrest of his friend and his exact description.

Such impudent boldness is more common than one would suppose. In no other way can be explained the rapidity with which fugitive criminals obtain such accurate details of the description given of them. But we cannot overlook the files of descriptions which would remain valueless if not published as widely as possible. Besides, they pass through the hands of so many people, that the individual described has little difficulty in obtaining the desired information.

The only remedy for this, is to prepare the description of the fugitive with great thought and minute care; so, in a given case, we can ask ourselves which details must be necessarily true, i.e., that cannot be changed, e.g., a stature singularly short, a missing limb, the colour of the eyes, the form of the nose, etc., and which are those that *can* be changed.

From the above, the number of the members of the former class is seen to be small and cannot be too restricted; in fact, it would be well to deem any characteristic unchangeable, more as an exception than the rule.

For all the other special characteristics, we must ask in what manner falsification has taken place. An approximate result will soon be obtained and we would stick to that description..

The most difficult task is that of the officer who. with the description given to him, must then search for the criminal throughout the whole town, in hotels, in passing trains, etc., without having the time to compare persons, one after the other, with a description containing characteristics, some disguised, but some actually real.

He can succeed only by practice and a gift for being observant. The task of the detective is made easier when an individual, suspected of being the 'wanted' criminal, is then brought before him. If the description does not agree with the appearance of the man, he will first bear in mind that almost the whole disguise may be false; he will then make sure that some mistake of observation has not slipped into the description when written down; and finally he will examine one by one, the signs which do not correspond and verify their intrinsic value. That is, he will see whether the divergence noted may or may not be the result of falsification. I am not saying that a definite decision must be immediately pronounced, for no change can be pronounced impossible, if the specialist has not been consulted.

We authors both have believed that certain transformations were impossible, but been speedily deceived by the doctor, the dentist, the maker of trusses, belts, etc., the hair-dresser, or the woman expert in the arts of makeup. Every experienced surgical belt maker can tell us how to conceal and how to produce, deviation of the spinal column, hunch back, deformity of the foot, etc. Every theatrical hair-dresser can furnish information on the changes wrought in the face, or as they call it, the mask.

Having just indicated how important it is for a detective to have an accurate and rapid and observant glance of identification, I here call your attention to a method introduced by M Alphonse Bertillon, of anthropometry fame. It is graphically described as the *portrait parle,* or speaking likeness.

We all know the remarkable descriptions which are found, even in these days, on passports, licences, in police gazettes, etc.: face, oval, chin round, nose medium, mouth moderate, etc. The officer, who, armed with a description of this kind, is sent in search of a criminal, may just as well stop at home. Even the aid rendered by a photograph, still is very much a matter of luck; failures amount to more than 60 per cent, and for various reasons: e.g, the defects of the photograph, difference in age, changes in hair, beard, corpulence, etc.

To M. Bertillon, however, belongs the credit of having devised a complete process, without the aid of photography, founded solely upon a precise and scientific description of a certain number of the features, which enables the officer who knows how to employ it, to find and identify in the middle of a crowd, and that with certainty, the suspect whose "*portrait parle*" he possesses.

The system is taught to the police of Paris, by a teacher employed by M. Bertillon. The instruction, theoretical and practical, lasts for two months, twenty men forming a class.

The theoretical course consists of lectures or classes in which the professor describes in exact and scientific terms, the various characteristics of the forehead; the nose, the ear, the lips, the mouth, the chin, etc. The walls of the lecture-room are covered with numbered life-size photographs of heads, so that when the description is finished, the pupils can look around and point out heads containing the characteristics described.

Here for instance, is the description of the nose, quoted from the table of descriptive marks, as entered in the new model descriptive card, which is a summary of the lectures on the "Portrait parle."

The Nose. Depth of the root: small, medium, large.
Profile: concave, rectilinear, convex, arched, irregular, sinuous.
Base: raised, horizontal, depressed.

Height: Projection: small, medium, large particularities. The root of the nose may be very narrow; or very large; high or low: the root may be broken.

The profile may be in the shape of an S: it may be flat, fine, or broad or the nose may be broken it may be curved to right or left.

The tip may be tapering, or thick, or bi-lobar, or flat; twisted to right or left; blotched and pimpled.

The partition (septum) may be disclosed or hidden.

The nostrils may be stiff or mobile, recurved, dilated, pinched up.

All the features and the general contour of the head are thus examined and described in succession, with perfect precision.

The next lesson is on colours; the colour of the iris, hair, beard, complexion; then morphological characteristics, first in profile, then full-face.

As the professor describes a trait, he draws it on the board, and asks the students to search for it among the photographs on the walls. The eye is quickly trained, and after a two months' course of five lectures weekly of 1-2 hours each, the student is able to construct a speaking likeness, or to search for a person by the aid of a speaking likeness, which he either has written on the card or fixed in his head.

Practical work also helps him. From the second month of the course, a descriptive card, serially numbered and drawn up in conformity with the principles of the *portrait parle*,' is prepared for every person arrested and brought daily to the office for anthropometric measurement.

These cards are given to the students, and when all the criminals, one or two hundred or even more, are assembled in the great hall, the students are ordered to go amongst them, and pick out and bring up the person or persons, whose card or cards they possess. In a very few days the students can pick out their men in two or three minutes.

At the end of the second month, on leaving the school, they are provided with a formidable and accurate instrument for the recognition of malefactors.

Section 2. False Names by Hans Gross.

The assumption of a false name or alias is one of the greatest difficulties encountered by the police; whoever can appreciate at its real value this difficulty and its troublesome consequences, will not perhaps be inclined to laugh at the counsel of despair, namely, to print painlessly but in indelible ink, on a part of the body not usually visible, the name and birth-place of every convicted criminal, and even of every individual in general.

But as this bold proposition has little chance of adoption, we must find other means of arriving at a solution in those troublesome cases where we cannot help suspecting some individual of passing under a false name. In every case, such people must be shadowed; for no one desires to move about in the world under an alias merely for amusement, or for some trifling offence as yet untried.

Generally speaking, the reasons for assuming a false name are the following: either our man has escaped from confinement, or he is obliged to fly in consequence of some serious crime committed, or he prefers to travel under a distinguished, high-sounding name, imposing upon and living at the expense of fools.

Sometimes we find in the same individual two of the reasons indicated or even all the three. Of course, no definite rule can be laid down for ascertaining with certainty the true name of such a person, but one can, and not so infrequently as might be supposed, establish a man's identity in round about ways, provided always one does not shrink from taking a little trouble regarding it..

First, we can see if the individual in question possesses any identification. If he has, thee papers must be examined for the purpose of seeing if they have been forged in whole or part.

If they be wholly false, or at least false as far as names and descriptions are concerned, they must be treated simply as non-existent; perhaps a starting point may be discovered by communicating with the authorities who have issued the certificate or letter of conformation, if, indeed, this portion of the document is authentic. It may be asked, for instance. on whose behalf the certificate was issued, and thus may be discovered the original owner of the paper, who can perhaps inform us how he lost it and into whose hands it has fallen.

Of course, the description of the original proprietor must be carefully compared with that of the man in possession of them, the height, corpulence, hair, etc.; but especially the trade recorded of them so that then the person in possession of the certificate may be examined by a specialist.

Thus. one can establish, with more or less certainty, that the individual is in illegal possession of the certificate, however loudly he may protest. If the suspect has got no letter of identification, or if the name found on a genuine certificate is false, we must never forget that almost every man in assuming a false name, tries to find some assonance or other relation with his real personality. Thus, the baptismal name is often preserved, or the family name is simply reversed or transformed in some manner.

The following are some examples of name transformation, drawn from the experience of the author. Sonnenberg becomes Sterhthal; Reimofier becomes Beinhuher; Herlog becomes Behgol (each syllable reversed); Maiidis (Slav) becomes by permutation Dasumi; Mailer reversed is Rellam; Mandl becomes Virl, Mundinger becomes Matihacher.

Such transformations are not discovered at a glance. Of those quoted, Dasumi was deciphered and Mauhacher suspected, but the others were not observed until the real name was known. In one case, a mother took her daughter's name, in another the name of the birth-place with the termination was assumed, and in two cases, the name of the illegitimate father slightly changed was taken: Hohnmaier for Hollmaier and Kreuziger for Kranziger.

Footnote by Sherlock Holmes.

Each individual case will give us some information as to how to proceed, to therefore discover the individual's real name. We can evidently only give some hints on important points. If it is of real importance to establish a person's identity, much time must be devoted to it. A method the author has found very successful is to make the suspect talk as much as possible.

This class of 'superior' gentry have in general travelled much and seen much. It is a good plan, when one knows how to tickle vanity, to make them describe their travels and their career.

Most often our man pretends that he was born on board ship, among gipsies, on a journey, or in some other romantic fashion; then perhaps, he joins a troupe of travelling comedians, rope-dancers, circus performers, etc., and traverses the world with them; then he takes an engagement as servant with a dealer in cattle or horses, or goes to sea as a sailor or stoker, the vessel bears some common name (Pluto, Neptune, Venice, St. Mary, etc.,) and the captain is dead, or perchance has remained in America; or else he was a disorderly sort of man who failed to maintain his registers in order. In such case, it is impossible to establish if the man has really been in the service, whether he pretends to or not.

One listens to all these tales, makes a note of them, or better still, takes them down in shorthand without being observed by the speaker; and little by little, a morsel of truth slips into the recital. Then come descriptions of countries and people that he has really seen, and at the same time come relations he has had with these people, in the reminiscences of his past life.

When his story eventually runs dry, the detective then interrupts the conversation and proceeds to gather all the information he can from books of travel, etc., as to the countries, people and things of which the man has been speaking. At the next conversation, he can dwell on these descriptions and thus draw out more precise details.

The truth will come to light by degrees, and perhaps it will be possible to form an idea of a man's trade, of his occupation, even of his origin, of his relations, and other ties. Meanwhile the detective investigating will be able, by noting his language and dialect, to limit, more or less closely, the area in which he must have been born. He will then have recourse to an expert. If, for example, he has been able to determine that the man is a Northerner, he will call in another Northerner to speak to his countryman; he should be able, within certain limits. to determine the district where the particular dialect is spoken. Then, on some pretext, a conversation is started, and if the agent is a clever man, he will always discover some of the countries with which the suspect has some acquaintance, and may, with good luck, light upon the exact neighbourhood of his birth.

When nothing further can be discovered by these means, the detective an then apply to the authorities of the supposed place of his birth, and will send them his photograph, his description, and all the details that have been discovered (his probable trade, travels, relations, etc.). When this has been carefully done with sufficient time and trouble, then the detective, if he has any luck at all, should easily establish the identity of the individual and have the satisfaction of rendering harmless a most dangerous person.

An instructive case follows. It is related here in detail from an esteemed colleague of mine, Dr Hans Gross, to whom I am greatly indebted.

Dr Hans Gross.

The author of this affair was a magistrate and friend of mine in a small town; and about three leagues from this town was situated a watering place, celebrated throughout the world.

One morning early, he rode over to this station on some magisterial business which was soon finished. But as the horse had cast a shoe and the only reliable farrier had gone out, delay in this watering place until late in the afternoon became compulsory. The Mayor and Inspector of the Baths was an old aristocrat, a retired cavalry officer, who had accepted the appointment as an interest. He was well educated and intelligent, a bachelor and a jolly fellow, who took an interest in everything going on.

The author spent the day in the Mayor's company, who pointed out to him a man, of foreign demeanour, who had been staying in the town for some time. Very tall, friendly mannered, extremely elegant, and dressed like a real dandy, he was to be found wherever anything was going on, and preferred to mix in the best society. He was not an invalid, and spent his money recklessly. He called himself the Baron, a native of Hanover.

This young man did not look like a genuine nobleman, as my friend also thought, who was most jealous of the reputation of his town and related all sorts of stories about him. We were both much interested and resolved to shadow him throughout the afternoon. We followed him in the park, in the saloon of the bathing establishment, in a restaurant, in a cafe, and carefully observed his strange behaviour. The most striking thing about the man was the way he spent his money; he appeared to take delight, not in making purchases, but in throwing his money about. Now this is an infallible sign of a man of little cultivation, who has gained without difficulty a fortune he has not always previously enjoyed.

This mode of spending is as characteristic as it is difficult to describe; it is best described by the words 'spending money for the sake of spending.' Further we were surprised to find our man boasting, without rhyme or reason, and often in an importunate manner, of his high and noble rank, while his manners appeared to show little confidence, and even to betray a certain disquietude, far from reflecting his boisterous gaiety. All this was so characteristic and at the same time so interesting, that we continued our study as long as possible; we came to the conclusion that our man was probably dissipating a fortune inherited from an over-selfish father, and that to fit in with his pleasures he had assumed a high-sounding and aristocratic name.

The incident had passed from the author's mind when, one day, a gendarme brought before him the Baron de V.

The gendarme had learned that De V. was gambling heavily and had invited him to establish his identity. De V. declared that people of his rank were not in the custom of carrying about papers of identification, dismissed the gendarme abruptly and rudely, and made preparations for quitting the watering place on the morrow.

This precipitate departure, immediately after receiving the invitation to establish his identity, appeared suspicious to the gendarme, who arrested him and brought him before the Court. This excessive zeal on the part of the gendarme seemed very unlucky, for the Court did not know what answer to make to the man just arrested, and who kept demanding to be informed what fault he had committed. He showed himself polite but indignant to the highest degree at the insult inflicted on him, talked loudly of the embassy, where, he said, the Magistrate would be obliged to justify his conduct and where much unpleasantness awaited him.

Soon, however, we began to talk more quietly. His father, he said, was a land-holder in Hanover; his family was descended directly from William de Lyon, and was closely connected with all the families which, little more than a dozen years after the annexation of Hanover, were still known throughout the whole world (Borries, Hodenberg, Hammerstein, etc). After the annexation, he added, his family emigrated and since then he had spent his time in travelling far and wide.

He related all this quite naturally and with barely sufficient explanation; he appeared really to speak the true Hanoverian dialect, and conducted himself otherwise like a gentleman. Nevertheless what made the Court doubtful, was his refusal to furnish the address of anyone who, by telegraph, could supply information about De V. He was ashamed, he said, to allow reference to be made through the Court to his relations and friends, many highly placed, a course which would ruin his future, etc. As he was absolutely guilty of no offence, proof of his innocence would soon be forthcoming; he would therefore rather remain under arrest than telegraph as suggested.

All this not being satisfactory, he was asked to describe his coat of arms: he replied with hesitation: "A helmet above, a shield below, arabesques all round, and plenty gold and silver everywhere." But in spite of precise questions, he could say nothing about his real armorial bearings, crest, colours, supporters, etc. That a "Legitimist, " who had with his king left his country, and his fatherland, should be ignorant of his own arms, was a certain proof of his birth. Fortunately, a copy of the *Almanach de Gotlia*, which gives the list of all the families of Barons, was at hand, and a reference to it showed that, while there certainly was a family of " Barons de V." there was no Otto, Baron De V." the name given by the prisoner.

The information he had given as to various members of the family was fairly accurate, but contained blunders which no genuine member of the family could have committed. This conclusion arrived at, he was remanded under arrest, in spite of his rage and repeated threats.

But what was to be done? All that we had as yet proved was that he was a liar passing under a false name, but he could not be accused of any grave offence justifying his detention.

On reflection, it was remembered that there lived in the town, an old master-turner, a native of Mecklenburg, who had somehow or other got stranded in the little place. He was sent for, and a fairly long conversation with the prisoner took place in his presence. The old Mecklenburger gave it as his opinion that, though the man spoke the Hanoverian dialect very well, yet he was in fact, a native of Hamburg, a place this expert knew from his infancy. Photographs, descriptions, etc., were then sent to Hamburg, Hanover, Bremen, Lineburg, and Oldenberg, and within a week, it was known that the man's real name was Otto H., that he had kept an inn in the neighbourhood of Hamburg, and was "wanted " by the authorities of Osnabrijck for manslaughter, and by those at Dresden for a great theft of valuable securities. Further inquiries showed that his mother had at one time been a chamber-maid in the family of the Barons De V., thus, he was able to know approximately all about the family; and he had retained his own Christian name, Otto.'

Besides the dialect spoken by the unknown, and which almost always, with a little trouble, betrayed the place of his origin, there are few devices or rather we should say, only petty devices, to fall back on. For the most part we do not succeed.

Comments by Sherlock Holmes.

It is a good plan to make the suspect undergo a medical examination, for such an examination may disclose exterior indications, such as a deformity, birth-mark, etc. One may perhaps discover signs of circumcision, indicating that the man is a Jew; perhaps also there may be tattoo marks on the arms or chest. These are very important, since they may show that the person belongs to the army or navy, and sometimes display his initials, etc. It is generally easy to discover signs, which are of importance as indicating the trade to which the person has belonged.

Thus, by constant handling of a plane, the joiner becomes lopsided; tailors and shoe-makers from the sedentary nature of their occupation develop a characteristic curvature of chest and shoulders; hairdressers have one shoulder higher than the other. Many striking instances are pointed out by Felix Hement in an illustrated essay, *La Photographie Judiciaire*, who further presses the point that photography can reveal what is hidden from the naked eye. Thus, handling the reins produces welts on the inner sides of the fingers of coachmen; the chisel causes thickening of the skin between the forefinger and thumb of engravers, etc.; the traces of the last are seen on the right thumb and upper part of the thigh of cobblers; the skin on the ball of the little finger of printers who have to tie type together with string is thickened; writers, students, clerks, and artists frequently have a wale on the right middle finger from holding the pen or pencil, as well as a perceptible thickening of the skin of the left elbow.

Seamstresses have plentiful needle pricks on the left forefinger; glass-blowers have baggy cheeks and the muscles are developed; Nine-pin players have a wale on the middle finger near the nail; the place where the handle of the brush comes can be easily seen on the hands of painters and varnishers.

A curious illustration is given by the criminologist, Crooke, as to the Malabar Nambudri:

'The Nambutiri Brahman men bathe three times a day; women and children only once. The men may be recognised by the thick, rough skin between the first finger and thumb of the right hand, where the loin-cloth is being held while being wrung dry.'

It is also very important to examine the man's clothes, being particularly careful over the seams, unripping those portions where the cloth is folded several times, as the coat-collar, waist-band, trousers-flap, etc.; we often thus discover papers that the suspect does not, for some reason or other, wish to part with, as letters, paper-money, even his true papers of identification, preserved for different circumstances.

A very curious discovery was thus once made. The male suspect had inserted in the lining of his hat, a piece of newspaper, folded several times, as is frequently done to make a rather large hat fit. This bit of paper, filthy with grease and dirt, contained among other things a short account of a highway robbery which had been committed by two persons several years previously. According to the paragraph, one of the robbers had been caught and convicted, the other had escaped and had not up to that time been captured.

One might easily look upon this as a mere accident; indeed the prisoner declared, in the most natural way, that he had been at school with the convicted robber, that the article in the journal had come into his hands by chance, and had been used to pack his hat, bought second-hand. Besides, he added, the sad fate of his old school fellow, fallen so low, had painfully impressed him.

But on forwarding the extract with the portrait and description of the unknown to the authorities where the robbery had been committed, it was found that the man was in fact the second robber, not found up till then ; he confessed he had preserved the article out of pure "interest in his case."

Another case (September 1879) made the round of the newspapers. In Paris a certain Lemot was murdered and the police had no knowledge of the murderer. A few weeks later, a policeman found a man asleep in the Jardin des Plantes on a bench, out of whose pocket a number of newspaper cuttings had fallen. The policeman read these, which were all about the case of Lemot; and when the man awoke and was questioned, in his half - waking state he confessed that he was indeed the murderer.

The psychological method is sometimes successful, but is more difficult to make use of. There are naturally enough.no rules for its employment.

We must observe the individual as closely as possible so as to know his intellectual qualities, dive in thought into his private life, and draw out conclusions from the particulars so discovered. Of course, luck must help us here.

One day a police officer came with a request to see an unknown prisoner, believing that he was on the track of an absconding cash - keeper. When he saw the man, his belief was confirmed, and he started a conversation. The suspected man knew of the theft, and when he saw that he was suspected of being the thief, he flew into a passion and declared that sooner than be taken for a thief, he would confess that he had escaped from prison where he was confined as a murderer.

Even for ' High Class ' malefactors, swell mobsmen, in cases which are so frequent and often difficult, no other means can be suggested. By this designation we these days understand the methods employed by men such as the forger and safe breaker, Mr John Clay, a man who knows how to give himself the manners of a person in easy circumstances and of good reputation. so as to be able under this guise to commit swindles, thefts, and other plants. Generally, they are men who have received a good education in their youth, or who at least have had opportunities of picking up the appearance of such. Without exception they are men of ability, full of dexterity and presence of mind, but with a love of an easy and idle life which prevents them turning to any regular and honest occupation.

The *modus operandi* of the 'swell mobsman' is well enough known from the daily press, which is always ready to give publicity to his exploits. Fashionably dressed, he steps into a jeweller's shop and steals while pretending to select, or he causes the valuables selected to be brought to his hotel, takes delivery, and disappears through another door; he goes to the banker and collects the amount of a forged cheque; he manages to get introduced to the highest social circles, runs up heavy debts and disappears; he cheats at play and that on a large scale; he becomes engaged to one or several wealthy young ladies, and makes off with the moneys borrowed from a presumptive fathers-in-law.

He then buys houses and estates without paying for them, also mortgages them, and then disappears. He gets into business relations with a merchant and runs up debts in his name; in a word, he knows marvellously well how to play upon that weakness of mankind that allows itself to be bluffed by a high- sounding name, fine clothes, easy and self-possessed manners. He knows there are fools to be found always and everywhere, and lives at their expense until he is caught.

The position of the detective in respect to this type of gentrified criminal is a delicate one. Especially when there is no specific offence to charge them with, the detective always has the fear of committing a mistake and arresting an honest man.

We repeat, that the only and safest plan is to observe whatever is not "quite the thing" in these people, and that does not as a rule demand much time; in his bearing, his dress, his way of introducing himself, his manners, his tales, his affirmations and denials, contradictions and inaccuracies; these can be speedily detected, and then the detective investigating the case can tranquilly set about his real work. The brassy gold, the gipsy coral, the sham ermine appear genuine, only at a distance to anyone knowing even but a little of such things; and the suspect can be easily upset by making him give a detailed account of his previous career; the improbabilities, the contradictions, the fantastic and concocted adventures. These are not difficult to recognize; the rest of the work may be safely left to the telegraph, photography, and perhaps by consulting a copy of Burke's Peerage.

The time expended in establishing the identity of an individual, or at least in making certain that he is not the person he pretends to be, is never lost, for usually the crime for which he has been arrested is already discovered and half proven. If the great land-holder, the self-styled "Chevalier de X.", has run into debt, he will be speedily convicted of swindling when he is proved to be a man without name or fortune; and if the self-styled "Countess Y.," suspected of cheating at cards, is no other than an ordinary prostitute, the proof of the cheating will not be very difficult.

In every case in which one has to do with a fashionable swindler, one naturally should endeavour to fix the exact scene of the crime; but the greatest care and the most trouble will be bestowed on the identity of the swindler. Above all this, one rule should be rigorously followed when a false name has been given or there is a suspicion thereof.

Our records show a shockingly large number of penal cases in which the most dangerous people have been mildly punished because they have chosen to conceal their real names and give themselves out as innocent. This deception succeeds beautifully when the accused is cunning enough to take the name and parentage of some real living and respectable man whom he has perhaps met in an inn and whose papers he may have purloined.

The law makes inquiries at the home of the supposed accused and receives the most satisfactory account of his previous life. The only thing to be done in such a case is to watch our man carefully. The old jail-bird belongs to such an easily recognisable type that the practised eye can scarcely be mistaken; but if there be the slightest suspicion that a false name has been given, then one must secure without fail at the alleged home of the suspect, a good photograph. If the name and the person agree, the question can be almost always settled with certainty.

The author recalls the following case. An honest artisan, a blacksmith, was in prison for rioting and likely to be punished, because the records of his own district showed two convictions against him for large robberies. The smith denied having suffered the punishments, but when it was demonstrated to him that name, age, birthplace, etc., were rightly shown, he was silent, and acknowledged the justice of the punishment. Through the circumstance that his work-book showed work done in Scotland, while according to the robbery he should have been in London, it was discovered that the convictions did not agree, and at last. the silent man admitted that a long time before he had lost papers proving his identity.

These had been found and used subsequently by a vagrant who had, as the supposed owner of these papers been twice convicted. The name, age and birthplace agreed but the conviction was wrong. It is well-known that such things happen very often.

THE CRIMINAL WORLD OF SHERLOCK HOLMES BIBLIOGRAPHY RELATING TO VICTORIAN CRIME AND CRIMINOLOGY.

The pauper, the thief and the convict: sketches of some of their homes, haunts and habits, Thomas Aboher. (Groombridge, 1865).

Bright Stars on a Dark Thread : being a narrative founded on personal adventures among the criminal classes. A. Mabsell. (London, Langley, 1873).

L'uomo delinquente. (Criminal Man). Cesare Lombroso. (Milan, 1876. Translated; Putnams, 1911).

A Book about Criminals. Mrs. S. M.

Abnormal Man: Essays in Education and Crime. Arthur Macdonald. (Washington, U.S.A., Govt. Printing Press, 1893).

The Study of the Criminal. James Devon. (Glasgow, 1902).

The Criminal Classes : causes and cures. D. R. Miller. (Dayton, 1903)

Les Criminels. C. Perrier. (Paris, 1905).

Criminals and Crime: Crime Facts and Suggestions. Sir Robert Anderson. (Nisbet, 1907.)

The Criminal and the Community. James Devon, Medical Officer, H.M. Prison, Glasgow. (John Lane, 1912, 1913).

How Criminals are made and prevented: a retrospect of forty years. Canon J. W. Horsley. (F. Unwin, 1913).

The E'nglish Convict. Dr. Charles Goring. (Wyman, 1913).

The Individual Delinquent: a text book of diagnosis and prognosis for all concerned in understanding offenders. William Healy, M.D. (Heinemann, 1915).

The Victorian Criminal: Neil R. Storey. Shire Books, 2011

The Victorian Detective: Alan Moss & Keith Skinner, Shire Books, 2013.

The Victorian Underworld: Donald Thomas, John Murray, 1998

Sidelights in Criminal Matters. J. C. Goodwin. (Hutchinson, 1923).

The Criminal as a Human Being. G. S. Dougherty. (New York, Apileton. 1924.

The Criminal [professional criminals]. Sir Basil Thomson . (Hodder & Stoughton, 1922, 1926).

The Soul of a Criminal. J. C. Goodwin, (Hutchinson, 1924),

The Underworld : a series of adventures and reminiscences in many lands. H. Ashton-Woles, (Hurst & Blackett, 1926).

A Book of Remarkable Criminals [Charles Peace, Robert Butler, Prof. Webster, etc. By H. B. Travino. (Cassell, 1918).

Queer People. Sir Basil Thomson. (Hodder & Stoughton, 1922).

The Sidelights of London. J. A. R. Cairns. (Hutchinson, 1923).

The Underworld of London. S. T. Felstead). (Murray, 1923).

Rogues and Scoundrels. P. W. Shrokant. (Hutchinson, 1924).

Mysteries of Police and Crime. Major A. Griffiths. (3 vols.; Cassell, 1898, 1903. Special edition, 3 vols., 1920).

The Byeways of Crime : with some stories from the Black Museum. R. T. Power- Berrey.

A Gallery of Rogues. (Crime and clairvoyance, Peace, Corder, Dr. Pritchard, etc.), C. Kingston. (Stanley Paul, 1924)

NEWSPAPERS SHERLOCK HOLMES MAY HAVE USED IN THE PURSUANCE OF CRIME INVESTIGATION.

"I read nothing except the criminal news and the agony column. The latter is always instructive." - Sherlock Holmes, 'The Noble Bachelor.'

"The detection of types is one of the most elementary branches of knowledge to the special expert in crime, though I must confess that once when I was very young I confused The Leeds Mercury with The Western Morning News." - Sherlock Holmes, 'The Hound of the Baskervilles'.

Sherlock Holmes was an avid reader of newspapers, both daily and weekly. He almost certainly had a subscription to *The Police Gazette,* which carried details of the most horrific murder cases and he was very familiar with the type fonts of all the national newspapers, admitting to Watson that he once mistook that of the *Western Morning News* with that of *The Leeds Mercury.*

Herewith, a list of the papers and periodicals that undoubtedly, he would have consulted and from which he compiled his news cutting files. For the Sherlockian researcher, they are an invaluable resource regarding the crimes of the period, and all may be viewed on the British Newspaper Archives Website. Please note this has a membership fee for access and all news cuttings are, strictly speaking protected in copyright as The British Library to whom an acknowledgement is sufficient. There is also an American equivalent.

NOTE TO RESEARCHERS. This is not a speculative list. All of the papers on this list have been checked to ensure that they were publishing during the periods when Holmes was active as a crime investigator.

LIST A -Most consulted (and many of which Holmes placed
 adverts in).
 Illustrated Police News
 Police Gazette
 Illustrated Police Budget
 Illustrated London News
 Lloyd's Weekly Newspaper
 Morning Post
 Murray's Magazine
 News of the World
 Night and Day
 Pall Mall Gazette
 Penny Illustrated Paper
 Punch
 Reynold's Weekly Newspaper
 The Standard
 The Star
 The Times

LIST B

DAILY PAPERS, INCLUDING NEWSPAPERS FOR
SPECIFIC LOCAL AREAS WHCH HE WOULD
HAVE VISITED WHILST ON A CASE.

'I am an omnivorous reader…' - Sherlock Holmes.
 Belfast Weekly News
 Bristol Times
 Burnley Express
 Chatham News
 Cornish and Devon post
 Coventry Evening Telegraph
 Westminster Gazette

Daily Telegraph
Donegal Independent
Dorset Country Chronicle
Dublin Evening Mail
Durham Chronicle
East Kent Times
Eastern Daily Press
Fife Herald
Folkestone Express
Galloway News
Glasgow Evening Post
The Globe
Gloucester News
Gravesend Reporter
Halifax Courier
Hampshire Chronicle
Hereford Journal
Huddersfield Chronicle
illustrated London News
Illustrated Police Budget
Ipswich journal
Irish Times
Isle of Wight Enquirer
Kentish Gazette
Lancaster Guardian
Middlesex and Surrey Express
Morning Post
Morning Chronicle
Naval and Military Gazette
Newcastle Daily Chronicle
Norfolk News
North British Daily Mail
North London News

North Wales Chronicle
Northampton Chronicle and Echo
Northern Daily Telegraph
Norwich Mercury
Nottinghamshire Guardian
Oxford Journal
Pearsons Weekly
Penny illustrated Paper
Peterborough Advertiser
Poole And District
Dorset Herald
Portsmouth Evening News
Reading Mercury
Rochester, Chatham and Gillingham Journal
Sheffield Evening Telegraph
Sherborne Mercury
Shrewsbury Chronicle
Somerset Guardian
South Wales Gazette
Stroud News
Surrey Advertiser
Taunton Courier
Cornish Telegraph
The Graphic
The People
The queen
The Scotsman
Mercury
Warrington Guardian
Welshman, The
Surrey Times
Western Daily Press
Wiltshire Independent

Wolverhampton Express and Star
Yorkshire Evening Post

THE PRIMARY SOURCES FOR CRIME RESEARCH (Relating to Sherlock Holmes and Crime).

Judicial and Government Records – (Primary Source)
Judicial Statistics for 1888
Reports of the Commissioner of Police of the Metropolis: 1887 – 1891
National Archives, CRIM
Old Bailey Proceedings, 1881 – 1913
(www.oldbaileyonline.org.

MANUALS, GUIDEBOOKS AND REFERENCE WORKS
WHICH WERE USED IN PREPARATION FOR THIS BOOK

Arrow, C., *Rogues and Others (1926)*
Ashley, F.W., *My Sixty Years in the Law (1936)*
Berrett, J. *When I was at Scotland Yard*
Berry, J., *My Experiences as an Executioner (1892)*
Bower, Sir J.W.N., *Fifty - Two Years as a Policeman (1926)*
Carlin, F., *Reminiscences of an ex-Detective (1927)*
Cavanagh, T., *Scotland Yard, Past and Present (1893)*
Cornish, G., *Cornish of the Yard (1935)*
Divall, T., *Scoundrels and Scallywags, and Some Honest Men (1929)*
Doyle, Arthur Conan, *The Adventures, The Memoirs, The Casebook of Sherlock Homes, His Last Bow, A Study in Scarlet, The Sign of Four, The Hound of the Baskervilles, The Valley of Fear.*
De Waal, Ronald B. – *The World Bibliography of Sherlock Holmes and Dr Watson, 1987.*
Fuller, R., *Recollections of a Detective (1912).*

Galton, Francis – Finger Printing, 1899.

Galton, Goldsmid, H.J.J., *Dottings of a Dosser (1886).*

Gross, Professor Hans – *Criminal Investigation, 1906.*
Criminal Psychology, 1909.

Jones, Kelvin I – *The Criminological Holmes, 2012.*

-The Sherlock Holmes Murder File, 1989.

-The Making of Sherlock Holmes, 1975.

-Sherlock Holmes, Consulting Detective, 2012.

-Sherlock Holmes And Poisons, 2012.

-Sherlock Holmes and CSI, 2012.

-Satyriasis: 'Walter's' "My Secret Life", the erotic memoirs of a Victorian gentleman, in six volumes, edited and with introductions by Kelvin I Jones.

-Sherlock Holmes and the Kent railways, 1987. (Contains several rail related railway cases referenced in the Holmes saga.)

Klinger, Leslie – *The New Annotated Sherlock Holmes (3 vols.) 2005.*

Krafft Ebing, Von, Richard - *Psychopathia Sexualis, 1902.*

Lansdowne, A., *A Life's Reminiscences of Scotland Yard (1893).*

Leeson, B., *Lost London: Memoirs of an East End Detective (1934)*

Littlechild, J.G., *The Reminiscences of Chief Inspector Littlechild (1894)*

Lombroso, Cesare – *L'uomo Delinquente (1875)*

MacNaghten, M., *Days of my Years (1914)*

Moser, M, and Rideal, C.F., *Stories from Scotland Yard (1890)*

Neil, A., *Forty Years of Manhunting (1932)*

Sims, G.R., *How the Poor Live and Horrible London (1889)*

Smith, Sir H., *From Constable to Commissioner (1910)*

Sweeney, J., *At Scotland Yard (1903)*

Wensley, F.P., *Detective Days (1931)*

OTHER SECONDARY SOURCES USED IN THE PREPARATION OF THIS STUDY

Allason, R., *The Branch: A History of the Metropolitan Police Special Branch, 1883 -1983 – 1983*

Altick, R., *Victorian Studies in Scarlet (1972)*

Begg, P., *Jack the Ripper: The Facts (2009)*

Bentley, D.J., *English Criminal Justice in the 19th Century (1998)*

Booth, C., *Life and Labour of the People in London (1889)*

Booth, William, *In Darkest England and the Way Out (1890)*

Browne, D.G., *The Rise of Scotland Yard (1956)*

Clark, R., *Capital Punishment in Britain (2009)*

Colquhoun, K, *Mr Briggs' Hat: A Sensational Account of Britain's First Railway Murder (2011)*

Conan Doyle, A., *A Study in Scarlet, (1887)*

Curtis, Jr., *Jack the Ripper and the London Press, (2001)*

Emsley, C., *Crime and Society in England 1750-1900 (2005)*

Evans, S and Skinner, K., *Letters from Hell (2001)*

Fishman, W.J., *East End 1888*

Gray, D., *London's Shadows (2010)*

Lee, W., *A History of Police in England (1901)*

Mayhew, H., *London Labour and the London Poor (republished 1968)*

Morrison, W.D., *Crime and it Causes (1891)*

Prothero, M., *The History of the Criminal Investigation Department at Scotland Yard (1931)*

Ross, E., *Love and Toil: Motherhood in Outcast London (1993)*

Walker, N., *Crime and Insanity in England (1968)*

Walkowitz, J.R., *City of Dreadful Delight (1992)*

Walkowitz, J.R., *Prostitution and Victorian Society (1980)*

Wiener, M.J., *Men of Blood: Violence, Manliness, and Criminal Justice in Victorian England (2010)*

CLASSIC CRIME CASES OF THE 18TH AND 19TH CENTURIES WHICH WOULD HAVE FORMED THE BASIS OF HOLMES' 'GOOD OLD INDEX.'

"Knowledge of Sensational Literature — Immense. (Holmes) appears to know every detail of every horror perpetrated in the century." — A Study in Scarlet.

Many collections were published in the 18th and early in the 19th Century: a selection has been made which, admittedly, is speculative.

The Terrific Liegwiser, or a Record of Criminals, etc, (London, Sherwood Jones, 1825),

The New mid - Century Newgate Calendar, William Jackson. 5 vols. (London, Alex. Hogg, 1828).

Annuls of Crime: a New Newgate Calendar, 2 vols. (London, W. C. (Lark, 1837).

The Chronicles of Crime or the new Newgate Calendar; being a series of Memoirs and anecdotes of Notorious Characters, **1841. 2 vols. Camden Publications. (London, Miles, 1841, 1886, 1891).**

The Complete Newgate Calendar, ed. by Capt. Charles Johnson, London, 1734, 1792;

Histories of the Lives and Adventures of various Highwaymen, Murderers, Pirates, etc., 1710.

The Tyburn Chronicle, 1708.

The Malefactors' Register, 1796.

Celebrated Trials, Geo. Borrow 1825.

The Newgate Calendar, by A. Knapp and W. Baltavin, 1824.

Strange Crimes. William Westall. (Ward & Downey, 1890).

Studies in Black and Red [10 tales of notable crimes : Arnold du Tilb, (Charles Peace, Madeline Smith, J. B. Rush, David Haggart, etc. Joseph. Forster. (Ward & Downey, 1896).

Mysteries of Police and Crime. Major A. Griffiths. (3 vols.; Cassell, 1898, 1903.

The Byeways of Crime : with some stories from the Black Museum. R. T. Power- Berrey, Greening, 1899).

Masterpieces of Crime. A. D. Vanoam. (Routledge, 1905).

A Greed Conspiracy. [The Fenian Movement], Sir Robert Anderson. (Murray, 1909).

A BIBLIOGRAPHY OF THE CRIMINOLOGICAL WORKS OF SHERLOCK HOLMES

Upon the Dating of Documents (pp. n.d.)
(An exhaustive examination of handwriting, its variant forms, etc. with a special section on forgery. The work also deals with paper manufacture from the 16th Century onwards).

Upon Tattoo Masks (London, pp.)
A guide to the varieties of tattooing both in the West and the Occident.

Upon the Tracing of Footsteps
(London, pp. 1878. Reprinted by Magico Magazine, N.Y. 1983, 9PP;
A short introduction to the subject of footprints with some remarks upon the uses of plaster of Paris as a preserver of impresses. A pioneering work which predates Hans Gross 's *Criminal Investigation*.

Upon the Distinction Between The Ashes of The Various Tobaccos. (London, pp.1879)
A highly lavish monograph listing 140 types of cigar, pipe and cigarette tobaccos. The colour plates help the reader to make distinctions between the varieties of leaf. The work contains a chemical analysis of the ash of each listed tobacco.

The Book of Life
(T*he Fortnightly Magazine*, March 1881)
An early magazine essay which discusses some of the premises of Holmes' method. The work owes much to the theories of Darwin. Part of the essay is quoted in STUD.

A Study of the Influence of a Trade upon the Form of a Hand (pp, 1886)
Holmes described this little brochure as "a curious little work" with "lithotypes of the hands of slaters, sailors, cork-cutters, compositors,

weavers, and diamond polishers. This is a matter of great practical interest to the scientific detective - especially in cases of unclaimed bodies" (SIGN). The work was rediscovered and reissued by Gilbert Forbes in *The Police Journal*, London, October - December 1946 and subsequently reprinted in the USA in *The Journal of Criminal Law and Criminology*, November - December 1947. (See G. Forbes' illuminating essay in BSJ 3, No. 4, 1948).

Malingering And Shamming (London, p.p.).

Holmes' own experiences as a protean actor suggested this monograph to him, as did his role in DYIN when his faked illness led to the arrest of Culverton Smith.

On the Variability of Human Ears

(The Anthropological Journal, September and October 1888)

These two short studies were later reprinted in The Strand Magazine for October and November 1893 and carry photographs of the ears of famous celebrities.

The Typewriter and its Relation to Crime (London, pp. 1890.)

This short work carries a comprehensive set of illustrations showing the type faces of typewriters in use in the late 80's and 90's. There is also an analysis of defective key marks, plus a number of photographs showing the occupational spatulate markings exhibited by typists.

Secret Writings (Vols. 1 and 2). London, pp.1896.)

A comprehensive guide to codes and ciphers.

Upon the Polyphonic Motets of Lassus (London, pp.1896.)

Said by experts to be the last work upon the subject, this obscure text was undertaken by Holmes on behalf of Queen Victoria (see Trevor Hall's Sherlock Holmes : Ten Literary Studies, Duckworth, 1969) and earned him the offer of a knighthood.

A Study of the Chaldean Roots in the Ancient Cornish Language. (Truro, Bell and Brown, 1898.)

An intriguing work which examines the popular theories of the late 19th Century regarding the Phoenician tin traders and the roots of Cornish. Holmes concludes that there is no factual basis for these assumptions.

(reprinted by *Oakmagic Publications*, 1997, edited by Kelvin Jones. Now republished in an extended format by *Cunning Crime Books*, 2019).)

The Use of Dogs in the Work of the Detective (London, pp.1905)

Holmes' preoccupation with dogs is widespread in the Canon. In this short work (intended as the first part of a series to be entitled The Whole Art of Detection) he examines the role of the dog in tracking, and the detection of organic substances (including drugs). The work was quickly adopted by the Criminal Investigation Department at New Scotland Yard.

The Use of Disguise in Crime Detection

(London, pp.1906. Reissued by *Magico Magazine*, N.Y. 1984, edited by Val Andrews, with an introduction by Hugh Pentecost,45 pp.)

The work comprises (i) General Observations on the Use of Disguise by the Detective (ii) The Detective's Make Up Box (iii) Accessories for Disguise (iv) Characteristics (v) Speech and Dialect (vi) From My Own Experience - Details of some disguises adopted by Sherlock Holmes during the course of his work (vii) A Few Concluding Observations and (viii), Epilogue.

Practical Handbook of Bee Culture, with some Observations Upon the Segregation of the Queen

(London, pp.1910. Reprinted by Magico Magazine, N.Y. 1982, with a foreword by Michael L. Cook, 16 pp.)

This short work was issued during Holmes' Sussex retirement.

The Adventure of the Blanched Soldier,

The Strand Magazine, November 1926; Liberty Magazine, October 16, 1926.

The Adventure of the Lion's Mane,

The Strand Magazine, December 1926; Liberty Magazine, November 27, 1926.

The Whole Art of Detection

Holmes' swansong, this work was to have been a major contribution to the literature pertaining to criminology and the forensic sciences, rivalling Grosse's Criminal Investigation.

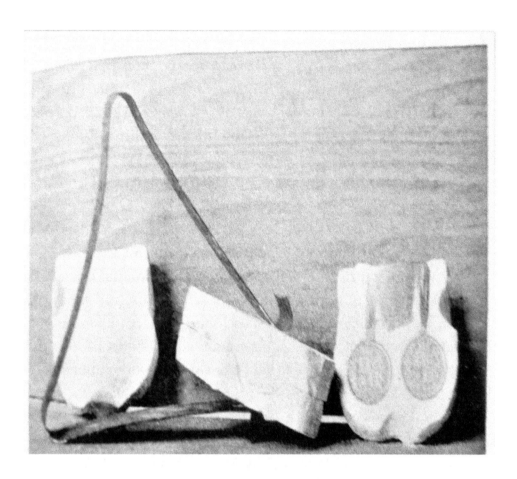

Fig. 42.   A late 19th Century coining kit. Formerly in Scotland Yard's Black Museum.

COINERS AND COINING

A SURPRISE FOR THE TAILOR.

Fig. 43. The coiner's shop is in the basement, The shop workers know this but so does the plain clothes detective,

This tongue - in - cheek article regarding the group of mainly men who earned a perilous but sometimes rewarding living as 'coiners' whose gangs populated much of the East End of London. There they developed into a self-regulating and widespread network as part of the 'cosier' aspect of the Victorian underworld. And as the article suggests, they were often seen by the middle class public for whom The Strand Magazine was largely aimed, as not wholly unsympathetic, possibly because the work they did, somewhat resembled in the public imagination the changing of base metal into gold.

However as we know from reading *'The Adventure of the Engineer's Thumb'*, this was not always the case. The tale of the unfortunate young engineer, Vincent Hatherley, whose thumb is completely severed as he attempts to leave the mad Prussian Dr Lysander Stark. who appears intent on destroying him, seems both bizarre and highly fanciful at first sight One begins to wonder if Conn Doyle had heard the story at first hand or read of it in his newspaper, but this does not seem to be applicable. In the following tale, from The Strand, "Tom the Tailor," was a tailor in the salubrious neighbourhood of Bethnal Green. The police made a raid upon the premises and discovered something like two pieces of base coin in the cellar below, and between the joists. some lamp black, plaster of Paris, and a spoon which had contained molten metal. The coiners were fairly caught.

'It was the duty of the gentleman in charge of the shop upstairs to give a certain signal with the bell, to warn the enterprising personages downstairs. A mistake was made, and the irrepressible Tom remarked, when told the charge: "Well, I have had a long run; but if they had given the signals right this morning, you would not have had me now." `

'It was, indeed, a long run. It took three years to find "Tom the Tailor" and a lady who helped to get rid of the coin to earth; and it was believed that the pseudo coat cutter had been making counterfeit coin for the last 17 years, and before that he had acted as coiners' agent. If time is money, Tom is still at his old occupation - fourteen years' penal servitude.

'New Scotland Yard has every reason to give it an ancient appearance. And the dirt? It is here quite handy. It is in a matchbox bearing a portrait of General Gordon, whilst another deposit is in a small tin whose label tells that it was originally intended for mustard. Both the match-box and the mustard-tin contain lampblack. The bellows is used for " blowing up" purposes. But George IV. is, or was, a great favourite with counterfeiters.

Fig. 44. The Coiner's kit.

There are such things in this world as lucky sixpences, and they are signalled out as such charms, should they happen to have a hole bored through them. Who would not give pence for one of these bringers of luck, and a George IV coin, at this. Echo answers 'Everybody.' We hope Echo will be more careful after learning the use of this little drill which we are now examining. It is used by counterfeiters to bore holes into sixpences, which they can warrant, seeing that they are their own make. The counterfeited brooch is not missing from the collection. It had its birth with the issue of the Jubilee coins, when those who could afford it had one of the gold Jubilee Five pound pieces - mounted as a brooch, and worn or treasured, as a souvenir of the anniversary of Her Majesty's accession to the throne.

Once again the counterfeiter had a chance. True, the Jubilee sixpences offered him admirable opportunities in the way of giving further point to the old adage that " All is not gold that glitters." But he went farther. He made counterfeit half crowns and fastened pins to them and put them on the 'quiet charging,' but a small sum for the supplementary fastener.

Fig, 45. The Jubilee coins.

"Well," argued the purchaser, "the coin will always be worth the money!" Permit to be proud of its counterfeit collection - it certainly has real and original samples of everything associated with this glittering profession, which we shall now proceed to specify. We do so without the slightest qualms of conscience, and without any fear that anything we may say may it lead to anybody admiring these remarks too greatly, and seeking to imitate. We are informed that years' practice are necessary to come up to the standard counterfeit coin of today.

Take this sovereign which is accorded the place of honour in one of the glass cases. It was made in Barcelona, and actually contains sixteen shillings' worth of gold in its composition-there is the true, honest, unadulterated ring about it. Its date is 1862. To those whom it may concern, that is, to those collectors of coins of those sovereigns of this date-this fact maybe interesting. Beware of Barcelonas! But this gold piece is an exception. There are two or three thousand gold and silver coins here- all arranged in the prettiest and most delightful of heaps, that would not deceive them as the easiest going of individuals.

Pennies, sixpences, shillings, two-shilling pieces, half-crowns, crown pieces, half sovereigns, and sovereigns are all here. The most popular, however, amongst the fraternity is the shilling, two-shilling piece, and half-crown; as people, when they accept change, are less likely to "try" these than coins of a higher value.

There are some coins here, however, which positively call for respect. These George IV half-crowns are perfect. The King's head is partially worn away by time and grit and dirt, from constant use of seventy years. These are lodged in the creases of the coin. But time did not wear the King's features away, or constant use to provide the dirt. After the coin was in a finished state, it was placed on a burnishing board of a piece of ordinary deal, with a few tacks stuck in to hold the coins in position-and rubbed over with an old scrubbing brush, in order to dull the coin.

COINERS SURPRISED.

Fig, 44.. 'Has he gone yet Fred?'

'Shhhh! I'm trying to listen.'

A GLOSSARY OF CRIMINAL SLANG

The criminal world of Sherlock Holmes had its own language. Although there is, in Dr Watson's elegant prose, infrequent reference to the terms used by the criminal classes of late Victorian London, Holmes himself would have been very familiar indeed with many of the words used by criminals and included in this glossary. Here is a selection of them:

APACHE – A lawless French ruffian or hooligan. Le Brun was attacked by Apache when he opposed Baron Von Gruner (ILLU)

ARAB, STREET – A homeless slum boy, a child of the street. Holmes used a gang of these street urchin to assist him in *The Sign of Four*.

BARKER – A pistol.

BERTH – A situation or appointment. Vincent Spaulding in REDH referred to his appointment as 'an easy berth.'

BETTY – A pick lock.

BHANG – A narcotic or intoxicant consisting of the leaves and shoots of hemp, or cannabis. (SIGN).

BILLET - A job. Duncan Ross referred to Jabez Wilson's job as a billet. (REDH).

BILLYCOCK – A bowler hat. Henry Baker's billycock hat was subject to an analysis in BLUE.

BIT FAKER – A coiner. Colonel Lysander Stark was one. See *The Engineer's Thumb.*

BLOB – Begging by telling a hard luck story. See Hugh Boone I n *The Man with the Twisted Lip.*

BLUDGER – A footpad. Holmes was attacked by a gang of

bludgers (EMPT).

BOAT, get the – be sentenced to transportation.

BIRD'S EYE – A tobacco where the ribs of the leaves are cut along with the fibres – See SIGN, CM h. 1.

BLUDGEON – A short stick, weighted at one end. Holmes was attacked by a 'rough with a bludgeon,' (FINA).

BRACELETS - Handcuffs. The notorious criminal John Clay was offered the bracelets by a Scotland Yard detective (REDH). Jonathan Small also referred to the 'bracelets on my wrists'. (SIGN).

BROADSMAN – A cardsharp. Sebastian Moran, who assassinated Ronald Adair, was one. (EMPT).

BUOR – A woman.

BUZZING – Stealing.

BLUDGEON – A short stick, weighted at one end. Holmes was attacked by a 'rough with a bludgeon,' (FINA).

BOB – A shilling (SIGN).

BOODLE – Money, property. Holmes told of claiming his boodle from the spy, Von Bork ('His Last Bow).

BRAIN FEVER – A type of delirium tremens or inflammation of the brain. Percy Phelps was thought to be suffering from this condition. (NAVA).

BUZZING – Stealing, especially picking pockets.

CARDSHAPER – A cheat, esp. at cards.

CASH CARRIER – A prostitute's manager, a ponce.

CHAFFERING – Haggling or bartering Holmes used the term when talking of his conversation with a receiver of stolen goods (NOBL).

CHAVY – A child.

CHIV – A knife or blade.

CHOKER – A clergyman.

CLY FAKING – pocket picking, esp. of handkerchiefs.

COB – A stocky, short legged horse. A pair of cobs escorted

Dr Watson and Sir Henry Baskerville to Baskerville Hall (HOUN).

COINER – Coining or the forging of coins was a large industry among the Victorian criminal classes. See ENG.

COP – To arrest. Sam Merton described his arrest by Holmes as a fair cop. (MAZA).

COOLIE – A derogatory, racist term for an Indian labourer. Holmes told Watson he was suffering from a Sumatran coolie disease (MAZA).

COPPER – A policeman – see above.

COSTER – Street trader specialising in fruit and vegetables. See REDH.

COVE – A fellow rogue. Sam Merton, prize fighter, used the term. (MAZA).

CRACKSMAN – Safe breaker. Beddington (STOC) was a cracks-man, as was John Clay. (REDH)

CRAPPED – Hanged.

CRIB – A job. Jabez Wilson referred to having for himself 'a nice little crib.'

CROAKER -A pessimist. A dying person, or corpse. See McGinty in VALL; 'You were always a croaker.' ((VALL).

CROW – A look out man.

CRUSHER – A policeman.

DARK LANTERN – Lantern with a sliding panel, enabling it to provide partial illumination. Essential for a burglar's kit. Mentioned frequently: REDH, STUD, SIGN, GREE, WIST, EMPT, REDC, SHOS, SPEC, MILV, SIXN, BRUC, CHAS.

DERBIES. A variant of darbies -handcuffs. (CARD).

DIDDIKI (Or diddikoi)– Gipsies – an abusive term.

DIPPER – Pickpocket.

DO DOWN – To get the better of, to cheat. Sam Merton told Holmes he would 'do him down a thick 'un') – MAZA.

DOLLYMOP – Promiscuous servant girl.

DOSS HOUSE – Cheap lodging house. See ILLU.

DRAGS - Nets drawn over the bottom of a lake for dredging. See MUSG.

DUFFER – A cheating hawker.

ELEY'S NO. 2 – A Webley pistol which took an Eley .320 cartridge. Watson had one in SPEC.

FLASH HOUSE – a public house, resorted to by criminals.

FLYING THE BLUE PIGEON – Stealing roof lead.

GARRET – Fob pocket.

GEGOR – Beggar.

GLIM – Venereal disease.

GONOPH – A minor thief.

GRIDDLING – Begging, scrounging.

HARD UP – Tobacco.

HAYBAG – A woman. (Abusive term).

JACK – A policeman. Holmes was described by Grimesby Roylott as a 'jack-in-office' (SPEC).

JEMMY – A housebreaker's tool, a long, curved bar. See NAVA, CHAS, SHOS, 3GAR, BRUC.

JEW'S HARP – A musical instrument, consisting of metal prong set in a pear shaped metal frame. Parker, the garrotter (EMPT) played one.

JINGO – An oath, uttered by Carruthers in SOLI.

JOLLY – A disturbance, a fracas.

JUDY – A woman, a prostitute.

JUMP – A ground floor window, a burglary through such a window.

JUNK – Salt beef. See GLOR.

JUNKER – A young German noble. See LAST.

KECKS – Trousers.

KIDSMAN – Organiser of child thieves.

KNAP – To receive stolen goods.

KNOCK UP – To arouse by waking. See ENGR, SIGN, SPEC.

LAG – A convict or ticket of leave man. Also to arrest. MAZA.

LAGGED – Sent to prison. SIGN, Ch. 11.

LASCAR – East End sailor. A rascally Lascar ran the opium den in TWIS.

LAUDANUM – Alcoholic form of opium in liquid. See TWIS.

LEARY – Clever, shy. See Sam Merton in MAZA.

LEG - A dishonest sporting cheat.

LENS – Holmes' preferred scientific term for a magnifying glass. See RESI, GOLD, THOR, SHOS, LION, BRUC, DEVI, VALL, Ch 4.

LIFE PRESERVER – Stick loaded with lead at one end. Some were made of whale bone and cane. See NOBL, GREE, BRUC.

LOAFER – An idler, often to be seen hanging around a pub. See STUD, ch. 3, EMPT.

LURCHER – A dog which is a cross between a greyhound and a collie. Toby, the dog used to hunt Jonathan Small, was half lurcher. SIGN.

LURK – A place of concealment.

LUSH – Alcoholic drink.

MAGSMAN – A cheat.

MASTIFF – A thick set, powerful dog. See HOUN, Ch 1 and COPP.

MENDICANT – A beggar. Holmes investigated 'the affair of the 'Amateur Mendicants.' – FIVE, ILLU.

MILTONIAN - A policeman.

MONKRY – A beggar's tricks.

MOT – A woman, especially a proprietoress of a pub.

MUG -A dupe, a foolish person. See LAST.

MUMPER – A beggar.

MUTE – A funeral attendant, often a child. See MISS.

NAB – To arrest. See Lestrade in SIGN.

NARK = An informer or police spy. See ILLU.

NEDDY – A cosh.

NEWGATE KNOCKERS – Heavily greased side whiskers.

NIGHT GLASS – A spy glass, with a concentrated lens or use at night.

NIPPER – A boy. BLUE.

NISKY – Nothing. See LAST.

OSTLER – Man employed at an inn to clean down horses. SCAN, SOLI.

OUTSIDER – Instrument for turning a key from outside lock.

PIG – Policeman

PIN FIRE REVOLVER – Revolver fitted with a pin that enables the hammer to strike the powder in the cartridge.

PLUG – Chewing tobacco.

POCKET LANTERN – A lantern of the same type as a dark lantern. Holmes owned one and used it on his way to the Lyceum Theatre.

PRUSSIC ACID – A colourless, deadly liquid with a distinctive almond smell. (VEIL).

RAMPSMAN – A footpad.

ROOK – A jemmy – see above.

RUFFLES – Handcuffs.

RUM – Odd, strange. VALL Ch.3.

SALT BOX – Condemned cell.

SAPPER – A trench or a member of The Royal Engineers. Mycroft and Sherlock spotted a sapper from the window of 221B.

SCABBY – One who breaks a strike. A union dissenter. A vile or contemptible person. VALL Part 2, Ch. 4.

SCALDRUM DODGE – Begging, using self-inflicted burns or wounds.

SCREW – A skeleton key. Also payment, as with 'to turn the screw', See STOC.

SCRIP – A preliminary certificate, as for allotted shares. Holmes used the word when referring to the affairs of the mysterious Mr Cornelius. See NORW.

SHAG – A coarse, strong, cheap, finely cut tobacco, popular among Victorian artisans.

SHEENY – Pejorative word for a Jew. Hall Pycroft referred to Arthur Pinner's nose as having 'something of the sheeny about it.' STOC.

SHALLOW, WORK THE – To beg half naked.

SHIKARI – A hunter. Colonel Moran was described as an 'old Shikari.'

SHIN OUT – American slang. To clear off, to run away. John Ferrier spoke of 'shinning out' of Utah. VALL.

SHIP'S TOBACCO – A strong, rough cut Dutch tobacco, popular among sailors. The proper name was 'Schippers Tabak Special. Watson and Patrick Cairns both smoked it (STUD Ch. 1, BLAC).

SHOFULMAN – Passer of bad money.

SHOVE THE QUEER – To pass counterfeit money (See VALL, Pt 2, Ch 2)

SINGLE-STICK – A heavy wooden stick 3 feet long, with a protected handle at one end. See ILLU, STUD, Ch 2.

SKELETON KEYS – Simple keys with serrated edges, used to pick locks. Holmes possessed a set. CHAS.

SLOP SHOP – A shop selling cheap clothes. The opium den in TWIS lay next to a slop shop.

SLUG – A bullet. GLOR.

SLUM – False document.

SMASHER – Passer of false money. REDH.

SMOKING CAP – A light, decorated cap. Culverton Smith had one. DYIN.

SNACKLED – Arrested. Jefferson Hope said he was 'neatly snackled' by Holmes.

SNAKESMAN – Lithe boy used in housebreaking.

SNIDE – Counterfeit money.

SNORTER – Anything exceptional. A tricky one. Expression used by White Mason in VALL Ch 2.

SPEELER – Cheat, gambler.

SPRING LOCK – Lock fastened by means of a spring action, similar to the modern Yale. 3GAB.

SPUD - Small digging tool. Holmes told Watson there

were instructive days to be spent in the countryside using one. WIST.

STIFF 'UN – A recalcitrant person. Billy the page boy at 221B referred to Lord Cantlemere as one. (MAZA)

STIR – Prison

STOOL PIGEON – A decoy or an informer. Word used by Holmes as part of his American slang in LAST.

STOVE – Broken. Jim Browner stove a plank to sink his wife's rowing boat (CARD).

SWAG – Goods.

SWEATING – Hard work usually performed by the poor or children. Jethro Rucastle referred to Violet Hunter's pay of £4 per month a 'rank sweating.' COPP.

TAIL – Prostitute.

TANNER – A sixpence. Holmes gave each of his Baker Street gang a tanner each. (SIGN)

TENEMENT – House divided into a number of living spaces. REDC.

THICK 'UN – A sovereign or crown piece. MAZA.

THREE CARD TRICK – A form of gambling involving three cards. 3STU.

TINKER – A mender of pots and pans, often an itinerant. See ILLU, TWIS.

TOFF – A rich or upper class person. See HOUN.

TOUT – A person who frequents racing stables to pick up useful information. See SHOS.

TRIM YOU UP – To thrash or knock someone into shape. (Steve Dixie to Holmes, 3GAB).

TWIRLS – Skeleton keys.

ULSTER – A long, loose woollen overcoat. See STUD, Ch. 5, SIGN, Ch. 10, SCAN.

VAMP – Steal or pawn.

VESTA – A wax stemmed match. See TWIS, SILV.

VITRIOL – Hydrous sulphate, containing concentrated sulphuric acid. Commonly thrown at victims in Victorian

England. See BLUE, ILLU.

WARD – Part of a lock so configured as to prevent it being turned in a particular way, See RESI.

WHISKEY PEGS – Glasses of whisky. See SIGN, Ch 12.

WIDE AWAKE – A low, wide brimmed, soft felt hat. YELL.

UPON TATTOO MARKS
By Sherlock Holmes

FOREWORD TO THE SECOND EDITION
BY DR JOHN H. WATSON, 1920

My friend, Mr Sherlock Holmes, passed away last year at his seaside residence in Cuckmere Haven, in Sussex. It had been my privilege to know him and serve as his chronicler over a series of decades. For very many years, I published in the publication known as the 'Strand Magazine', accounts of the several adventures I shared with him concerning the criminal fraternity. Among the many papers, which I had to deal with, contained among my battered tin box was a collection of privately printed monographs on various aspects of criminal investigation, and published by him, the first of which I present here to the reader In the chronicles, which I recounted, the subject of tattooing appeared on several occasions. The reader will probably remember that the central character of what I subsequently wrote as 'The Adventure of the Gloria Scott,' Mr Trevor senior sported the initials "J B," which had been tattooed in the bend of his elbow and which he had attempted to obliterate.

In 'The Adventure of the Redheaded League,' I described a fish tattoo, which appeared, on our client's right wrist, which Holmes described as quote 'quite peculiar to China.' Holmes also noted a large blue anchor on the back of a retired sergeant of Marines' hand, described in my account, entitled a 'Study In Scarlet' which was most popular during that late Victorian period.

As Holmes observes, tattooing was equally popular among female of our generation. My own first wife, Miss Mary Morstan, had a most beautiful tattoo which had been inscribed on her left arm, depicting a precious stone which was lost to her when her casket of jewels was dropped into the River Thames, an incident that was related in the chronicle, later entitled as 'The Sign Of Four.'

Upon Tattoo Marks (London, p.p. 1898) (A guide to the varieties of tattooing.)

INTRODUCTION
By Sherlock Holmes,
Private Consulting Detective, Baker Street, London.

In my experience as a private consulting Detective, I have frequently been asked by members of the Metropolitan police to offer my opinion regarding the nature and significance of tattoos, relating to bodies, which have been retrieved, from the River Thames and elsewhere.

The frequency of complexity of tattoos, especially among the lower classes of society and especially those which occur on corpses of former or current members of the Armed Forces has often been remarked upon by those detectives who have consulted me.

Tattoos have become very popular, especially in the last decade, when the application of these decorations has been more easily facilitated by electronic means, a development which originated in the USA. Now, it is not uncommon for persons in the middle and upper classes to decorate their bodies with tattoos, and within the last five or six years such phenomena have become increasingly fashionable with women. In my role as a consultant Detective, I worked closely with members of Scotland Yard during the so-called 'Jack the Ripper' murders and was quite frequently asked to examine tattoos, which had been obtained by some of the suspected victims of the anonymous criminal.

Tattooings which exist or which have existed on the bodies of living or dead persons may be very important in determining identity; they must therefore be examined and described in detail. Let it also be stated that attention must be paid to tattooings which are no longer visible; there is no doubt that they may disappear from view; they fade away either through lapse of time or, if the work has been badly done or unstable colours have been used, even after a short time.

They may also be made to disappear artificially by submitting them to the corrosive action of an acid, especially indigo extract (*indigotin disulphonic acid*), (Patent Deuchatel).

Dr Variot mentions a device whereby nothing but a scar is left; the application of a paste containing salicylic acid and glycerine (for about a week's time) will make the tattoo mark disappear). Another method has lately been suggested as the best.

A strong solution of tannin is put on the tattoo mark, which is then treated with a needle in the same way as in tattooing, and finally a strong solution of nitrate of silver is used.

The French criminologist, Tardieu, also tried the following: acetic acid and fat, then potash, hydrochloric acid, and finally solution of potash. But the result of all these methods must always be that a scar, however slightly visible will be left.

If for some reason or other one suspects that tattooing now invisible has existed upon the body of a living man, the medical expert should be asked to carefully examine the place where, thanks to some indication or other, we may hope to find it, in the places where tattooing is most usually found (forearm, breasts etc.)

If it has been artificially removed, even the naked eye will discover very noticeable cicatrices, the form, size, etc., which are easily described.

In regard to the time which tattooing takes to disappear, Caspar Liman says that even on old invalids, he found the marks clearly noticed after 40 or even 50 years.

Amongst 36 tattooed persons, he found 2 with the marks faded, 2 half, and 4 completely disappeared.

A similar comparison is given by the German criminologist, Hium, who found among 3000 invalids more than the sixth part were tattooed.

Tardieit found even more striking numbers; as the people he examined mostly had used chalk, 96 % of the tattooed marks had not vanished. The materials employed will disappear in the following order, cinnabar, gunpowder, washing-blue, ink; chalk mixed with lampblack will keep longest.

About the age of the tattoo mark in general, not much can be said. The scar, after the operation, is soon healed and does not change much for a long time. Partial strength in the colouring does not prove anything. A fresh tattoo with little pigment and an old tattoo with much pigment look nearly alike.

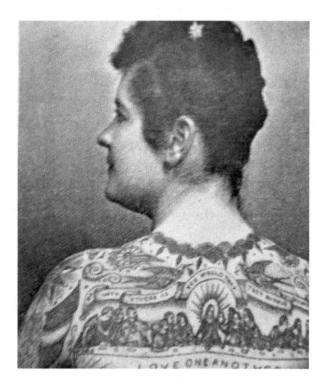

Fig, 47. A French female prostitute, wearing an elaborate tattoo.
The criminologist Cesare Lombroso has demonstrated their
Popularity, among certain classes of Italian prostitutes.

Only in a few cases can one judge this, i.e., if a child has been tattooed on the back, the design will lose its form as the child grows up, so the same will happen with a circle tattooed on the arm of a strong young man, as he becomes old; the mark of the inoculation will often move far away from its original place as years pass.

Lately, a young American girl was shown in many European centres with beautifully tattooed designs over the whole body. These were certainly genuine and interesting, but it was false to state as was done to the audience that her father did them when the lady was a child, as the designs would have lost their correct forms and become irregular and distorted as they had grown with her.

All the dictionaries and encyclopaedias I have consulted, suggest that among Europeans, tattooing is largely confined to seamen, and sometimes soldiers. The first permanent tattoo shop in New York City was set up in 1846 and began a tradition by tattooing military servicemen from both sides of the Civil War. Samuel O'Reilly invented the electric tattooing machine in 1891, after which time the creation of tattoos became more accessible, and frequently by members of the middle and upper classes in England.

In 1861 French naval surgeon, Maurice Berchon, published a study on the medical complications of tattooing and after this; the navy and army banned tattooing within their ranks.

In some cases this circumstance might be important, if the age of the tattoo mark is desired to be ascertained.

If the tattooing has disappeared naturally the medical man will in most cases be able to discover, with a strong magnifying lens, the cicatrices in the form of pricks or marks of a needle, or stitches. In many cases these cicatrices are so well preserved that it is easy to reconstitute the whole design; this reconstitution is rendered easier if the part of the skin in question is vigorously rubbed with some colouring matter such as ink, lamp-black, or oil, etc.; the colouring matter will adhere better to the cicatrised places which, becoming blacker than the other parts of the skin, causes the tattooing to show up distinctly.

In proving the existence of tattooing upon a corpse, the same method is followed; we have even a further important proof in cases where it has disappeared long before. As Follin, Markel, and other reliable criminologists point out, the small colouring particles penetrate as far as the lymphatic glands nearest to them, where they remain and go no further; they lodge for preference in the periphery of the gland and on enlargement, may be observed as much in the whole gland as in certain sections of it.

They can, naturally, be better seen through the microscope, but the cinnabar so often employed as colouring matter looks reddish when rays of light fall upon the gland, and has a black aspect when they traverse it (see the German criminologist, Hofmann's work).

The examination of the gland should in such cases be always made by a medical man. It must also be remarked that tattoos upon wet corpses and on mummified and dried up corpses are not easily recognisable; in the first case the parts of the skin in question must be taken off and dried and in the second, they must be soaked in water.

Let us now call attention to the general importance of tattooing.

It is not necessary to go as far as a number of criminological specialists such as Marro, Macassagne, Batut, Salillas, Drago, Ellis, Greaves, Bergh, etc., who, following the example set by Lombroso in 1874, by considering tattooing the characteristic sign of habitual criminals

Be that as it may, tattooing is very important. Kurella has clearly demonstrated this in finding tattoo marks upon 14 per cent, of his subjects.

It may indeed be attested *as a general proposition* that tattooing is almost exclusively revealed among people of an energetic disposition, a disposition already revealed in the career such people have chosen. Tattooing will generally be seen upon soldiers, sailors, butchers, fishermen, wood- cutters, smiths, etc; but rarely, in the working classes, on tailors, weavers, or, for example, waiters.

Not only can energetic people better support the pain caused by tattooing, but their character leads them to the display of something uncommon and difficult of acquisition. In this connection, sexual motives play a dominant ad important role -- precisely why, it is difficult to say; but the motive seems to be that strong and sensual natures certainly do find pleasure in placing their bodies on view; they admire their own persons and love others to also admire them, when they are in a state of partial or complete nakedness.

It is for this reason that among persons of the feminine sex, tattooing was in Europe, until very recent times generally only found among prostitutes; though it should be noticed, that women of the cultivated classes are now also frequently tattooed; in Bosnia, for instance, a girl or woman of the Catholic peasant class is seldom to be found without it. It mostly consists of a more or less decorated cross on the forehead, the chest, or the upper part of the arm.

A curious circumstance is mentioned by the criminologist, Mashka. He examined all prisoners before and after the period of detention , and found that most of them were not tattooed before but only *after leaving* the prison. This surely shows that the chief reason is the tediousness of the incarceration. Also, the criminologist, Giuiter, asked 24 tattooed persons for the reason of undergoing this operation, and the reply in nearly all cases, was 'an imitation'.

If we add to what we have stated that this rude body toilet is found chiefly among common people (Lombroso says among people of Celtic origin, but this in my mind a gross exaggeration,) we shall have collated all that concerns tattooing among criminals.

We are able to conclude that we only meet with tattooing among criminals who are people of energy such as murderers, hooligans, house-breakers, etc., and on the other hand. also among people of a sensual nature such as bullies, sodomites, ravishers, prostitutes and others who commit crimes against morality, but not, interestingly, among cheats and thieves.

It should further be noted that the simple and honest man is content with certain characteristic figures; the sailor, however, carries an anchor or dates and initials; soldiers, swords or rifles; the butcher, crossed axes, etc.; and the tattooing is generally placed on the inner aspect of the right forearm.

A grosser and less honest nature is not content with that; it adorns itself with allusions to its crime or has signs of vengeance, accompanied with resigned or frivolous indications of its probable end, e.g., *"le bagne m'attend"* or a gallows illustration, etc.).

If the person is, by nature, possessed of an obscene imagination, it is revealed by the character of the design, or by the place in which he is tattooed (the sexual parts, or the buttocks, near the anus, as in certain classes of narcissistic homosexuals, or in some female prostitutes,, near to the labia, where they also, in some examples, Lombroso observed, exhibit small rings which some women interviewed by him admitted, heightened sexual pleasure).

Now it is very natural, that among people of gross and energetic natures and doubtful morals, there are therefore many criminals who are tattooed, it is for the same reason: natural grossness and immorality. In this lies the whole correlation existing between tattooing and a criminal; and because of this, every tattooing upon a prisoner ought always to demand our interest and be thus recorded when on entering prison they are required to remove their clothes and submit to examination.

That not only criminals and those of criminal instincts tattoo themselves is shown by the fact that to-day among the young English nobility, tattooing is the height of fashion and has grown in popularity among certain types of the more exhibitionistic homosexual men and women. It should also be noted that several youths recently arrested at the Cleveland Street male brothel in London, were found by detectives to display elaborate tattoos placed in and around their genitalia, backs, buttocks and even close to their fundaments. When asked why they had in these positions, one youth explained that he had placed them there 'for the entertainment, interest and stimulation of my clients.' Tattoos are not now done in the usual way with hot needles, but by professional artists, with the help of an electrical apparatus (the galvanometer system).

The age of the tattooing custom is shown by the fact that the criminologist, B. Karl Blind, for example, tried to prove that the old Germans paid homage to this custom and that it was a sign of the nobility. In 787 a law was passed in Northumberland against this heathenish custom. See also *Tractatus de Superstitionous* by Magister Nicol, 1405) in which he prttests against the custom of "pricking", as a superstitious and forbidden practice.

I conclude by enclosing examples of some of the more recent and complex female tattoo photographs sent to me by Mr Harry Lellenberg of The New York Police, and in addition, I have also thought fit to include some recent examples exhibited, in an issue of 'The Strand Magazine', by way of further illustration. Those taken by police in the Cleveland Street raid may be examined by detectives at the Black Museum, Scotland Yard, by letter of application only.

NAKE, TATTOOED IN GREEN AND BLACK, RO
AUTHOR'S NECK, BY MR. MACDONALD.

Fig. 48. An elaborate tattoo, devised for the author of a fascinating article in The Strand Magazine, concerning tattoos, Vol 13, 1897.

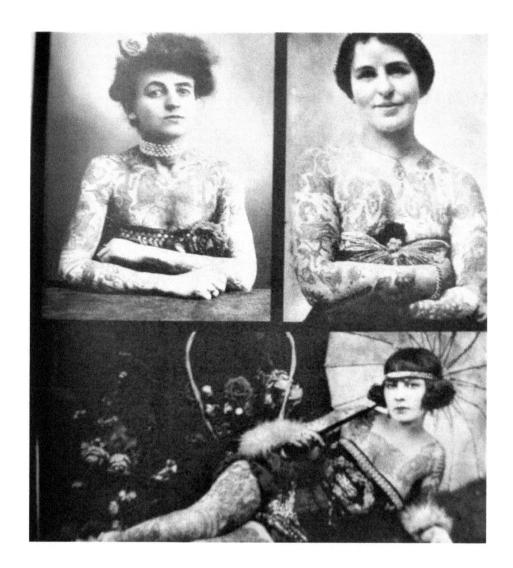

Fig 49. Examples of American prostitutes' tattoos.

Fig 50. Eastern European gentleman. Photo supplied by Inspector Lestrade of Scotland Yard. This man had been arrested by police for operating a bawdy house in Rotherhithe, London.

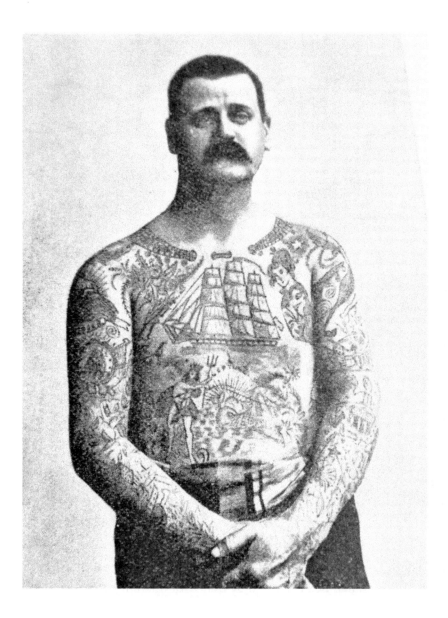

Fig. 51. Only known photograph of Huret, the Boulevard assassin, This gentleman had an unfortunate end, being cudgelled to death by French *apaches*. Courtesy of Scotland Yard.

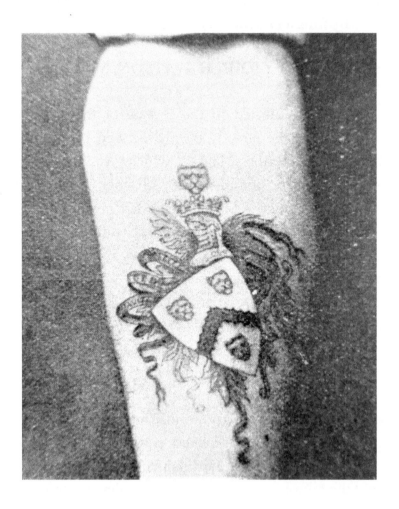

Fig 52. A particularly detailed example of an arm tattoo of considerably complex pattern, featuring an heraldic design. From a German criminal who was a confederate of Professor James Moriarty, and who had been suspected of three gruesome murders, arranged by members of Moriarty's gang.

THE SCENE OF CRIME INVESTIGATION
By Sherlock Holmes,, London 1897.

INTRODUCTION BY JOHN H. WATSON, M.D.

The circumstances connected to the reissue of this series of brief monographs by Holmes have already been described by me in the first volume, entitled 'Upon Tattoo Marks,' which was my friend and colleague's first foray into the complex study of what is, these days, now termed 'forensic science.' Holmes himself regarded his method as wholly scientific in its application, but in origin, akin more to artistic inspiration. In his own words, 'art in the blood can take the strangest of forms.'

The present volume of this series deals in depth with the strategies that a first rate detective should employ when relating to the investigation of the scene of a crime. When Holmes began his private consultancy in the early 1880s, he informed me then that the regular police force at Scotland Yard were often at their wits' end in connection with certain complex murder cases.

I shall never forget his remark, on entering the crime scene at Lauriston Gardens, Brixton, to the effect that it looked as if a 'herd of buffaloes' had trampled through the place. The cardinal rule espoused in Holmes' monograph about the importance of preserving evidence at the scene of the crime, had yet to be understood by Scotland Yard detectives and Holmes often would remark that the fault lay not in their lack of desire to apprehend criminals but in their lack of training and knowledge,

Of course, much has changed since then, and for the better, since that bygone and somewhat random period of policing.. Nowadays, murder investigations and scenes of crime are controlled in a far more rigorous and observant manner. The 'herd of buffaloes is far less apparent than it used to be, when Holmes and I first shared rooms at 221B Baker Street.

The subject of footprints is of course, an exact science in itself, but I was intrigued to read in the present volume, of Holmes' opinions and advice concerning the use of dogs. I was of course at once reminded of the dear dog Toby, who led us a merry dance across the rooftops and down the narrow lanes of dockside London, before losing the scent of our quarry, Mr Jonathan Small, and his diminutive south seas accomplice, Tonga.

Over several decades, in my past capacity as an assistant to a private consulting detective, I also have been of some not inconsiderable assistance to Scotland Yard, especially regarding the investigation of a scene of crime. During my first dealings with members of the detective force in London, I realised, as Holmes did, that their methods at scenes of crime lacked a singularity of purpose.

It seemed to me, as a practising doctor of medicine, that the more one knew about the subject being presented to one for analysis and observation, then the better able one might be, in determining the cause of an illness; or in the case of a serious crime, such as murder, the more complete the picture could then be gained, of the steps which might lead the investigator to the culprit, However. to assume that the evidence at the scene of a crime will not be liable to change, either before or after the event in question, is merely to deny one of the principle law of physics: that our physical world is in a constant process of change, and therefore, the way we often regard those surroundings - as fixed, or immutable, or bounded by time, may be decidedly unrealistic.

It is my cherished belief, that if Mr Holmes' view of the perishable nature of evidence at a crime scene had been adopted at those places where the murderer, known popularly as 'Jack The Ripper,' dealt his fatal blows, the criminal might have been apprehended before now. The wiping clean of the slate board in the case of one of the murder victims, for example, may well have been ordered from a desire to avoid community unrest, but if it had been seen as what it actually was - a vital element in the crime - then much more progress might have been made in providing a swift conclusion to the whole affair.

- John H. Watson M.D.

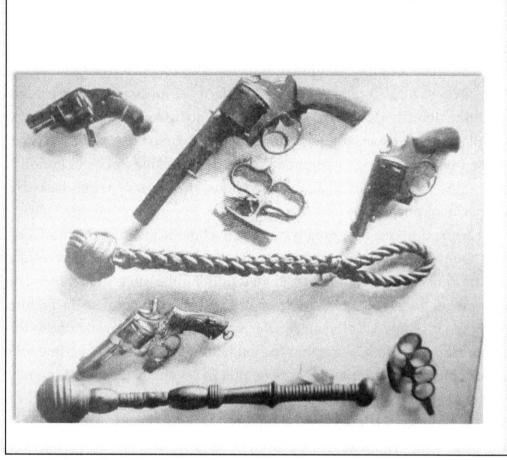

Fig, 53. Often criminals will leave weapons at the scene of a crime. When discovered and examined by detectives, these most often yield vital clues as to the identities of the perpetrators, as in the recent case of the 'Lewisham gang.'. Each one of the examples shown above, in fact led to a successful prosecution.

Over the past few decades, Scotland Yard officers have regularly asked my advice regarding the handling and interpretation of evidence. I therefore was able to assist them by drawing up a number of strategies in order to preserve evidence at the scene of crime by the use of scientific method. These are my observations, which have already been of considerable assistance to other investigators, especially to Professor Hans Gross, that foremost Austrian criminologist, who tells me that he uses many of the examples cited by me when lecturing to his students on the subject.

On arrival at the scene of crime, certain things must be attended to, which are common to all cases, be they of murder, arson, robbery or some other crime. The first duty is for the detective to preserve an absolute scientific detachment at a scene of crime, for without this, nothing can be regarded as truly objective and everything is possibly compromised.

The assigned detective who sets to work aimlessly, and begins a plan only to subsequently drop it, or asks everyone present questions, giving out orders, only to then cancel them, makes the most painful impression on those engaged with him in the enquiry, and thus destroys any confidence about the handling or processing of the investigation.

Equally, if the detective shows a strong measure of confidence and no apparent trace of any excitement, but acts with sure and certain awareness and a clear prevision of the results, then everyone will then submit to his orders and each do his best to see the conclusion of the enquiry.

Thus, when the detective reaches the spot, he must beware of speaking at random, or starting to do something without apparent good reason or motive; issuing orders in a wholesale fashion, and then subsequently altering them, will simply cause confusion.

The first endeavour, therefore, is for the detective to quietly and attentively take stock of the situation, and then to find his bearings and modify his plans accordingly.

As soon as the detective arrives at the scene of crime, he should immediately make a mental picture of the case and all those connected with it, with very precise details. When travelling to the scene of crime, he may offer to himself a theory as to how the offence may have been committed; and then build within it, his mental picture of a plan of enquiry to be subsequently pursued by his team.

The idea may take root in his mind to such an extent, that he cannot rid himself of it when the scene is frequently displayed before his eyes, and it may, therefore, cause him to go wrong in his reckonings. For this reason, the force of a first impression must be corrected on the spot and his plans then modified accordingly. Otherwise, he will simply interpret every piece of evidence relating to that *a prori* standpoint.

The scene of crime must then be inspected both in its general aspects, and then *in considerable detail*. But it must be considered as far as possible, in relation *to the very obvious facts before him*.

The time given to this close examination is far from being lost, but the results will invariably compensate for any apparent delay.

After this, the detective must find out the persons best able to give information about the case, which will then enable him to become approximately acquainted with its circumstances.

If it is an initial enquiry, with reference to an important crime, such as murder, arson or even a large accident concerning a railway collision, for example, he should try to find a representative of the authorities, a policeman, or person directly interested in the matter, e.g. a relation of the murdered man, the sufferer by the fire, and so on. He will then learn not to waste time over details, and will then forget nothing of importance.

However inexperienced he might be, he should always remember the old maxim:

Quis, quid, ubi, quibus, auxiliius, cur, quomodo, quando?

Who, what, where, with what, why, how, when questioned:
What is the crime, who did it, when was it done, where was
 it done, how was it done, with what motive; and who shared
in the deeds?

If these words are kept prominently before you, the words will be impressed on your memory and imagination.

The next consideration should be to make a careful selection among people interested in the case. The detective must watch all who have given or who can give information to remain upon the premises, or near to the scene of crime. If possible, it is as well to submit the witnesses to some degree of surveillance, so as to prevent them from gossiping uselessly with each other.

For witnesses, and more especially, for people with merely a basic education, or women, children, etc., who cannot help discussing the case and telling each other what they have see; this process of the exchange of speculation may extend to such an extent, that they don't precisely know, in the end, what each thinks or may believe they know; in other words, they mix up what they have themselves seen and heard, with what has been told to them by others.

It is often the case that the witnesses may have talked to each other and heard each other's stories beforehand; but in every case, nothing leads them to talk, to such an extent, exclusively about the case, if they are actually corralled together on the scene of the crime by the detective; thus making the affair stand out in full relief to them and, by this means, obviate confusion.

While taking these measures, the detective should see to the preservation of the existing physical parameters of the crime and take care that they are interfered with as little as possible.

He must establish, e.g., whether the corpse of the person who has been murdered is still in the same position, as when the crime was actually discovered.

He must then distinguish any marks of footsteps, comparing those made before the discovery, from those afterwards by the curious, etc. The exclusion of everything happening after the moment where the crime is committed, is a very special task for the detective, especially so, as *the most regrettable errors may arise from the neglect of this.*

There are known cases where the detective has described, with the utmost accuracy, the position of the corpse, and drawn from this the most remarkable and ingenious conclusions; while, unhappily, the evidence points out that the corpse has been interfered with several times by different people *even before his arrival.*

The exclusion of everything that was happening, after the moment when the crime was committed, is a very special task for the detective, although sometimes, most regrettable errors may arise from the neglect of this.

The criminologist, Bayard, as far back as 1847, told of a case where a physician who was summoned, then stepped in blood, and walked all over the building, leaving bloodstains everywhere. This subsequently caused so much trouble and confusion as to utterly spoil the investigation. Here is an example, surely, where the consequences might have been much greater.

Fig. 54. (above) A French scenes of crime officer, pictured here in Arthur Griffiths' authoritative three volume series on Victorian police, crime and police methods; *Mysteries of Police and Crime,* essential reading for the Holmes enthusiast.

In a case of arson which I investigated; a footprint was discovered which corresponded with that of the accused. It was indeed his, but it had not been made at the time of the crime, but subsequently, when, on his speedy arrest, he had been taken to the place of the murder by policemen.

There is one golden rule which needs to survive; and that is: *never alter the position of, or pick up, or even touch, any object before it has been minutely described in your report.* The detective must never forget that this very rarely actually happens, i.e. to find anything clear and distinct from the beginning. As a rule, the detective has not the slightest idea of the outcome of the case, and does *not* know what may be important or what will be denied, and therefore these things have to be proved.

At this early stage, *everything* may be of importance, and *nothing* will be too small or insignificant to have a decisive bearing on the case. The situation of an object – an inch or two to the left or the right, to the front or the back – or a little dust, may all turn out to be of the utmost importance. The natural impulse is to immediately touch an object of apparent significance, e.g. an object left at the scene of the crime by the criminal. It is laid hold of, then moved about, and only afterwards does one recognise that the object itself signifies very little, *but that everything depends on its position, which,* alas, can no longer be fixed.

The involuntary impulse is at first to seize the hands of the person present and to examine them, to see if there are any hair or scraps of clothing of the criminal on them; but it may turn out that there are some small but significant details, such as a smear of blood on the hands. In fact, in seizing them heedlessly, you might destroy evidence which might have been of greater importance.

Now in order to follow important rule; *"Never change any part of the condition of the scene before it is described in the report,"* it is necessary to make sure of the preservation of trace elements.

Footprints should be protected by coverings of small boxes or planks resting under three stones. Traces of blood, or discarded objects, should also be carefully covered up, especially if they are in the open air and the hour is late. Moreover, a line should be drawn round objects which may be confused with others, such as footprints etc. But if all this is in order, then everything irrelevant can be eliminated, and the report can be then commenced.

No one supposes a report will be a model of style, but certainly, grammatical accuracy and logical sequence are useful. This is, in the first place, important to the person who dictates the report, for he will only be able to do good work if he's convinced of the accuracy of the evidence, and without having to wait for confirmation afterwards. If he deals carefully with each point, on its own merits, and without connecting it with those that follow; and lastly, if his method proceeds logically, according to a determined plan, passing from the general to the particular, it will *then* avoid the treatment of the same point made twice over.

Secondly, the arrangement of ideas in a report is of importance to the reader, for he will only understand the matter clearly, only if the style of the report is lucid and logical. Anyone who has perused many police reports is often struck by how difficult it is to make use of them when they are so badly drawn up, or how easy it is to miss important points from the difficulty in attempting to understand what the officer intended to express.

In all cases, a general description of the spot *must* be set out, stating where it is and how it is reached; then, state whether it is a house, field or wood, etc., that is in question. Next, briefly indicate the neighbourhood, and then describe the actual scene in detail. *Always* have regard to the possible connection with the case under enquiry.

The extent of the description in the first place depends on the nature of the crime, but in all cases, the following truly must be observed and described;

1. The place itself.

2. The direction from which the guilty person came.

3. That direction in which he went away.

4. The places whence the witnesses have seen or could have seen anything significant.

5. The points where traces of the crime were found, or whether they might be expected to be found, or if in fact, if there are simply none.

6. The notification of purely negative facts should *not be neglected*. On the one hand they may lead to possible inferences, and on the other, they

may reassure the reader of the evidence and show him that they were not forgotten altogether.

For example, suppose traces of blood are mentioned, as having been found in the room of the murdered man. It is not merely sufficient to state what has been found, but also to mention what has *not* been found. It can be stated, for example, that there was no bloody water in the wash hand basin, nor were there any imprints of bloodstained fingers or hands.

Or if the report concerns the search for compromising papers, a search which has been so far without a useful result; it must be expressly stated, therefore, that no ashes were found in the fireplace.

The special circumstances attached to each particular crime must be clearly set out, e.g. in cases of arson, mentioning the objects more especially exposed to danger or impeded by the wind; or for example, in the case of a riot – places from which weapons have been taken. Again, the actual place of occurrence must be described in detail, e.g. in cases of murder, the room containing the body of the victim, and in cases of burglary, the place or the house which has been broken into; and here, a certain, specific order must be preserved.

For example, with a room which may be adjacent to an enclosed space, the door should be taken as the *starting point*; then, following in the same direction as the hands of the clock; - that is, standing in the entrance facing into the room - you must start from the left hand, and go around the room towards the right. In this way it will be certain that *nothing has been forgotten*.

First, describe the size, shape, height and other peculiarities of the space in question. Then, go from the entrance to the nearest left corner; then proceed to the left-hand wall, then the wall facing the entrance, the right-hand wall and then, finally, to the object in the middle of the room. In the description provided, the windows and the doors will be noticed and described.

Always describe alterations to the state of the movables in the room relating to the crime in question; damage done by blows, bloodstains, or changes in the situation of objects, or damaged windows and doors, etc; *and finally, include in your account of the subject matter of the crime, all the particulars necessary to a detailed description.*

In doing this, the detective will then proceed step by step, examining minutely his description before it is written down.

Here is a good example I have often employed.

By lying on the ground, I am usually able to primarily describe the scene of crime according to the impression it produces when first observed; e.g.,

'Near the corpse, an inch from the left hand, a red cloth rolled up in a ball, small in size, a pocket handkerchief; one end sticking out, lying on the ground in the direction of the head of the body. On picking up the cloth it was found not to be cotton but silk, a three-cornered scarf with hemp borders on each side, 17 inches in length, and unmarked. There is also a hole in the middle, about the size of a small coin, probably due to use. Under the scarf there was no trace of blood or anything remarkable. And, moreover, it was not identified by anyone present. Probably therefore, it did not belong to the murdered person.'

In these subdivisions, as well as in the general preliminary description, an unvarying order must also be adhered to; the same order or direction followed at the beginning, must be continued when examining and then interpreting these details.

If, for example, the description of the corpse has been commenced by proceeding from head to feet, it is best first to describe any important objects found in the neighbourhood of the head, and then finish with those that are near the feet. In making an abstract of these details, a measuring stick must be used when possible, and distances calculated exactly; for no one ever knows at the time what subsequently may be of use.

Expressions like "not far from there," "some little distance away," "a little higher," "further behind, "or "away at the bottom," *must on no account* be allowed to recur in a report. Expressions should only be used if they are easily understood, for the detective has everything in front of his eyes and such an expression as "quite near," is quite clear to him, but the person who has to read the report may have very different ideas of distances.

Anyone who has paid attention to these details will agree that there are few reports where these expressions are not to be found, and that they have often made it very difficult for the detective to properly comprehend the case. Expressions like "on the right" and "on the left" may only be used when they admit of no ambiguity, as, for example, "on the right hand of the corpse," or "on the left bank of the river." In all other cases, these words must be discarded, for expressions like "to the left of the entrance," may give rise to ambiguity, if the position of the spectator is not stated, and it is not certain whether the detective is within, or without the entrance; and also, naturally, what direction he is actually facing.

To conclude, *be exact*.

The points of the compass should be used as far as possible to describe positions of objects, but there can be no doubt that the description can always be checked subsequently.

If in a building, or in a room, it is, in certain cases, much more convenient to choose fixed points which have already been noted and to say, for example, "on a line extending from the head of the corpse to the corner of the room, where the fireplace is situated, at a distance of two feet from this latter."

In this case, the distance should, without exception, be taken from a starting point which remains fixed. It will *not do*, for example, to say something like "on a line extending from the head of the corpse to the corner, with a stove situated, and three feet from the head of the corpse," for the corpse will probably have been removed and on subsequent measurements being taken, it would prove difficult to find the point again.

In addition to this, the direction of measurement must be, in most cases, indicated. Again, *it is not good enough* to say "twelve feet from the apple tree in question, there was found," but instead to say "at twelve feet from the apple tree in question in the direction of the corner of the house, and situated to the north-west, there was found…"

This may necessitate a very long description, but the detective must not be disheartened by this fact. It might be necessary to say, therefore, at length, something like this: –

"This door, single, not double, is 8'3" broad, starting from the hinge side, and faces towards the north. Going towards the lock side, which is towards the south; it measures one inch from the bottom where the door touches the floor. From that point, then one must draw a perpendicular to the line, formed by the bottom of the closed door, and from this perpendicular, measure off seven inches, starting from the door. At the spot thus indicated a piece of watch chain was found."

When the precise position of an item is of importance; for example, splashes of blood on the wall from which the position of the accused person attacked may be deduced: in this case, where horizontal and vertical measurements are involved, the floor should *always* be taken as the horizontal.

The vertical may be found with the aid of a thread to which a knife, stone, or some such object is attached. e.g., for a drop of blood on the wall, a plumb line should first be constructed; the plumb line must be held at the point where the bloodstain is to be found, taking care not to touch it, and then by making a mark where the line touches the ground.

Before completing the description of an enclosed space, the detective must be sure of evidence connected with the corpse, which otherwise might have been neglected. It is *not sufficient* to throw a rapid glance around the area, but every object must be *carefully reconsidered*, to make certain that nothing important has been missed, and that the latter does not bear a different aspect from that which it might have been previously; or that a detail which at first appeared to be of some consequence is not now important.

In a recent case, which I personally was asked by police to investigate, a cigar holder with an amber mouth piece was found near the corpse of a murdered man, and the marks of the teeth on it brought about the detection of the murderer.

It is impossible to notice everything which may subsequently turn out to be of importance, and there will always be certain details which will be passed over.

In one case, it turned out to be of great significance to know whether the sun shone into a certain part of the room at a certain hour of the day, and for this purpose, the locality had to be specially revisited, though it was very far distant from the place where the court was subsequently sitting. In another case, *everything* depended on whether any sand was strewn about on the floor of the room, a point that no one had thought it worthwhile to notice. Such an omission will never act as a reproach to the detective, for only chance would make him think of noting down these details. The old axiom of the civil law: *"re minimis non curat lex"* does not hold good for the detective.

The following cases are now cited from my own experience.

On one occasion, everything rested on whether or not, at the hour of the crime, the splashes that lamp oil will consistently make; on another, whether a half burned cigar was in an ashtray or on the floor; again, whether there was a spider's web near a nail in the wall; on another, whether there was still some kerosene in a lamp; that is, whether it had been extinguished or had burnt itself out.

In another murder case, the assailant would certainly have gone undiscovered, if the detective had not thought of examining the top of a wooden partition, about eight feet in height. On not reaching the ceiling, he then saw that the top of the partition was covered with a thick coating of dust, save in one place, where the dust had been displaced, and naturally, he therefore concluded that someone recently must have, climbed over the partition spot. He made a search, and discovered the accused, among people living in the room, but separated from the scene of the crime by the partition in question.

When the description has to be made in the open, the same method should be followed. In reading certain reports, one can clearly see what trouble the detective has taken in writing down the results, and how painfully he has made his description.

If the detective has a principle and remains faithful to it, not only will the description be comprehensive and useful, but his task will be greatly facilitated. One thing will then follow necessarily from another, and he will not have the trouble of making additions and references which he himself has brought about, by having to face difficulties of his own construction.

It will be easier for the detective to decide what his *modus operandi* must be, by first making a sketch plan, which should always be done before the written description. With this always before his eyes, the detective will soon find out what is the best method to follow in each case.

The Search for Hidden Objects

In the search for hidden objects, there is little probability of finding anything of importance, if the attention is confined to beds, boxes, chimneys, or safes. *Absolutely everything* must be examined for there is no place where important objects cannot be hidden.

The following, for example, are a few of the hiding places discovered by myself and my Scotland Yard colleagues: – the horsehair stuffing of the sofa, a birdcage, the space between the back of the picture, and its protecting board; the manger in a stable; the contents of a soup boiling on the fire – this contained gold coins;– a prayer book, old boots, a dog kennel, the space between two upright millstones; wine barrels; a spectacle case, a pillbox, old newspapers, a cuckoo clock, a baby's clothes; and, on one

Fig. 55 (above}. If only Holmes had been able to examine this victim of 'The Cornish Horror' and ascertained evidence of the cause of death… The removal or tampering with evidence also included the corpus delictus, in Holmes view.

occasion, the criminal himself was actually discovered in a dung heap; a small opening having been made to give him air in the side nearest to the stable wall.

Moreover, the accused himself must always be carefully searched. This is something that the detective often may neglect to do, either from regard for the accused, or from a certain timidity.

Certainly, a personal body search, or strip search is often regarded as a grave affront to the liberty of the suspect, and such a measure should only be resorted to after consideration; but, if resolved on, it must be carried out energetically, and not only the house, but the man or woman in it must be searched. Sometimes such searches will require a doctor, e.g, the secreting of a murder weapon or evidence concealed in a suspect's rectum or vagina, a method of concealment most frequent among some criminals..

In the great majority of cases, the hidden object will be found, for everyone is naturally inclined to carry on his person, suspicious objects – just as he is wont to carry objects of value – believing they are secure. The task is greatly assisted, if it is known what is to be searched for, for then many places where it cannot be hidden may be excluded.

Unfortunately, the objects searched for are often small and easy to hide, such as: money, jewels, papers, poison – such things can be hidden almost anywhere. The presence of the accused may make the task easier, for his face and glances often indicate to a keen observer, whether the search is an unlikely place or whether the evidence is "hot or cold." In a case I investigated in Surrey in the village of Reigate, for example, much depended on the detailed observations I had made regarding the expressions on the faces of a family.

If objects of any size are sought for, and it is ascertained that they are hidden in places easy to be got out, they must be looked for in the structure of the building itself; but it is, of course, scarcely practical and thorough to search by demolishing the building, so the detective may employ certain artifices of the simplest kind and keep his eyes wide open.

Just suppose that the objects have been walled up. It is useless to take into account those parts of the wall which can easily be seen or discussing that anything is hidden there – at least, where there is no reason to suppose that the plaster had time to dry.

As a rule, the walling up, where it is behind low mirrors or boxes, or in cellars, will often be significant, and the place may be recognised by the freshness or inequality of the plaster. If the place is not found thus and there is still room to believe the objects are hidden in the walls, nothing else can be done but to knock and tap the walls and then listen for the hollow sound, indicating a cavity.

The most remarkable, and perhaps famous example of this. was described in the narrative which my friend Dr Watson entitled as 'The Adventure of The Norwood Builder', where a small part of the room had been partitioned off to accommodate the suspect in question.

The search for a hiding place under a wooden floor is more difficult and, as the floor cannot be completely taken up in most cases, indications of a recent disturbance must be sought; such indications do as a rule exist. In fictional terms, the late Edgar Allan Poe describes such an event in his story entitled "The Tell-tale Heart.'

On an ordinary plank of wood, the heads of the nails driven into the boards must first be examined. When the floor is first constructed, the nails holding the planks to the cross beams are driven in as far as possible, so that the heads of the nails are slightly below the surface of the floor, to prevent the feet from catching on them.

This being the case, it is difficult to pull out the nails, especially if the floor has been often scrubbed and the nails have become somewhat rusty with the wet. With the nails holding tenaciously to the floor, it is impossible to extract them without damaging the wood round them, and traces of such damage cannot be erased. If, therefore, the wood around the nail appears to be bruised or damaged, it can, with a certain degree of confidence, be presumed that something is out of place; but it is useless to lift the planks where no such indications can be seen.

The eminent criminologist, Hans Gross, cites a case in India, where something had been buried in an earth or mud floor. Here also was poured, in fairly large quantities, a liquid on the suspected surface: the place where the water filtered through more rapidly than elsewhere and where, at the same time, bubbles made their appearance, this was also the same place where the soil was broken and where digging had recently been carried out. He concluded that the same would be true when the covering was of bricks or flagstones.

In time, the quantity of dust or sand gathered between them, by its own weight and humidity then formed a kind of firm cement. If water was thrown over the paving, he reasoned, it would sink in very slowly, being, as it were, soaked up little by little. But if the flagstones had recently been taken up and laid down again and the interstices had been filled up by sweeping in of dust, which does not usually hold together like cement, the water would therefore penetrate rapidly, and air bubbles would then be seen mounting to the surface.

When the objective is to discover a corpse, there is one possible expedient: to make use of a good bloodhound.

One cannot underestimate the use of dogs in detective work; however, it is useless to take the first setter or bloodhound that comes along. Few dogs have a good enough scent. If the detective needs help in such cases, it will be of little good for a team to issue forth an order for a hunting dog, for you will be pretty sure not to get one of any use. In this case, as I have observed before, preparation is essential.

A tanner was the owner of a quite common watchdog, having absolutely no resemblance to a hunting dog, but it was a wonderful dog which could even from a great distance, scent and track any carrion. The local sportsmen used to borrow him after each shoot to look for the game kills, which had been undiscovered by the pack of dogs.

The tanner's dog would find anything animal, whether alive or dead, producing the corpse just as quickly as a recently killed deer. One day, when police were seeking the body of an idiot who had disappeared, and who was suspected of having been murdered by his brother-in-law, the dog discovered the body, a long way off in a wood.

At that moment, it was yet possible to establish that the idiot had succumbed to an attack of epilepsy; but some days later, a post-mortem was unable to prove that no violence had been used, and the brother-in-law would have gone through his subsequent life with the suspicion of murder hanging over him.

In some European counties, every year, an astonishing number of people disappear, especially children. The police often now keep dogs which are trained like the bloodhounds of Cuba, who once were employed for tracking fugitive slaves. In such cases, clothes belonging to the person to be caught are placed to the nose of the dog, which is then brought on the trail; if the trail is fairly fresh, the dog will follow it without caring for the hundreds of other trails, crossing the right one, until the fugitive is finally reached.

A short time ago, a dog was mentioned in a Paris newspaper, *Le Monde,* as having succeeded in finding for police a lost child. If we compare this with the splendid results of the Austrian and German war dogs, as related in Professor Hans Gross' book, entitled *Criminal Investigation,* for example, it must be admitted that dogs can help us in many cases. We do not claim that the government should keep official dogs of this kind, but if a detective should show special interest in the training of dogs for this purpose, government authorities should provide him with some canine assistance.

A great number of murdered people are injured and killed in rather deserted places, especially in areas of jungle. A great number of these are often dug out by jackals and other animals, who easily scent out such spots. When a corpse is not completely covered, it is easy for dogs or even men to find it. In 1867, in Prussia, two murder cases were discovered through the murdered bodies having been uncovered by foxes. Moreover, crows and ravens and above all, vultures, will at once collect, so it is not unprofitable to watch them for this event.

The body of a murdered woman was once found in the following way.

The teachers at the surrounding schools had told children to report as soon as they saw crows or ravens gather anywhere. Some of them made this report, with the successful result that the murdered person was then traced.

An interesting incident arose in 1871, during the search of a residential house. A man had fired on a gamekeeper, who thought he recognised his assailant. The house of the suspect was searched, the principal object sought for, being the gun used to commit the crime.

The search was carried out with the greatest care, the house being turned out from top to bottom, but no trace of gun or ammunition was found. The enquiry was then repeated and during the search, a heavy rainstorm came on; so the search party remained in the house, waiting for it to stop.

The house had a ground floor, divided by a corridor, at one end of which was the front door, and at the other, the back door, while the doors of the kitchen and the living rooms opened onto the front. The front and back doors, except in winter, remained open all day.

It was in this corridor that the search party awaited the end of the storm. The rain, now coming down heavier and heavier and beginning to come in at the front door, they then shut the latter doors; and there they found, hanging on the inside of the door, which had up till that time been leaning against a wall, the gun and a pouch containing powder and shot.

Clearly, from all these examples which I have quoted, and from the precise strategy of investigation which I have recommended, the detective who leads an enquiry should be well armed with strategies which can seek to further strengthen his powers of observation and deduction. Much depends upon consistency of approach, the logical and precise accuracy in applying methods, and, above all, the collation of detail at the scene of crime.

A scene of crime should never be disturbed, but its contents *always* preserved for further analysis.

In my opinion, the detective should have overall and complete control of the scene of the crime, and he should take such steps as are necessary to analyse its contents.

Only by this painstaking and precise method, can all the evidence be collated; then, that which is relevant and irrelevant can be distinguished in the course of his investigation.

There is an old maxim of mine which my erstwhile companion at scenes of crime has, I think, been referred to in one of his chronicles of my numerous cases:

'You have seen everything, Watson, but you have observed nothing.'

For the Scotland Yard detective, let this never be the case. - Sherlock Holmes.

AFTERWORD BY KELVIN I. JONES

The circumstances relating to the discovery of this series of monographs are explained in the prologue to my volume, entitled *Sherlock*

Holmes: The Plagues Of London. The editor of this narrative explains how, when her aunt died in 1979, she inherited a large country mansion, named Marsham Manor in Norfolk, some 10 miles from the city of Norwich. She had visited the Manor as a child with her mother, but now retained only fleeting memories of the place, with its long winding drive, mullioned windows and Palladian frontage.

She did recall, however, the tall, corpulent figure of her uncle, Mycroft Holmes. He is described as a pipe smoking, reserved man, with prominent eyes and an aquiline nose.

In the years that followed her mother's death, she received a letter from her solicitors, informing her that she was the sole beneficiary of the Holmes estate. After travelling to Norfolk to supervise the house clearance of the Manor, she was astonished to find that the attic of the house was crammed with books and papers. She then made a unique discovery.

In the far corner of the attic, under a pile of books, mouldering music scores and broken furniture, lay a battered foreign office dispatch box, marked with the initials "MH". When opened, inside was discovered a collection of leather bound notebooks, filled with Mycroft Holmes' neat, copperplate handwriting.

She was even more astonished when she read the contents. Interspersed with many original documents, giving details of some of the most celebrated and shocking criminal cases of the late 19th century, was a bundle of short monographs of pamphlets on various aspects of criminological investigation.

One of the pamphlets was especially devoted to crime scene investigations and clearly had been privately printed sometime in the late 19th Century.

The author's name was Sherlock Holmes, and it became immediately clear that this was a rare, but forgotten publication by the famous Baker Street consulting detective.

Re-reading this pamphlet today, I was indeed struck by the thoroughness and clarity of Sherlock Holmes' methods, which are given in detail. The basic strategy of a crime scene investigation is laid out in very clear and precise terms, and is very close to the standard procedure which is in place to ensure that a modern crime scene is handled in an appropriate manner.

Sherlock Holmes explains in depth, how the crime scene must be preserved, along with all vital pieces of evidence, plus entrances and exits, and the physical barrier which is required to be placed around the scene.

Those who enter the scene must today exclude all non-essential personnel, and a log is produced, noting all individuals who cross the barrier, plus the times at which they enter and exit.

The use of clean cardboard boxes to cover the relevant areas, which Holmes suggests in his monograph, has become a standard practice in today's forensic examinations of scenes of crime, and the simple searching, on a room by room basis, of an interior, plus the search pattern employed for exterior scenes of crime, is identical to the Holmes method.

The use of general notes regarding the crime scene, including environmental details, information on the state in which the scene was found, and any other details that may be relevant; all of these are predicted by Sherlock Holmes; they also include the use of sketches, dimensions and orientations of objects of significance, found at the scene of crime, plus relevant measurements.

At the time during which Holmes wrote his monograph, photography was in its infancy, but now, in the 21st century it is regularly relied upon by forensic scientists to form the centre of crime scene documentation. In other and subsequent monographs, Holmes also discusses the uses of photography in remarkable depth.

We can best sum up the Holmes contribution to scenes of crime in the French phrase: *'Plus ca change: plus c'est la meme chose.'*

The monograph is astonishingly predictive and it provides us with a vivid insight into how advanced the methods of this unique consulting detective truly were, at a time when in the UK, at least, fingerprinting was only of an embryonic nature.

Fig. 56. A scene of crime from the late 1890s, when photography was starting to become used more regularly to accurately record evidence. The body of a man was found here in this outhouse. A public domain photo, from a series of fascinating shots of murder scenes taken slightly before and just after the end of the 19th Century. Courtesy, *Daily Mail online.*

Fig. 57. Camden Place, Chislehurst.

The Curious Case of Camden Place: A Sherlock Holmes Investigation

This 'Trifling Monograph'
Being A Gift to my Several and Most Loyal Friends in
The Sherlock Holmes Society of London,
The Bootmakers of Toronto,
And All Generous,
Kind Sherlockians Everywhere,
Living And Not Living,

Who Have Assisted Me
Over the Past 50 Years,
To Discover The True Meaning of
Being A Sherlockian.

*This limited edition was devoted to my very good friends,
the Sherlockians, who between us all, keep alive, in every
country of the world, 'The Immortal Memory.'*

The Curious Case of Camden Place

In his consummately recorded story of the savage murder of an abusive, alcoholic husband, *The Abbey Grange*, set in the freezing winter of 1897, Watson describes with shivering accuracy how, on a bitterly cold January morning of that year, Sherlock Holmes and he travelled via the Old South Eastern railway to Chislehurst, Kent, to a grand mansion in nearby Marsham. Chislehurst is and has been for many years a wealthy suburb of London, being only 11 miles away from the capital. Nevertheless, it still retains a number of picturesque Victorian houses which might have served as the original of 'Marsham Manor', then, in the Holmes tale, home of the brooding alcoholic, Sir Eustace Brackenstall and his down-trodden, infatuated wife, Lady Eustace Brackenstall.

A long time ago, in the early 1980s, I suggested in one of my 'trifling monographs' that two buildings possibly would fit the location in the story. The first is a large affair, called Frognal Place that stands about 2 miles from Chislehurst Railway station, but whose distance is probably nearer to 3 miles. It does conform with Watson's description of it. It is also known that Conan Doyle actually stayed here before the writing of the story of the Abbey Grange. However, I am inclined to dismiss the identification because in fact, it is nearer to the Suburb of Sidcup than it is to Chislehurst and, secondly, the house has no avenue in front of it, as it is clearly described in the story.

However, the second choice, Camden Place, *does* bear a close resemblance to the description, since it is approached through an avenue of ancient trees; it lies 'in a noble Park;' and in the story of *The Abbey Grange,* the Grange itself is described as a house widespread, with Palladian pillars at its front. Moreover, the Victorian print which I obtained of Camden Place shows that it has a large pond in the park, just as is described in the story, where it was rumoured that the valuables, the plate, silver and the like, were thrown into the waters here by an infamous family of burglars from Lewisham, bearing the surname 'Randall').

The only single objection to this choice is that it is only a mile away from Chislehurst station and not the 2 miles drive as mentioned in the story. We may assume though, that Sherlock Holmes and Watson got out at Petts Wood Station, which is in fact. precisely a 2 mile drive from Camden Place.

In the story of *The Abbey Grange*, the murder victim, Sir Eustace Brackenstall, a beast of a man who clearly intends to beat his wife, declares he will also annihilate her lover, when he discovers her affection for the seafaring gentleman of her forbidden, but anticipated congress, with Captain Croker. They fight, Croker hits his assailant hard with a heavy poker, his head being horribly injured by the force of the blow which strikes him and which consequently bends the poker into a curve. To do such a thing would have required a great deal of strength, as was clearly evidenced by two other sworn opponents in the case of 'The Speckled Band,' when the incestuous and overbearing Dr Roylott has the audacity to beard Holmes in his inner sanctum, and bends the poker to make a point of what might become of the detective. should he persist in interfering in his affairs. Of course, Holmes being Holmes, who's always open to a challenge, thinks no more about the matter, unbends the poker, then puts it back by the coal scuttle, where it is then no longer resembles a phallic symbol, becoming once more a mere poker.

In The Abbey Grange, Doyle's tale of passion, anger and unconsummated love, with its obvious undertones and references to the illicit love affair of Conan Doyle's own life, it was declared by the wife that a family of burglars called the Randalls had broken into the premises, and then murdered her husband.

The use of the name 'Randall' as the name of the gang, suggests how much Conan Doyle knew and read many of the area newspapers of the early 19th century, which very often would carry a full account of the murder like the one at Camden Place. A newspaper known as the *Belfast Telegraph,* for example, on Wednesday the 31st of May 1810, provided a full account of the coroner's court hearing, which took place at Camden Place just after the owners, Mr and Mrs Bonar had been murdered. This then is part of the account that appeared in that newspaper.

Report of a terrible double murder

'… Mr and Mrs Bonar of Camden Place, Chislehurst were attacked last night. It appears that both the Bonars had been beaten heavily. There were terrible gashes across their faces and the husband has now been declared dead. When the banker Mr Bonar went to bed that evening someone, it appeared, left open one of the doors to the outside of the house, though no one could recall who that was. During the enquiry that followed, it was then revealed, said one of the servants, that Mr and Mrs Bonar had left the library around midnight and retired to bed in the upstairs property where they slept together. One of the maids said to her mistress that the footman had not fastened the door and she had offered to do this, but the mistress said it did not matter to her as the bedroom door was left open as usual.

'The next morning the maid was woken by the housemaid who said there was a terrible smell coming from her mistress's room and when the two entered they beheld a dreadful spectacle. The mistress was in a terrible state and labouring for breath, whilst Mr Bonar was already a

Fig. 58. Frognal Place, the second contender for the Abbey Grange story.

corpse and lying on the floor. He had been badly wounded and his right wrist was so hurt the witness said that she only assumed this must have been sustained when he was attempting to defend himself. His wife pointed to the weapon, the poker that was found near the body, The footman entered shortly thereafter then soon left again, with a sheet which was stained with blood which he had taken from the room. Both the groom and Mr William Evans reported that the last they had seen of Mr Nicholson was at 7:30 a.m. When he saw Nicholson sitting on his bed immediately after he had come down the stairs he recalled him holding the bloody sheets. He noted that the man was very keen to take a horse in order to go to London.' Philip Nicholson was an ex - serviceman who had come from another employment in Ireland.

Although there is no surviving record of the events compiled by Conan Doyle, fellow Crime Club compatriot, Major Arthur Griffiths, suggests that Mr Bonar displayed to Nicholson some satisfaction at the passing of a controversial anti-Catholic bill the night before, and, since he was himself a devout Catholic, members of the household may have noticed a grudge against his master.

It was soon discovered by police that Mr Nicholson had disappeared shortly after the murders been committed. A warrant was issued for his arrest by the mayor and he was arrested subsequently in a public house in Whitechapel.

In his statement to the police he claimed he had been the first to discover the dying couple but he could not account for his abrupt departure from Camden Place. He was then stripped and examined for bruises which might indicate a struggle between himself and the two victims.

The coroner's court announced the verdict that the Bonars had been knowingly and intentionally killed by Nicholson. Among the witness depositions which was given at Nicholson's trial, when the family coachman declared that he 'had come to the house about half-past seven, and went to call Nicholson, found him sitting on the bed-side; almost immediately he came down stairs with bloody linen, then wrap it up in a sheet in the servants' hall. And the name of that witness, I hear you ask? Why, William Randall, of course.

After he had been imprisoned and was awaiting trial, Nicholson subsequently attempted committing suicide, by trying to slash his throat, but he lived long enough to face his own execution, which took place on Penenden Heath near Maidstone on a cold and windswept 23rd of August in 1813.

To the many fans of the Sherlock Holmes stories, and of course to the detective's creator, Arthur Conan Doyle, a keen criminologist himself, who on two occasions contested the prosecutions of men innocent of very serious crimes for which they stood trial, and then were quite mistakenly found guilty, Sherlock Holmes would have been very interested in examining the methods shown by the two investigating officers. In this case the first officer

William Lavender found a pair of blooded shoes in the suspect's bedroom wardrobe, which he managed to compare with traces of bloody footprints in the anteroom, and which corresponded precisely with the impressions that were recorded by the investigating officers. These shoes, interestingly, happened to be odd sizes. The accompanying officer agreed with him that the shoes were very odd, one being common - healed variety and worn at the toe, the other having a Spring Heel. Thus it appears that the art of tracing footsteps about which the master of all forensic consulting detectives wrote that famous lost monograph in the 1880s, about footprints and their significance, even as long ago as 1810 proves to us that there were detectives who, like Holmes, were both keen and observant at the scene of a crime.

What also is vividly clear from reading the details of the Bonar case, is that, not only had Conan Doyle read theses account of the crime himself but that he'd absorbed and remembered much of the detail of it. Otherwise thee are just too many coincidences. For I am most certain that we who love our Sherlock Holmes, will all recall his return to the Baker Street menage; and we remember also that Camden House was also the name of the empty house in Baker Street, directly opposite 221B, where Colonel Sebastian Moran, late of the Indian Army crouched by an open window in that deserted house, aiming his hydraulic air rifle at the wax bust of Holmes, preparing to shoot Mr Sherlock Holmes, It is also worth noting, I think, that the nearby Frognal Place, which might have served for 'The Abbey Grange,' was once the seat of the Marsham-Townshend family, proving quite clearly that this is where Conan Doyle got the name from.

POSTSCRIPT

In the case of Camden Place these 'coincidences' are not altogether surprising, for we know for a fact that Conan Doyle investigated serious cases of miscarriage of justice in the Oscar Slater case and the one regarding George Edalji, What we do not know is the extent to which he may well have been intrigued by some of the other, but less well publicised murder cases of his time which fascinated him as a writer and doctor. Conan Doyle received many letters asking him to assist people who had suffered as a result of either criminal or fraudulent actions against them. He wrote that, at a certain time in his life, when he felt he had enough of Holmes, 'from San Francisco to Moscow I continue to hear of Mysteries which I could only not solve but I had no idea, for there were so many mysteries in existence.' Nevertheless, though growing tired of his creation he still kept an interest in some of the curious and outré murder cases and he was also quite clearly interested in what we now call 'criminal psychology.'

Fig.59. Holmes and Watson examine the mere in *The Abbey Grange.*

Figs. 60/61. *The Abbey Grange*, a comparatively late story, and based on a violent, real-life murder. Sherlock Holmes listens sympathetically to Lady Brackenstall narrative about the intrusion of burglars at her family home. Known notoriously as 'the Lewisham Gang' by police, the two brothers Randall, partners in violent crime allegedly beat her husband to death with a poker. However, a detailed forensic examination by Holmes reveals a very different story.

THE MURDER LAB: A STATISTICAL ANALYSIS OF MURDER IN THE SHERLOCK HOLMES STORIES.

This is a murder list, or homicide list, if you prefer the American version, of murders which occur in the Sherlock Holmes stories. I find myself at slight deviance with the conclusions of Diane Madison in her excellent reference book, entitled 'Cracking the Code of the Canon,' where our numbers are at odds, but, I believe, for what I believe are obvious reasons. I have included also in my list additional attempted murders, so therefore, this means the figures are slightly higher in number.

What follows is, therefore, a list of all attempts at murder, whether successful or not, whether by intention or from accidental or non-intentional design, off which, the latter could be argued as manslaughter. I have also included a list of the weapons or methods, used to achieve the outcome of the murder.

THE MURDER LIST
The conclusions are as follows; (REFERENCES TO STORIES, USE THE FOUR LETTER ACRONYM SYSTEM invented by Dr J. Finlay Christ)).

Ronald Adair EMPT.
weapon. Air rifle, operated by hydraulic means.

Baldwin, Ted VALL.
Weapon. Shotgun blast caused by a dumdum bullet, resulting in a head trauma and death.

Blessington, alias Sutton RESI.
Weapon. Strangulation. By means of a temporary gallows being constructed, in order to hang Sutton in his quarters.
Brunton, R. MUSG.

Method. Asphyxiation.

Peter Carey. BLAC.
Weapon, Harpoon. Death by either major organ failure or loss of blood.

Lady Frances Carfax. CARF.
Attempted murder, method, chloroform. Not successful.

Cubitt, Henry. DANC.
Most probably an American Webley (see picture), revolver, successful, bullet to brain.

Cushing Mary. CARD.
Blunt trauma to skull or possibly drowning, Weapon, wooden oar., Attacker removed an ear, probably post mortem.

Drebber, Enoch. STUD.
Weapon, poison. Probably of strychnos variety, uncertain which.

Ernest, Ray. RETI.
Weapon, coal gas inhalation leading to asphyxiation.

Fairbairn, Alec. CARD.
Weapon, wooden oar.. Either blunt trauma or drowning.

Ferguson, Alec. SUSS.
weapon, Curare, administered by means of a blowpipe.

Fournaye, Henri. SECO.
weapon, Indian dagger, probably curved type (see picture).

Garcia, Aloysius. REDC.

weapon: sandbag, or, conjecturally, cosh. Death by blunt
object trauma, thus causing brain haemorrhage, using,
as mentioned above, repeated blows with a sandbag, otherwise
known as COSH (see picture).

Gibson, Maria. 3GAB.
Weapon; revolver that had a .2 bullet from probably, a
Webley (see details, in this section).

Giorgiano, Guiseppe. SIXN.
Waepon, knife, probably slashing carotid artery, judging by quantity
of blood found.

Heidegger. PRIO.
Weapon, heavy stick, possibly Penang lawyer or similar
, conceivably bulbous-headed. See photo.

Holmes Sherlock
All attempted murders, non-successful, including: a bludgeon,
sticks (unspecified, but see photo for likely possibility),
bricks, bacterial poisoning, air rifle - hydraulic (see
note earlier). Contexts as follows:
FINA, DYIN, ILLU, EMPT.

Kirwan, William,
weapon, revolver, unspecified., probably Nigerian, Western
revolver type; result, successful murder.

Kratides, Paul. GREE.
Weapon, charcoal burner fumes causing slow asphyxiation by
carbon monoxide.

McCarthy, C,

Gun butt to head, trauma, brain, soft tissue damage etc.

Milverton, Charles Augustus. CHAS.
weapon, Webley number two, undoubtedly. Small model, popular
with women and easily concealed in handbag etc. (see illustration).

Prescott
Weapon, gun, unspecified.

Ronder, Eugene. VEIL.
Weapon, club with nails attached, therefore blunt force trauma.

Savage, Victor. DYIN.
weapon, bacterial poison, uncertain as to which.

Selden. HOUN.
Criminal madman who lived on Dartmoor & probably fell to his
 death, possibly an accident.

Sholto, Bartholomew. SIGN
Weapon, strychnine tipped thorn.

Smith, Willoughby. GOLD.
weapon method, sealing wax knife, probably hitting carotid vein
in the neck.

Stangerson, J.
weapon, knife.

Stoner, Julia. SPEC.
Weapon, snake bite, not known which species, but certainly of
 type whose venom has a neurotoxic effect, thus causing
rapid respiratory failure.

Tregennis, Brenda and Mortimer. DEVI.
Killed deliberately by two different people, both planned as
act of revenge, drug of unknown origin. probably one of the
tribal ordeal drugs used in Western Congo.

Venucci, P.
Weapon, Knife, uncertain which.

Watson, John
Weapon, revolver, specific weapon not specified.

West, A,
Weapon, life preserver, AKA usually a lead -tipped cosh
(see picture).

Number of times weapon or method used

Firearms 9
Variety of blood instruments 12
Sharp instruments e.g., short knife 7
Poison 11
Rope once with Sutton in RESI.

Motives for murder in the Sherlock Holmes stories

Self-defence in BLAC, 1.
Murders as result of love triangle, . Relationship with
man and woman.12.
34% of all 12 murders, have as motive some monetary gain,
Only 9% of the 23 stories published until 1893 involve murder.
The conclusion we draw from this, is that as we move
forward in time, many more of the stories are actually to do with

or are connected with attempted murder or actual murder thus showing the gradual change in Conan Doyle's conception of the crime story.

SPECIFIC ANALYSIS FOR MURDERS
AS DEFINED BY THE VICTIM

GAIN
CARFAX, F.
SAVAGE, V,
STONER, J.
TEREGENNIS, M.

REVENGE
ADAIR, R.
BALSWIN, E.
BLESSINGTON
BRACKENSTALL, E.
DREBBER, E.
MCCARTHY, E..
MILVERTON, C.A.
RONDER, E.
STANGERSON,A,
TREGENNIS,B

JEALOUSY
AMBERLEY, MRS.
ERNEST, RAY.
CUSHING, M.
FAIRBAIRN, A.
FERGUSON. J,
FOURNAY, H.

SELFDEFENCE (MANSLAUGHTER)
CUBITT, H.
CAREY, P.

ELIMINATION FOR OTHER REASONS, PARTLY OR MOSTLY FITTING ONE OR MORE OF THE ABOVE

GARCIA, A.
GORGIANO, G.
HEIDEGGER.
HOLMES, S.
KIRWAN, W.
KRATIDES, P.
OPNSHAWS.
PRESCOTT.
SELDEN.
SHOLYO, B.
SMITH, W.
VENUCCI, P.
WATSON, J.
WEST, A.

THIEVES, LOCKS AND SAFES.

An extract from an article from the Strand Magazine, and attributed to Sherlock Holmes, Volume 8, July-December, 1894

Ever since man has been possessed of anything worth keeping. Some other man has been at work to get it away from him without paying for it. When the property was cattle and tents, then he who could took who had the power and with a club or other means of solid argument. But when jewels and money came into fashion, and people used houses with doors to them, things became more orderly and a gentleman who wanted another gentleman's portable property had to go about the matter quietly.

As experience taught him that it saved trouble to select a time when the owner was out or asleep for making selections in a strange house, the owner, naturally, began to fasten his door. He would put a staple in his door post and two more on his door and slide a wooden beam through the three.

We do precisely the same thing now with an ordinary iron bolt on the same principle. This was a capital arrangement to sleep behind, but didn't admit of going out shopping with security. So that soon a hole was made in the top of one of the staples and another corresponding to it in the bolt. Then a pin was dropped through these holes and held fast.

This was done from outside through a hole in the door- the forerunner of our own keyholes. With an instrument, conveniently shaped both for dropping and lifting the pin, here was the ancestor of our own familiar key of the street. With a handle to slide the bolt to and fro, the primitive lock was then complete.

Wooden locks of this kind are even now in use in certain remote parts of Austria and in the Faroe Islands. Whence it may be inferred that in those happy spots, man has a singular trust in his neighbour.

Almost anybody could open a lock of this sort so that an improvement was then wanted.

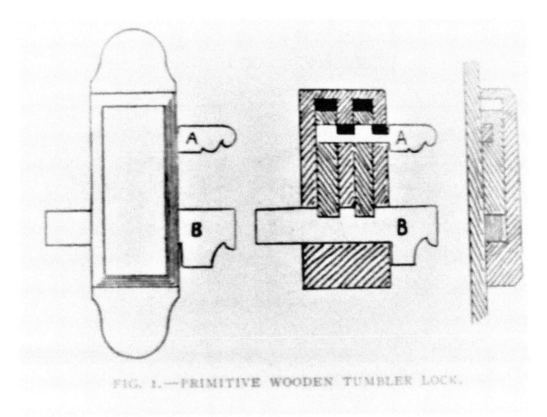

FIG. 1.—PRIMITIVE WOODEN TUMBLER LOCK.

Fig. 64 A tumbler lock..

The illustration at figure one shows the first improvement. Two or more falling pins were used and they were afterwards called Tumblers. And these pins and the part of the bolt into which these fell, were enclosed in a box shown in the outer view. The key at figure one was provided with certain projections which fitted into notches cut into the bolts so that, when inserted at the side of the box and lifted , it then raised the tumblers from the holes in the bolt and allowed the withdrawal of the latter.

Now it is obvious that unless this wooden key were made with its projections at such a distance apart, as exactly to correspond with the notches in the tumblers and of that same number one or more of these would not be lifted. And the bolts would then remain immoveable. So that here was some sort of security against other keys than those held by the owner. Identical in principle, though rather neater in application is the wooden Egyptian lock still in use and shown in Figure 2.

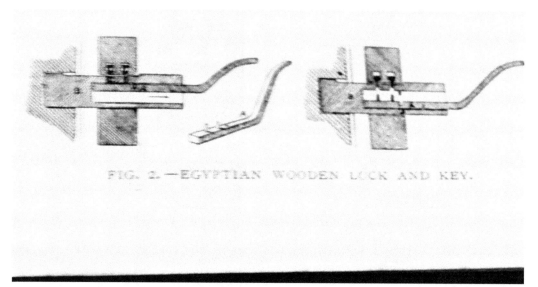

FIG. 2.—EGYPTIAN WOODEN LOCK AND KEY.

Fig. 65 Egyptian lock and key.

Here the bolt at B is made hollow and the loose key at A is provided with small pegs with which the Tumblers are pushed up when the bolt is drawn back in the direction indicated by the arrow. This is all done with the key so that this lock possesses the advantage over the previously mentioned requiring the whole of one hand to work it. Although it was possible to make these locks and keys in any number of different patterns, it required the expenditure of very little ingenuity on the part of the Bill Sykes of early ages to dodge them.

A simple picklock with a movable peg or two and a little patience were all that was required. The Romans made a gallant attempt to defeat these picks by making the tumbler's of all sorts of sections triangular, square, semi-circular et cetera. But the device was scarcely worthy of the Roman genius. Obviously, a mere peg, if only thin enough, was enough to lift a tumbler, no matter of what section. One improvement, however, the Romans did make. They kept the tumbler's down by the springs instead of allowing them to rest by mere gravitation. And thus, with the addition of a revolving key produced in all its essential parts. The common Tumbler lock which we modern people use went back within the last century or so. But in order to secure these locks against picks, it became customary to interpose all sorts of obstacles, of many different shapes and sizes. Cutting each key to a shape to pass these obstacles, then gave rise to the system of warding which during the Middle Ages was almost exclusively relied upon, tumblers being scarcely used then.

Fig. 66 The death of Milverton, the blackmailer. It was during this bold and highly illegal burglary attempt that Holmes admitted to Watson that he possessed 'a first class burgling kit' and that he have made 'a highly efficient criminal.'

A revolving key was made to act upon and shoot a bolt direct, but the way to this bolt was guarded by a complicated system of wards.

Now it is impossible to devise wards which skeleton keys and pick locks cannot defeat. You make a great key; it cuts into a perfect fretwork. And then the Lock provides complicated wards, which this fretwork just passes.

Immediately there comes a burglar along with a mere wire frame of a key which overcomes all these wards by simply ignoring them, passing its thin frame round behind or before the whole system and easily shooting the bolt.

So that,150 years, ago or more the old Tumbler system, though modified, was then returned to.

Here the tumblers were mere horizontal pegs pressed down by a spring in two notches on the bolt. This was still guarded by certain simple wards and such a lock.

And this is the ordinary cheap door lock of today, scarcely more secure, however, against the pick lock and the skeleton key rather than a simple warded lock.

The illustration here is from a photograph of certain skeleton keys and pick locks actually used by burgers burglars on ordinary modern locks.

The more common skeleton key. Is in fact an ordinary key, with all the warnings filed out of the bit, as is the specimen on the right of the wire picklock thus shown in the centre of the group. In making a skeleton of this sort, it is a principle to file down the Shank and bit as thinly as possible. Consistent with strength these parts maybe than those on the proper key.

They will still do their work. While the least excess in thickness will either prevent the instrument entering the lock or cause a jam.

For this reason, a barrel Shank is filed down flush with the last arm of the bit as is seen here in the two small keys represented in the picture. because no matter how much thinner they appear to be, these parts maybe than those on the proper key. They will still do their work. While the least excess in thickness will either prevent the instrument entering the lock or cause a jam.

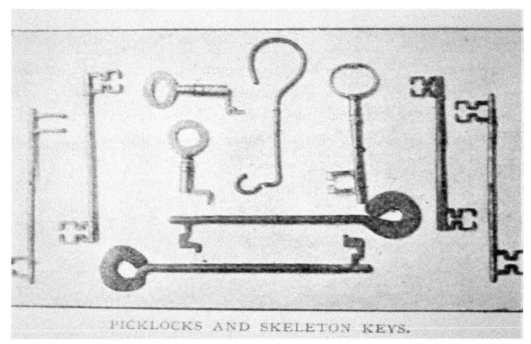

PICKLOCKS AND SKELETON KEYS.

Fig. 67. Skeleton keys and picklocks,

. For this reason, a barrel Shank is filed down flush with the last arm of the bit as is seen here in the two small keys represented in the picture. The double bitted pick locks shown on either side in this picture are specially made for portability and convenience and designed, of course, to suit the various usual types of warding.

The two bits of instruments are commonly of very similar patterns, with a little variation in size or measurement of warding, so that when a lock is tried, which one end will almost pick, but not quite. The other end is then handy and almost certain to fit. The principle of keeping all the parts thin, as well as some strong and stiff is well exemplified in these double bitted pics. A pic of stiff bent wire is a very handy, quickly prepared and commonly used thing. The one shown here is used for shooting the plainer kind of bolt, lock or latch.

This variety is also convenient for pushing through the keyhole of a small latch and then moving the finger catch up on the inner side. Skeleton keys are of course to some extent defeated by the well-known modern leverlock. In this, a number of small levers affixed at one end are then held down by a spring.

These must each then be lifted to a certain different height before they will then allow the bolt to be withdrawn. Any number of combinations is possible. And the least inaccuracy in any part of the key will cause it to prevent action since one or other of the levers must be lifted too high or too low.

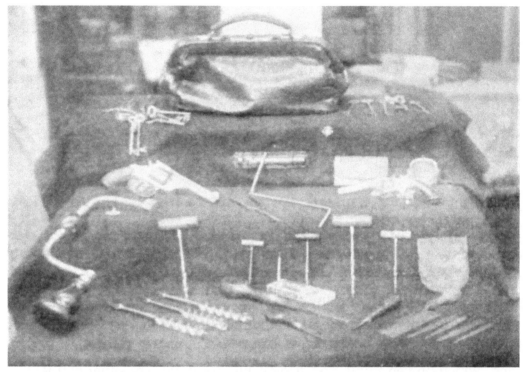

Fig. 68 A collection of lock breaker's tools.

But a skilful man will then get out the bolt and applying pressure to free it back deal with each lever in succession with a wire pick until the projection from the bolt will pass. But he will probably prefer in fact to break the door. A much simpler task; which then brings us to the matter of safes.

Fig. 69 A rare photograph of the inside of a safe maker's factory
taken around the late end of the 1890s and reproduced here in
the *Strand Magazine.*

An impregnable lock is useless on a weak box or a door. And in almost
any case, it is a simple matter to use force in breaking or cutting through a
door, or by breaking the lock away from it, than to use the patient guile in
picking the lock, so that over time, safes and strong rooms then came into
being. At first these were the coffers of Ramus, the pharoah, where there
were strong oak boxes with bindings of iron. Orsome were made entirely of
metal. And fastened usually with a padlock. But in these days, these later
days, criminals became much more effective, and systematic workmen, and
so the safe, which, over time and for convenience had been now set on one
end with a door instead of a lid, assumed the shape now familiar to us;

being made of various designs in iron and steel and fastened as to the door, with many bolts shooting from every side.

The tools of the modern housebreaker are many and varied, and they consist of many things besides skeleton keys. Here on the page above you can see a copy of a photograph of a very simple set taken not from a burglar, but from a mere hotel thief, whence the practise was to take a bedroom in such an establishment and then to pay quiet visits during the night to other customers' bedrooms.

One of his most useful tools are the small pair of pliers shown here in the middle of the group near the muzzle of the revolver on the left. This was a long nosed instrument with a cylindrical grip. When a visitor with valuables in his possession locked his bedroom door on retiring, and like a careful man left the key in the lock to prevent anybody trying a picklock e saved our burglar a lot of trouble. That worthy simply placed the long nose of his pliers in the keyhole, gripped the shank of the key, and then turned it.

The door was immediately open. And, moreover, quite free for him to enter quietly and make his selection. After doing this, it was only necessary to retire and then lock the door again with the victim's own key in the same manner. The surprise of the said victim, on rising and finding the door locked and the key on the inside, but all his valuables disappeared, may well be imagined.

The crooked metal rod almost touching the pliers is another very interesting implement. It was used to unfasten small bolts. The small brass bolts fixed halfway up a door. At the angle near to the pliers is a hinged joint so that the two pieces may be straightened out like one rod. This was then thrust through a keyhole. The hinged end is allowed to fall across the bolt fastening. A very little firm and skilful handling is then only necessary to push back the bolt.

The small bolts shown here by the way were used to fix temporarily on the door of an unoccupied room in which the gentleman might be pursuing his profession in order to prevent the possibility of intrusion or surprise.

The other articles shown are comprising silent matches, a brace, and bits, gimlets, a saw, screwdrivers files, picklocks, pistols and a very neat crocodile hide bag to hold them in all of which have uses too obvious to need any explanation.

None of these tools, however, are designed for the attack on an iron safe. Here, then, is a very different group - a group of tools of the very first quality.

They were found hidden in a suite of empty rooms in Cannon Street, London, over a post office, together with a quiet little syndicate of two or three gentlemen who were then anxiously awaiting nightfall.

It is sad to observe that not only were these gentlemen deprived of the possession of these admirable instruments, but that an unsympathetic administrator of the law sent them then to gaol.

The long article at the top is the most splendid Jimmy ever captured. Five feet in length, it is made of the best tool steel procurable, and in three pieces. This is partly for convenience of carriage and partly to enable 'beaks' or business ends; or various shapes to be used on it.

The three additional beaks are shown on the ledge below. And the joints are fastened by collars and set screws; these being then tightened by a little steel 'Tommy,' so called. which lies in the picture close by the point of the extra beak in the centre.

So well is the whole thing made and fitted, that mere screwing with finger and thumb will suffice to hold the entire 5 feet as rigid as a single rod.

There is also a brace with bits for drilling iron or steel. A carpenters chisel, a cold chisel. I have screwdriver and half a dozen still wedges of graduated sizes. Certain staples with which to improvised or fastenings and guard against intrusion a bullseye, London.

And the next, a neat brush with which to remove any unseemly dust caused by the operations being contemplated.

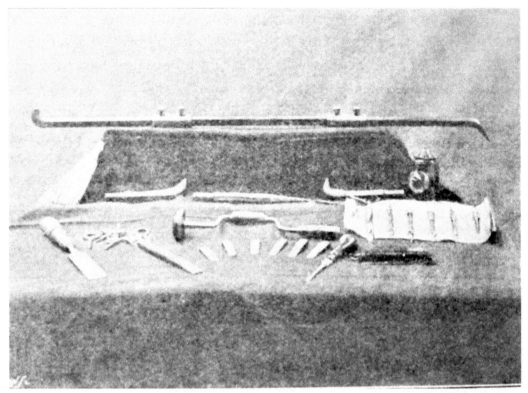

Fig 70. The complete burgling kit..

Charming little set, isn't it? You see, by drilling a hole or two in any ordinary safe, suppose it to be of the sort known as fire proof only, and inserting the jemmy with one of the loose Beeks shown on the right here and the left which both have sharp edges, the sheet steel can then be ripped open like the lid of a sardine tin.

Fig 71. Victorian criminals being photographed.

And finally….These fine, upstanding citizens, waiting at Scotland Yard to have their photo mug shots taken, look forward to your company once more, in volume 3 of *The Criminal World of Sherlock Holmes*. I'm off to get my latest tattoo done.

From *Mysteries of Police and Crime* by Arthur Griffiths.

LIST OF ILLUSTRATIONS

Bush villas, where Doyle practised as a GP in Southsea. iv

1. Conan Doyle in 1902. v.

2 Doyle poses at his Norwood home with the agent from Lippincotts 5.

3 The Mystery of the Hansom Cab, best-selling crime novel 6.

4 Edgar Allan Poe, who greatly influenced Doyle. 10

5, Ripper victim scene, from *The Illustrated Police Gazette*. 14.

6. The railway arch, location of a Ripper murder. 17.

7. The PC who discovered the railway arch victim, Francis Coles . 20.

8. Montague James Druitt, suspected of being The Ripper. 22.

9. Conan Doyle, by now a popular crime writer. 24.

10. Richard Von Krafft Ebing, psychiatrist who heralded profiling 28.

11. The Thames River Police in action. 30.

12. The handwriting of Jack the Ripper. 35

13. Police profile of H. H. Holmes, thought to be Ripper. 38.

14. Murder scene in The Cardboard Box. 40,

15. Ripper bloodstain examination in *The Police Gazette*. 48.

16. Dr Forbes Winslow, psychiatrist, who thought he knew the Ripper. 51.

17. Holmes examines tobacco evidence in *The Resident Patient*. 62.

18. Holmes' chemical lab at 221B. From *The Naval Treaty*. 63.

19. Dr Joseph Bell, the inspiration for Sherlock Holmes. 64.

20. Curved briar pipes. 65.

21. Victorian clay pipe. 67.

22. Actor William Gillette, the first man to play Holmes. 68.

23. An addicted Sherlock Holmes in Cornwall. 70.

24. William Gillette, populariser of the bent briar pipe. 74.

25. Holmes, smoking a straight briar pipe. 76.

26. Watson, wounded in the Afghan war, smokes for pain relief. 77.

27. Frank Wiles picture of Holmes in a pipe reverie. 80.

28. Sherlock Holmes' short, straight clay pipe. 81.

29. Thomas De Quincey, opium eater. 90.

30. Oscar Wilde, the illustrious Bohemian.   94.

31. Sigmund Freud. 104.

32. Charles Altamont Doyle with his son, Arthur. 117.

33. The Brighton train murderer, Percy Lefroy. 122

34. Ladies often fainted n Victorian times. 127.

35. Dr. Roylott throws the village blacksmith into a pond. 138.

36. Sherlock Holmes beats the swamp adder. 139.

37. Dr. Roylott with the snake curled around his head. 144.

38. American newspaper drawing of the death of Dr. Roylott. 146,

39. The phallic and aggressive Dr. Roylott. 147.

40 The Baker Street Boys. 148.

41. The Duke of Clarence, involved in the rent boy scandal. 156.

42. Victorian coining equipment. 197.

43. A detective arrives at the coining premises. 198.

44. Jubilee coins. 201

45. 'Have they gone yet, Fred?'.

46. French female tattooed prostitute. 215.

47. An elaborate tattoo. 219.

48. American tattooed prostitutes. 220,

49. East European tattooed man. 221.

50. Huret, the tattooed French assassin. 223.

51. Ornate tattoo worn by German criminal. 224.

52. Array of weapons left at crime scene. 238.

53. French gendarme officer guards a crime scene. 230,

54. Holmes, with Watson, examines crime scene evidence. 238.

55. A Victorian crime scene. 248.

56. Camden Place, the real Abbey Grange. 249..

57. Frognal Place, where Doyle played golf. 250.

58. Holmes & Watson examine The Mere in *The Abbey Grange*. 256.

58 . Holmes gathers evidence in *The Abbey Grange*. 256.

59, As above. 256.

60 A tumbler lock. 265.

61 An Egyptian lock and key. 266.

62 The death of Charles Augustus Milverton. 267.

63. A rare collection of lock breaker's tools. 268.

64. Skeleton keys. 269.

65 A photograph of the inside of a safe maker's factory. 271.

66 A complete set of housebreaking tools. 274

67 Reluctant criminals being photographed by police. 275.

THE CRIMINAL WORLD OF SHERLOCK HOLMES:

INDEX TO VOLUME TWO

A

Abbey Grange 230

Albert, Victor Eddy in male brothel 141

Adam, A.L. Book on Scotland Yard 60

Albert, Victor Eddy in male brothel 141

alcohol 87

Anderson, Robert 7

Anderson & Jewish identity of Ripper 36, 53

Apaches 99

Arabs, Street 99

B

Baker Street 125

Baker Street menage, 94

Bell, Dr Joseph

Bertillon, Alphonse 153

Bibliography of Sherlock Holmes' Writings

Black Museum. Conan Doyle interestedd in 44

Blackwoods Magazine 37

Bloodprints 41

Bond, Thomas, Dr, 20

Burgling kit 246

Burgling tools 243-24

Bush Villas, Southsea iv

C

Camden Place, Chislehurst, murder case, 223 et seq.

Cardboard Box. 41 -42

Cedars, The 148

Central Press Agency 38 42

Cherrywood pipes

Clarence, Duke of, 140-142

Clark, police surgeon 56

Clarke, Russell, sea stories 94

Cleveland St. Scandal 145-146

Coiners and coining 180 - 183

Cocaine 23-26, 178

Coles, Frances 58

Coles, Frances, relationship with Sadler 58-59

Crime Club and Conan Doyle 44

Criminals being photographed

Criminal slang 184 - 202

Criminals, identification of 153

Criminals identified by medical examination 160-161

D

Daily newspapers Holmes used, 93

De Quincey, Thomas 83

Dickens Charles, *Our Mutual Friend*, 28

Description of Jack the Ripper 3

Detectives at Scotland Yard 7

Devil's Foot 119

Disguise & deception 147 etc

DOYLE, CONAN

Doyle & criminology iv

& crime library 44

as GP 5

& Black Museum

Doyle & Lippincotts 5

Doyle and Edgar Allan Poe 19

Doyle's father in asylum, effect on 99-100

& Hornung, writer 7-8

& Jerome K. Jerome 7

& Jean Leckie 22

Doyle novel, *The Sign of Four* 7

Doyle's female characters show courage 100

Doyle male characters predatory, 100-108

view of Ripper as foreigner, 48

opinion of De Quincey 83

& profile of Ripper 50

& view of police 53

and Vienna 8

& *The White Company* 7

Doyle studied Krafft- Ebing & Havelock Ellis

Dracula and madness 114

E

Edwards, Owen Dudley 93

Egyptian lock 239

F

Fainting 128-19

False names used by criminals 177

Forbes Winslow, psychiatrist, 109

Fraud, a story of by Gross, H 176-180

Freud, Sigmund 104 et seq.

Freud's Lectures on psychology 114

Freud's method similar to Holmes' 105-106

Frognal Place, Kent 253

G

Gikbert, Dr, 44

Gowers' *Bible of Neurology* 190

Great Eastern Railway 15

Griffiths, Arthur *Mysteries of Police and Crime* 44

Gross, Hans, criminologist 149

Gruner, Baron Von 30

H

Holmes

Alternating moods 109-110

And breakdown 110

and cocaine 108

and depression   108-110

and drugs 53

and newspapers 186 -b189

and psychoanalysis 92 et seq

Holmes H.H., murderer 39

For bes Winslw, psychiatrist,

See under Winslow

forensic methods of 65

oedipus complex 111

inductive analysis 98

oral personality 99

Pipe assiction 73-79

works on criminology 194-198

and monograph on scenes of crime 293-222

and Sigmund Freud 56

use of drugs page 53

I

Idee fixe,, See Aloensr

Innocence, seduction of 142

Jack the Ripper. See **Ripper**

Jerome K. Jerome 44

K

Kelly, Mary. Ripper, murder victim 28, 40 et seq.,

L

Lascar opium den 92-93

Laudanum, Victorian   attitudes to :95

Lauriston Gardens 133

Etter from the Ripper 35

Leman Street, Whitechapel 9, 13

Leatherhead 132-136

Leckie, Jean 22

Letter from Jack the Ripper 35

Lockbreaker tool 272 etq seq,

M

Man with the Twisted Lip 76

Macnaughton, murderer thought mad 113

Macnaghton, Chief Superintendent 12

Manuals and reference books on Victorian crime 95 - 96

Mapleton, Percy 108, et seq.

Mental asylums 113

Mental illness, 112-123

Milverton, death of, 267

Moore, Chief Inspector 25

Manuals and reference books on Victorian crime 184-185

Mobsmen, strategies of 181

Morphine, actions 99

Morphine as sedative 100-

Morphine, bibliography 100

Morphine, effects on brain, spinal cord & stomach, 100

Morphine effect on eyes 101

Morphine, used to treat gunshot wound 87

Murder cases in Holmes stories 258-263

Murder, Victorian, classic cases 6-9

Mystery of a Hansom Cab, 6

N

Names, false 172

New York Herald 17

Notting Hill murder 110

O

Old Scotland Yard 44

Opium 76

Opium, among Bohemians 84

And Chinese 88

In *Silver Blaze* 93

In *Wisteria Lodge* 94

P

Phillips, Dr 11

Pinchin St. Torso Case 21

Poe, Edgar Allan   10, 73-79

Portsmouth & Doyle 5

Portsmouth Evening News 14 , 31

Profile of Ripper killer 50

Psychopathia Sexualis 40

R

Ratcliffe Highway murders 91

Railway arch murder 17

Research, crime, causes 190

Reid, DCI in Ripper case 55

Reich, Wilhelm 129

RIPPER

Ripper 53, but see also 'Jack The Ripper'

Ripper as an American 34

Ripper as homicidal maniac 56

Ripper & Hanbury St murder 48

Ripper, handwriting 35

Ripper as a Jew 35

As psychopath 138-145

Ripper suspect Druitt, unlikely 22

Sadler, James, suspect 50 58

Ripper used River Thames 29-32

Ripper victim Anne Chapman 32

Ripper victim Frances Coles 8

Suspect Druitt 23 27

Research, crime, primary sources 172-173

Roylott, Dr. Grimesby 100 et seq.

as Gothic villain 129

as psychopath 124-125

S

Sadler, James 57-61

Safe makers' factory 271

Satyriasis 75

Secondary sources, re criminology & late Victorian Society

192-193

Selden, madman 117 et seq.

Six Napoleons 50

Sexuality in Victorian England 27

Skeleton keys 269

Speckled Band 132-146

Shelley, Percy: laudanum hallucinations 95

Smoking in Holmes stories 65-81

Somerset, Lord Arthur in male brothel 142 - 143

Skin, discolouration of by 214

Stoke Moran identity of 134 - 136 et seq.

Straker, John see *Silver Blaze*

Swindlers 177-178

Syphilis 130

T

Telegraph boy scandal 138 et seq.

Thames, River 28

Thames River Police 32

Thieves, locks and Safes 237

Trevelyan, Dr. And nercous lesions 76

Third Generation, story 26

Titbits, magazine 49

Tumbler lock 238

Transportation of juveniles 138

U

Upper Swandam Lane 80

V

Veiked Lodger, The

Victorian crime cases , classic 175

Vigilance, Committee, and kidney 58

W

Wagstaffe, farm labourer 123 - 126

Wainwright 7

Watson, Dr. 77, 85

Whitechapel Vigilance Committee 41

Wilde, Oscar 89

Winslow, Dr., believed Ripper was of foreign origin 49, 51, 56

Wisteria Lodge 84

Lightning Source UK Ltd.
Milton Keynes UK
UKHW031518221222
414315UK00007B/106